ORANGES FOR MIRANDA

ANNETTE BOWER

SOUL MATE PUBLISHING
New York

ORANGES FOR MIRANDA

Copyright©2021

ANNETTE BOWER

Cover Design by Rae Monet, Inc.

This book is a work of fiction. The names, characters, places, and incidents are the products of the author's imagination or are used fictitiously. Any resemblance to actual events, business establishments, locales, or persons, living or dead, is entirely coincidental.

All rights reserved. No part of this publication may be reproduced, stored in a retrieval system, or transmitted in any form or by any means (electronic, mechanical, photocopying, recording, or otherwise) without the prior written permission of both the copyright owner and the publisher. The only exception is brief quotations in printed reviews.

The scanning, uploading, and distribution of this book via the Internet or via any other means without the permission of the publisher is illegal and punishable by law. Please purchase only authorized electronic editions, and do not participate in or encourage electronic piracy of copyrighted materials.

Your support of the author's rights is appreciated.

Published in the United States of America by
Soul Mate Publishing
P.O. Box 24
Macedon, New York, 14502

ISBN: 978-1-64716-260-3

www.SoulMatePublishing.com

The publisher does not have any control over and does not assume any responsibility for author or third-party websites or their content.

For Meradith

with whom I first travelled

to the Portuguese Algarve.

For Cam

who returned with me and our friends

so very many times.

Acknowledgments

Huge thanks to Debby Gilbert, founder and senior editor of Soul Mate Publishing, LLC, for helping my book shine and publishing my fifth novel with her company.

Rae Monet, my cover designer, who tells this story with her inspired images.

Janet Corcoran for her editing and knowledge, bringing Oranges for Miranda to a higher level.

Roy and Beth, Bob and Anita, Nick and Becky, Ron and Madeline, Bob and Dorothy contributed to many happy Algarve memories.

To the Saskatchewan Romance Writers for their constant encouragement and support, especially Mary Balogh, Karyn Good, and Jessica Eissfeldt.

To The Saskatchewan Writers Guild who supports writers and provides opportunities for readings.

To my family who supports me with continued unconditional love and joy.

To my readers who tell me how much they enjoy my stories and ask me about the next book.

PONYTAILS AND PROMISES
Uncaged Review

Two dreams become one. A realistic and beautiful look at a family of farmers and the love and loyalty to each other. Emily is taking over the family farm, but it's tough when she also has her older uncle with dementia to keep watch over. Emily hires her best friend's brother Max, who is a nurse with a dream of his own. If you don't know anything of a farming life, you will learn a lot in this book, of the struggles, the hard work, and the unique intelligence of a farmer's life. It will also show you a realistic look of the progression of dementia, and the family that is devoted to each other. And if that's not enough we find a love story.

Emily is outgoing and outspoken and Max is a bit more reserved, watching how the two navigate their growing attraction to each other, specially knowing Max will only be around for the planting and then he will move on to his new position. I went into this book with a bit of trepidation – as so many contemporary romances seem the same to me, but this one is a wonderful surprise and is highly recommended.

~Reviewed by Cyrene 4.5 Stars

Chapter 1

The bubbles floating across Miranda Porter's abdomen and covering her breasts reminded her of the retro photos of women in clawfoot bathtubs. She inhaled the scent of lavender and wiggled her toes against the worn brass taps. *Who should I be today in this new place? What name would reflect a woman in this bathroom in this whitewashed stucco home nestled among the other houses sheltered by red-tiled roofs in Albufeira?*

Arriving in the southern coastal city in Portugal late in the afternoon after a long and tiring journey from Regina, Saskatchewan, Canada, she'd admired the stylish women walking along the cobblestone streets in their stilettos. Women with names like Raquel, Sofia, or Lusia all sounded softer, more romantic. Indeed more European than Miranda. Miranda was in Shakespeare's play *The Tempest*, where father and daughter were stranded on an island. But not her story, just her name. She wasn't stranded. She chose the Portuguese Algarve to be the place of winding down and redefining the woman she was now. Not the Miranda of the Canadian Prairie, award-winning realtor and mother of two adult children.

A bubble tickled her nose. She reached for the box of tissues on the wicker table positioned next to the tub and sneezed with abandon.

A concerned, carefully annunciated voice followed the gentle tap on the door. "Miss Miranda, are you well? Will you be out soon? I need to clean your room and the bathroom before I hang out my Monday laundry."

"Please don't be concerned about my room, Maria. I will tidy it. And I will rinse out the tub." Miranda yawned, still feeling the effects of so many hours travelling and the eight-hour time difference with her internal clock.

"But you pay me to do these things for you." The heavy accent slid around the hinges and under the door.

"Just for today?" Miranda said. "Please?"

"As you wish. I will be in the kitchen when you are ready for breakfast."

Miranda heard the bedroom door squeak against the timber frame. What would a woman named Raquel answer?

"Maria, you may come and clean the sink while I bathe."

The imagined Sofia would call, *"Maria, come back after lunch, you know I am not an early riser. I will come down for my coffee and croissant when the water is cold."*

Ahh, a gentle Lusia might call, *"I'm sorry, Maria, the time has gotten away on me. I'll be out in a moment."*

Would these women be accustomed to other adult women moving freely in and out of their private lives or having someone do things for them? Miranda's parents had taught her to be self-sufficient. She had depended upon her ingenuity and organizational skills to be on time and ready to meet the circumstances of her school days, part-time jobs and finally, her very own Porter Real Estate company. If someone called when she was in the shower, her bright, cheery answering voice would ask them to leave a message, and she would be back to them in ten minutes. If her focus were on another client, her business voice would inform the caller that she would personally return each call. If a friend called for a chat, she'd set her timer and listen attentively for a quarter of an hour and then agree to a lunch date. If her children called, and that was a big if lately because she saw them each day in the office, she would drop everything.

Miranda and her children, Stacy and Nathan, were a solid unit. Even though Miranda might remain in Albufeira for up to three months or more, she had no qualms about leaving the business in their capable hands. Stacy and Nathan were her business succession plan, and they were ready. The office would run smoothly. Miranda's absence would give them space to carry the real estate business into the next generation. The planets had aligned and she had found the perfect spot, Maria's guest house, Casa O Mar, warmer weather, and the sea.

But now she had to get her life back. For the first time since she could remember, she was without a definite plan.

Miranda poked the rubber stopper with her toe, and it slipped out of the drain. The lukewarm water gurgled away before she tapped the plug into place and added more hot water. Her eyes drifted closed.

When the bathwater had cooled again, Miranda examined her puckered fingertips. While late for many, it was time to start her day. She would join the people meandering the markets and strolling to the sea.

Miranda dried and slathered lotion and sunscreen over her body before wrapping herself in the terry towel robe. She bent down and wiped out the tub as she had promised Maria.

Although it was January and the low tourist season, the street noise below and the spicy scents of food cooking wafted through her open window. The oranges on the tree in the front courtyard caught her eye, the sunlight on their dimpled skin, reminding her of sweet, candied orange peels.

She opened the wardrobe and chose a loosely fitted blouse, mid-calf flowing pants, a pashmina, and comfortable walking shoes. Today she would be open to new experiences.

"Maria, Maria, something you are cooking smells marvelous," Miranda sang out as she entered the kitchen.

"Miss Miranda, the bread is just out of the oven. Now come and sit down and eat while it is hot."

"This is too late for breakfast, Maria. I came to tell you I was going out."

"The bread is fresh. Sit down, please."

She had never made something so essential to survival. In all her years she had allowed others or commercial bakeries to provide this staple for herself and her children. Miranda sat at the large plank table. "Will you teach me to bake bread one day?"

"Any time after my holiday, it is not that difficult. When you look for a place to live, make sure there is an oven in the backyard. There are still many houses with this, and then you find the man who brings the best wood for bread or pizzas. He will tell you which to use for either."

Miranda's tentative plan was to find a place for three months, to stay until spring arrived on the Canadian prairies. She held her arms out. "I may never move away from here."

"But you must. I told you when you phoned that I will be going to Canada to visit my Lorenzo."

"Yes, your brother, who lives in Calgary."

"Eat."

Miranda surveyed the fresh slices of bread begging for the butter to melt into it, and jars of orange marmalade and honey. "A meal fit for a queen," she said, not knowing what to sample first.

"Coffee or hot chocolate?" Maria indicated the pots on the stove.

"Coffee, please, Maria." Miranda relaxed in her chair and watched Maria reach for the pot. She wasn't much older than Miranda but had a stillness about her, a quality that Miranda wanted to learn. For too many years, life had been ruled by a clock, watching peoples' reactions to the properties she showed them and then negotiating and closing deals for someone's dream home. Her work kept a roof over her family, food on their table, and provided the best opportunities for her children.

"Maria, will you join me and tell me about your village?"

"What is there to know?" Maria poured herself an espresso and sat across from Miranda. "I have lived here all of my sixty years. My father was a fisherman and my mother a lacemaker." She pointed to the valance across the window. The hibiscus flowers poked their heads across the open windowsill. "She made those for all of the windows in her house, then my house, and Lorenzo's house, but I don't know if he uses them in his fancy, modern place."

"Did you fish or be a lacemaker?"

"No, fishing was for the men, and my hands were too big and not flexible enough to move the spools. I stood at my avó's, my grandmother's, side when she cooked for the family. She always sang and danced around the kitchen. I liked that happy place. I wasn't so convinced that sitting and watching the sea from the top floor of the house while flinging spools of different threads was a good choice for me. My mama was an artist with an artist's temperament. She liked to be alone." Maria's eyes searched the bottom of the small cup while her large fingers twirled it in the saucer.

Maria and Miranda could be sisters, but their lives had been so different. "There was you, your mom, your dad, and your brother Lorenzo in your family?" She slathered a generous portion of butter and orange marmalade on the piece of bread.

"Oh no, there was also my grandmother and grandfather on my father's side, and my cousin, Miguel. We are people who live together. Mama came from away. This way of life was strange to her, but I think my parents were happy. We are a country that has seen many sorrows. We have learned to recognize and accept a little sorrow in everyone. Like you, Miss Miranda."

A coldness settled into her chest. She slid her plate away and concentrated on steadying her hands while lifting her cup to her lips. She prided herself in keeping her emotions behind a professional demeanor.

"Do not be concerned. We don't pry."

"Thank you." Carefully placing her cup in the saucer so she would not stain the beautiful linen tablecloth, she took a deep breath. "Which way should I walk this morning to learn about your town and look for a place to live when you go to visit your Lorenzo?"

"If you want to see the ocean, go to the square and then chose one of the streets that wind up and around. Look high for the signs that say *Venda*, to sell, or *Aluguel*, to rent."

It would be a change to be the client instead of the realtor. Miranda pushed away from the table and stacked her dishes and cup, ready to carry them to the sink.

"No, no, you are a guest." Maria reached for the dishes.

"But I asked you to join me, and now you're behind in your duties for today. We're of a similar age, and I understand how it is to have a business with many details to accomplish that the customer cannot see."

Maria nodded. "This is true. I heard the washing machine stop a few minutes ago, so I must hang the sheets and towels on the line."

"Can I help you, please? It will be a new experience for me to stretch and clip sheets to a line where they snap in the wind and dry by the sun."

"You are a strange guest, but come, we will do it together." Maria led the way down stone stairs into a basement with blue and white tiled walls and modern appliances. "My cousin, Miguel, sells appliances, and Lorenzo builds and is a tile layer. They fixed this for me."

"It's beautiful."

"And convenient. Before this, I had a wringer washer, which took a very long time. But when Avó was sick, they did this for me because I was here to care for her."

"That was kind of them."

"Kindness had nothing to do with it. The family is

responsible for those who look after the older generation. We all do our part."

It was rare in Saskatchewan, but Miranda had occasionally sold homes to customers with different generations who shared the same house. Miranda had ached for the support of an extended family, but that wasn't her life.

"I'll empty the machine with the sheets. Come, we'll go out that door. There's a nice breeze today. They should dry quickly."

A stone wall fenced the property. The clothesline stretched between two trees. Miranda recognized the lingering scent on her pillowcases had come from this space in the sun.

Chapter 2

A blue and white tiled stairway leading up to the second floor of a house caught Miranda's eye. She positioned her phone and snapped photos as she thought about the amenities she would prefer in her perhaps forever home or home for a while.

Orange trees in yards were stunning. Back home in Regina, residents planted fast-growing poplar trees in front of a row of fir trees, which would be mature when the poplars had reached their life span. Her mind leapt. Stacy and Nathan were her fir trees. Her parents started the business and expanded it for her, and she, in turn, developed it for her children. She shook her head, no more thoughts of her Canadian life to ruin this beautiful day with the azure blue sky, the white stucco buildings and the red tile roofs.

Miranda stepped onto the corner café's patio and sat on the blue-tiled bench attached to the blue-tiled table. A young woman, dressed in black, appeared from a dark interior and gave her a menu with different flags denoting the various translations of the food items. She ordered black coffee and a glass of brandy as a treat she had read that many locals enjoyed during the day. While she waited, she searched in her guidebook to discover the tiled pavement in the area was called calcada. Then she listened as a couple behind her discussed train and bus schedules to visit Mount Foia, the highest mountain in the Algarve.

When her order arrived, she sipped her coffee and then cradled the snifter in her palm. When the aromas wafted out of the glass, she knew she wasn't sitting in Starbucks drinking a mellow latte in Regina. An older woman, also dressed in black with a scarf covering her head, standing in the dark doorway caught her eye. She stared at Miranda before she hoisted her basket and turned toward the rear of the building. Did she find a woman tourist alone unusual? It was what it was. Miranda was alone.

Miranda savored the amber liquid while watching the traffic flow toward the sea. Some cars jumped the curb and parked with tires on the sidewalk. Pedestrians strolled around bumpers pulling their carts crammed with umbrellas, beach chairs, and towels. Two scooters whizzed by with baskets filled with groceries, and one had a baguette poking out from the saddlebag.

That's what she could use for her Algarve transportation. She had thought about a small car, but the narrow streets were a challenge. A scooter was just the ticket. Or was it the brandy talking? Miranda signaled the proprietor and asked if she spoke English.

"Yes, Senhora."

"Do you know where I can purchase a scooter?"

The woman tilted her head and studied Miranda. "What you asking?"

Miranda didn't know the Portuguese word for scooter and she certainly didn't want to embarrass herself. But if she was going to live here, she should try to improve her phrasebook Portuguese. She pointed to the lovely aqua-colored scooter chained to the palm tree, opened her wallet and pointed first at the Euros and then herself. *"Para mim."*

"Ahh, *o minute, por favor.*" She went to the front of the store and brought back a map of Albufeira. With her red pen, she marked an x. *"Aqui."*

Miranda laid the tourist map flat on the table and studied the streets. The server placed her finger on a spot and pointed to the restaurant and then drew a line on the map. *"Aqui.* Here."

Miranda had long since given up using a paper map. In her early days of real estate, she would leave early and make a few U-turns and stops to ask for directions. When GPS came to her area, she quickly adapted to the technology. One of the first items on her list of purchases would be a local smartphone with a GPS app. If she were planning to stay, she would also enroll in language classes. Although many Portuguese spoke English, she wanted to improve and increase the few phrases she knew. "Aqui. *Obrigada*."

A woman dressed in a business suit approached the scooter. She unlocked the chain, opened a side compartment, lifted out an aqua helmet, dropped in the chain and lock, closed the latch, and within minutes, she was helmeted and riding down the street. Miranda had practical pantsuits for climbing stairs to top floors and descending into basements to show the most basic workings of the furnaces and water heaters. She wore timeless dresses for conferences. But now, Miranda could choose to be as elegant as often as she wished. But she'd carry a wide-brimmed straw hat and large sunglasses in her compartment, for when she strode away from her scooter, she would become a mysterious *turista*.

The sound of shoes clicking toward her across the stone floor pulled Miranda from her daydream. The older woman had returned and now stood staring down at her. She tilted her head and then plucked two oranges, stems and leaves still attached, out of her basket and offered them to Miranda.

Tears clouded Miranda's eyes. Women knew. This woman sensed she was at a crossroads and needed a friend. "*Obrigada*," Miranda said while she cradled the fruit still warm from the sun.

The woman reached over and patted Miranda's cheek. "*Bela*."

Miranda leaned into the woman's palm, rippled with tendons and the lingering citrus aroma. She could have stayed there for a few moments more, but the woman swung her basket up and strode into the restaurant. She had called her beautiful. Miranda stashed the word into a corner of her mind. She folded the map into her purse and slung it across her body. Cradling the oranges in her hand, she continued down the winding black and white paved sidewalks toward the sea.

Tucking her oranges into the pocket of her billowy trousers, she toed off her shoes, removed her socks, and padded down the stairs and onto the beach. A rock, eroded and pocked from the wind and seas, was the perfect place to stop. With her toes in the sand and her eyes closed, the scent of salt and the sound of seabirds engulfed her. A wave lapped cold over her feet. Miranda lifted an orange to her cheek.

As a shadow blocked the warm sun, her body momentarily chilled. A deep voice whispered close to her ear, "Por favor, Senhora."

Her eyes flew open, and she jumped away from the sound. Her shoes slipped from her hand, and she reached to catch them at the same time the man did. They bumped heads, but his hands were quicker and larger and rescued her shoes seconds before the ocean foam of a retreating wave could swallow them whole.

Miranda didn't know whether to rub her head, reach for her shoes, apologize, or sink into the sand in mortification. "I'm sorry," she stammered.

"I must apologize to you. My head is so much bigger and harder. Are you okay? You aren't dizzy. Come, let's sit over here on the rocks." Long, thick fingers curled around her elbow as she allowed him to guide her.

When he let go of her arm, he swiped sand away from the surface of a rock and then motioned her to sit. Her orange. Miranda turned and saw her orange lying in the sand at the base of the rock she had been leaning against. She ran back and scooped it up before the next wave would have taken it out to sea. She tucked it in her pocket along with the other one.

Walking back, she surveyed the man who had scared her, bumped her head, and then shepherded her to safety. Tall, with a large frame and short-cropped, thick hair graying at the temples. He wore a golf shirt, shorts, and sandals. He appeared to be a visitor, too. But why had he spoken to her at all?

"Miranda." She stretched out her hand.

His hands were hard. "Renato." The lines around his brown eyes were crinkled. "Renato Monteiro."

"Was I in danger?"

"Perhaps of falling asleep in the sun, but no. You captivated my imagination, and I wanted to ask your permission to take your photo."

She was still basking in the *bela* compliment and now this. Her heart sped up. This strange city was a balm for a shaken spirit. "Are you a tourist?"

"Almost. I grew up in this city, but I moved away years ago. I'm back for a visit. You?"

"I'm visiting as well." She leaned against the rock and brushed the sand from her foot before tugging on a sock and then slipping into her shoe. She felt him watching and glanced up at him. "Are you a photographer?" She looked around for his camera.

"Amateur." He held up his phone.

She shrugged and reached for her other sock.

"Stop."

She stopped moving at his whispered insistence. "Like this."

"Please."

She watched his feet as he moved closer and changed positions. He seemed to snap many photos.

"Thank you."

"May I see?"

"Of course." His significant presence filled the space on the rock. He opened his photo app, and there was a mysterious woman doing something very ordinary while balanced on a rock on a beach. But he had captured the sun and glistening water perfectly.

"Would you like me to email you a copy?"

Now that was a pickup line she hadn't heard before. "No, thank you."

With both shoes on, Miranda felt the oranges in her pocket. They were her touchstone from a woman who called her bela. "I must be going."

"Thank you. I'll treasure these photos."

"By the way, thank you for asking my permission before you took my photograph."

"You're welcome. I wanted you to know I was capturing your spirit, Miranda."

"Goodbye, Renato." She rolled the r as he had and winked.

Chapter 3

Miranda lifted her head and glanced at the square tower of the old church. Tears filled her eyes. She wiped them away before putting on her sunglasses. It happened like this. Suddenly, she was assailed by the finality of leaving her life's work, her identity for decades. She needed this break more than she had realized.

Lifting her face to the sun, she pushed one hand into her pocket and cupped the oranges. Such a silly thing that comforted her. From the blossom of a tree to a fruit, a new life continuing on its journey. She'd keep them whole for as long as she could.

She pulled her hand from her pocket and squared her shoulders. Enough. Just as the fruit was continuing through life, so would she. Time to locate the scooter business and do something new.

Taking the map from her purse, she placed her finger on the image of the church, drew a line down the streets that branched off and then counted the intersections. She was close.

As she walked the short distance to the scooter shop, she itemized everything she would need to ask. Driver's license, where to take lessons, parking. She would use her organizational skills honed from running her own business to break down the task that could, if she let it, overwhelm her, and have her slinking back to Marie's Casa O Mar.

When she arrived, the absolute most beautiful, mint green scooter with a matching helmet stood with a painted scenery that suggested adventure from the shop window.

And then there was a bright shiny red scooter at an ocean's edge that suggested 'pick me'. What image did she want to portray while riding around the streets? She had always shown her strength. That's what she wanted.

"*Bom tarde*, Senhora." A young man in pressed pants and a polo shirt approached her.

Miranda smiled back and held up her palms. "Do you speak English?"

"A little." He had a lovely smile.

"I am interested in learning about scooters. Can you assist me, *por favor*?"

"Senhora, you have come to the right place."

Miranda showed him the café on her map. "This woman told me to come here."

"Intelligent woman. She is a friend." He winked. "Come inside, and we will speak about what you want and perhaps what you need." With his hand on his chest, he said, "*Chamo me*, Eduardo."

"*Chamo me*, Miranda."

"*Bom*." He stepped aside, and she entered the gleaming showroom.

He guided her to a leather, tub chair beside a low table. "May I bring you coffee, tea, or *água*, ah, water?"

The oranges in her trouser pocket pressed against her thigh. The coolness in the air, the brightness of hope, and the kindness of this stranger put her at ease. "Tea would be lovely, please."

He offered her a selection of teas. She chose one. "Milk and sugar?"

"Yes, please." Miranda breathed deeply and settled back. Miranda, a businesswoman, knew the routine. But now she was a customer, not the salesperson.

Eduardo returned with a tray. He placed a china teacup before her.

"This is a lovely pattern."

"Then, I chose the right cup for you." Eduardo settled into the chair next to her. He sipped from a large cup. "Cappuccino." After another sip, he rotated his chair. "While we have our refreshment, why don't you tell me what you would like."

Miranda turned and surveyed the gleaming scooters. "To be honest, I hadn't considered a scooter until this afternoon at your friend's café." The scent of oranges rose from her tea. "I watched a woman return to one like that." She pointed to the mint green and white scooter. "She was stylish and professional. But when she shook out her hair and donned her helmet, she looked free. Possibly for only a few minutes while she traveled to her next destination, but happy." She paused. "I would like that feeling."

"So, you are not experienced in riding a scooter?"

She lifted her chin. "No, but I ride a bicycle." She, Stacy, and Nathan had included a bicycle tour as part of their last trip to France. Granted, they always had a van with them for emergencies.

"But of course. *Sim*. Would you like gas or electric?"

"Can we discuss the pros and cons of each model, por favor?"

"Bom." Eduardo reached for a remote and an informational video appeared on the screen in front of them. A man spoke succinctly, in English, about the engines while a woman pointed out the features.

Miranda passed her cup to Eduardo when he offered more hot water. She considered the differences. "Because I don't know where I will be living and the availability of an electrical source, I should consider a gas engine."

Eduardo nodded.

"Although I like the idea of the mint green and white body, I might want to explore a more vibrant color. One that drivers and pedestrians will notice. I'll be new to the area and unsure where I am going."

"Sim."

"May I ask if there is a driving school, or perhaps I could hire a teacher?" Her heart raced at the thought of navigating the narrow streets down toward the ocean. She looked forward to adventures in this next stage of life, but was she putting herself in unnecessary danger?

"Miranda, may I ask, how long do you plan to be in our beautiful country?"

"I haven't decided." She twisted the teacup on its saucer. "This is probably a silly idea. I shouldn't take up any more of your time. You have been so kind."

He placed a hand on her arm before she could rise. "I only ask the question because we have an excellent rental program."

"Oh."

"I have a cousin whose English is very good, and she's driven a scooter for years. If you like, I can ask if she has some time to take you to a place in the city that has a big empty space. I will arrange for a scooter to be delivered, and she can teach you. You can see if it is the freedom you are picturing."

She swallowed hard. "Even if I don't purchase?"

He extended both hands toward her. "But of course."

She placed her hands in his and took a deep breath. "Obrigada."

"Where can I reach you after I speak with my cousin?"

"My phone number is Canadian, but I'm staying at Casa O Mar."

"Bom. I will call there."

"And I'll purchase a local phone as soon as possible."

Chapter 4

Renato had hurriedly returned to the city of his youth for his avó's funeral last week. Now he sauntered along streets that hadn't changed in all the years he had been gone. Perhaps the storefront had changed or the owners, but not the foundations, nor the religious plaques adorning the walls next to the doors asking for protection. He wanted his avó to be waiting at her home behind *Igreja de Santana* where the bells tolled, calling the faithful to worship inside the whitewashed walls. But the house was no longer her home but his, bequeathed to him. Hopefully when he opened the door, most of the family who were choosing a few of Avó's things and calling out memories, would be gone. Their whispered questions, would he stay or would he sell, had chased him out hours ago.

He had invited his avó to Canada. She wouldn't come, so he cared for her from afar by sending money every month to supplement her small pension, making sure there was someone who would take up fresh milk and bread and anything else she needed when she could no longer walk to the market every day. But her faith was her solace. Just steps out of her door and down the street to the back door of the church. He knew she lit candles for him, perhaps so that he would find his way home. When things were tough in Canada, he'd known she was in his corner. He was her especial Renato. It was hard to be unique when every other male in the community had the same name.

After his tile apprenticeship, he left for Regina, where

Uncle Tomas taught him a great deal more about tiles until Renato was a master-tile layer just like his uncle.

Now he wandered the streets with his phone and recorded the places he had taken for granted. Had there been women in his circle who he had dismissed when all he thought about was leaving? If only it were as easy today to attract a life partner, as he believed it had been when he was young and naive. There had been special women in his life, in his apartment for months at a time. These women professed their love for him until he couldn't bring himself to talk about their future. But he knew there was still something for him to do before he found the right woman.

He stopped to catch his breath. The streets that climbed from the ocean's edge to the town's center were different from the flat terrain of Apex, Saskatchewan, on the Canadian Prairie. Taking his phone from his pocket he scrolled through the photos he had taken. He stopped and examined the photo of Miranda on the beach. She was beautiful but something about her seemed to pull him toward her.

Ren focused his camera on the worn center of the concrete stairs where thousands perhaps even millions of feet had run, stumbled, strolled, or plodded until they reached the top.

Renato opened the door to his avó's home, and his heart hurt, every corner of the small house held memories of when he last felt unconditionally loved.

He was sure he could hear her heeled shoes clicking on the porcelain tiles. She would always call out to him.

"Ren, Ren."

He turned toward the sound, but it was his grandmother's oldest daughter, "Renato, you should be making this your home, not acting like a tourist in your town."

"You're right, *Tia* Ester." He didn't have the strength to argue with this strong-minded woman who had never left the boundaries of her country. She would not understand that a man could have a home away from here.

"It's time you settled down and had a family." She nudged him with her shoulder. "If my sister, Isabell, were here, we'd find you a woman. Isabell cries on the phone because she missed our mother's funeral. Mama knows."

His right woman was somewhere. But how much longer could he wait, he was almost fifty-five, and he was without a family of his own. He had thought he might have children one day, but it was too late now.

The familiar scents of tomato, oregano, paprika wafted from her like perfume the women he occasionally dated wore. Except Tia didn't dab it behind her ears. Instead, the scent was a lifetime of living with the ingredients. Like his avó. He put his arm around her. "I'll be an old papa to a child, Tia. Right now, I have many decisions to make for my future. I must return to my job at the end of the month. We have many homes to tile before I can leave Canada."

"Mama gave this place to you. It cannot be empty. Her spirit will cry." She lifted her apron and wiped the tears from the corner of her eyes. "You are not the only Portuguese man who can tile in that big country of Canada. There are many of our countrymen who went there to work."

"Like we set the tiles. One row at a time. One problem at a time." He squeezed her shoulder. "Any messages for me?"

"Your cousin phoned."

"Which one?" He chuckled.

"Katia. She said you are to phone Eduardo. She said to tell you that she's too busy, it must be you who helps him." Tia Ester shook her head. "That one. She's always speeding around from place to place on her scooter. She weaves in and out of traffic like a devil."

"Hardly anyone drives scooters in Canada. Everyone is in a car protecting themselves against the cold, and it gets cold." When he walked out of the airport in Regina all those years ago, he was sure he'd landed in the North West Territories by mistake. The cold mist hung in the air like smog. Uncle Tomas slapped him on his shoulders so hard, he almost skidded across the slick road into oncoming traffic with his leather-soled shoes.

The next morning, he had tucked his dress pants and cotton shirt into his suitcase and dressed for his new job. He wondered how he would ever cut and set tiles in the bulky coveralls and the hat with earflaps. It turned out, that he wasn't laying tiles that winter but rather helping build apartment buildings. Until he found a place of his own, he rode on the construction bus around the city. The men on the bus came from many countries, but the language they had in common was building. They soon learned to communicate with hand signals and through the weekly English classes.

Renato had been lucky. He had studied English in school and Albufeira was a British tourist destination, so he practiced often. Some of the men in Regina laughed at his British pronunciation of words.

Tia Ester patted his shoulder and moved toward the kitchen. Renato stood in the foyer and stared at a picture of himself on the table, a photo he had sent to Avó when he moved to Apex. He had been there for two years and felt like a local. He'd even ridden on a snow machine and ice fished. Thank goodness for the ice shack. And in spring and summer, he also trolled on Last Mountain Lake, the longest and deepest lake in the area. He never did see the last mountain on the prairie. That was on his bucket list before he left Canada.

Away from the ocean shore and where the older men sat on the bench outside his avó's window, the white stucco buildings crowded up, and he had a pang for the limitlessness horizons of the prairies.

The familiar lament from the fado singer on the radio sleeked through the house and nudged him away from memories of his new home. Here was where he was. His avó always told him to enjoy where he was, not try to run away to some other place. Tia Ester sang along to the mournful tune about his country's soul. His heart sped up with the traditional longing.

The house phone rang. He absently picked it up. "Hello."

"You've been away too long, Ren," his cousin Katia said in Portuguese.

"Como?" He heard her panting as if she had just run a race.

"Stop kidding around. This call is important."

"Katia, everything is always important to you. Tia said you called."

"Eduardo needs someone to take a customer out to the fairgrounds parking lot and teach her how to ride a scooter. She thinks she wants to purchase one, but good old Eduardo wants to make sure she is safe."

"Eduardo, old? He's younger than both of us."

"But he's an old soul. He's taking fado singing lessons, the mixed-up monkey brain."

"Katia, can't you do this? Tia Ester says you weave in and out of traffic like a demon."

"This is my busy season. Tourists come and they love it here, they want to buy a property."

"Where are you?"

"Running down the street to meet my next buyers."

"Okay, I'll call Eduardo, but you owe me."

"You're not thinking of selling Avó's house, are you?"

"No, not that at all. Good luck." Even if he wanted to, his family would disown him if he sold this magical house. Their avó had been there for every one of them.

"Lunch," Tia Ester called.

He entered the kitchen and found the table laden with salads, chicken, and the ever-present bottles of red and green sauces.

"I hope you haven't lost your taste buds for peri-peri sauce?" Tia Ester said while she placed a plate of batatas fritas on the table. "It's the last of your grandmother's recipe. I found it in the back of the fridge, as fresh as the day she made it."

"You haven't made all of this for me?"

"Of course not. Your uncle will be here and Eduardo. I heard you talking to Katia. I texted her, but she's busy, busy."

As if the bells tolled calling the workers to lunch, Uncle Joseph and Eduardo knocked and stepped into the kitchen. "I smell those chilli peppers from the street." Eduardo pecked Tia on the cheek.

Eduardo put his arms around Renato and whispered, "How are you holding up?"

Ren shrugged. "The mass and the funeral were what our avó would have enjoyed attending."

"She always donated food for funerals in her parish." Eduardo bowed his head for a moment.

They sat, and after everyone had helped themselves, they raised their glass of wine. "*Para a Avó.*"

"Pass the sauce. Ester, did you put any spice on this at all?" Uncle Joseph splashed the peri-peri over his chicken and fries.

"Of course I did. Your mouth is thick from all the years of eating these chilis." She snapped her serviette at him.

Renato's gaze flickered around the table. It had been too long since his last ordinary family meal. Maybe he should send an email to Will Cleaver and tell him he wouldn't return? He bit into a piece of chicken and his eyes watered. His tongue was on fire. "Milk, quick."

The others guffawed in laughter while Tia wandered toward the refrigerator. She carefully poured a tall glass of milk and strolled back toward him. "You have gotten soft. What do they feed you there in your Canada?" She reached for the piece he had taken a bite from and moved it off the table.

"You did that as a joke?"

"Welcome home."

"I may never be able to eat again."

"Drink your milk. You will survive."

He glanced at his uncle and cousin who nudged each other and concentrated on their plates.

"Were you in on this?"

They shook their heads and bit their lips.

"Eat," Tia said.

Renato inhaled deeply. The scent of cayenne pepper and garlic floated off the chicken. He took a tentative bite and savored the crispy outside before he chewed, remembering all of the dinners around this table. Avó in her apron, jumping up and serving each of them whatever they wanted. Could he sell this home full of loving memories to a stranger?

His memories were in his heart and his mind, not in the four walls, or the table and chairs.

Perhaps Katia would help him find a renter while he thought this through. Or he asked, "Is there anyone in the family that would like to live in this house for a few months until I can decide where my future is going to be?"

He was bombarded with Portuguese as they spoke to and over each other. He struggled to keep up. But in the end, they didn't have any suggestions.

Eduardo tipped the last drops of wine from his glass. "Enough about you. The problem you are going to help me with, yes? Katia called you, yes?"

"I was going to call but here you are."

"This lovely woman would like to purchase a scooter. I believe she saw our Katia riding. The way she described the woman on an aqua and white scooter with a helmet to match can only be her. I sold her that scooter after her one hundredth house sale."

Joseph beamed with pride. "A hook from the same tackle box."

Ester barked, "What are you talking about? You sell fish."

"True, but don't I sell enough to give you everything you need?"

"Sim. Always." She touched Joseph's shoulder. "But poor Katia, she doesn't have time for a man or a family, she only has time to dream big dreams. As if it isn't enough to be close to family." She put her hand on Renato's shoulder.

"Sim, Tia. *A familia.*"

Eduardo smiled at Renato. "You will help your family, right?"

"Katia said something about going somewhere." He wasn't going to make it easy for his cousin who had been part of the hot sauce trick.

"The fairgrounds is a good open place to try out scooters. Tomorrow isn't the market day, so it's empty." Eduardo placed his hands, palms up on the table and looked directly into Renato's eyes. "You just drive a scooter to the parking lot with a spare helmet and when she arrives, you show her how to start, balance and be safe. And don't damage my scooter."

"Is it going to be one of those feminine colors I'll have to drive all over town?"

Eduardo coughed into his palm. "Pink." He laughed at Ren's curled lip. "You always tell me that you are confident in your masculinity."

"I'm confident, but that's not the issue. It's those drivers on the road that may not respect me." He motioned to his size. "I wouldn't want to get sideswiped or have to ditch your possible sale."

"No, really, it will be okay. I'll take my chances."

"Does this woman look as if she will be capable of purchasing or is she just looking for an adventure?" Ren hoped Eduardo would reconsider, he hadn't driven in a long time. "Those rental places often just give the tourists a few minutes of instruction and then send them on their way."

"She's older, like you," Eduardo said. "And unfortunately she hasn't learned much Portuguese, yet, but I think this one will. Sancha sent her to me."

Ren's heart paused for a minute, thinking about Miranda and her attachment to the fruit. An older woman, obviously a tourist with little Portuguese. Could it be? "Did she have an orange or two?"

"I didn't notice. This lady was comfortable asking questions. She's staying at Maria's Casa O Mar. She must be looking for someplace longer-term because she's going to buy a local phone."

It couldn't be. "What time do you want all this to happen tomorrow?"

"One o'clock."

"Tell her I'll be on the pink scooter." Ren gave an exaggerated shudder. "I'll come to the shop an hour before that, to give myself time to remember how to drive those things. It's been a few years."

"Then I'll have to give you a lesson. The technology has come a long way since you were a kid."

"They're not popular in Canada, or at least the part I'm in. Too cold. Too far between places. Too many bugs between your teeth when you drive." He smiled wide, showing off his bright teeth against his olive skin.

Chapter 5

Miranda rested on the window seat in her room and intermittently scanned the streets below while reading about the area, customs, and food. Her fingers itched for a keyboard, but she had promised herself she would not open her laptop for every little thing, and she had added a few gigabytes on her new phone plan. Her goal was to slow down life and how else but to page through books with a highlighter and sticky tabs, the small things she packed into her case.

Glancing at her watch, she calculated the time back home. She wanted to reach out to Nathan and Stacy. She loved them with all her heart and left so that they could soar, find their heights in the business. Her time was here, and she was responsible for herself, but one text would show she was thinking about them.

The discarded book slipped off her lap when she opened the app and decided the best message would be her number for the new local phone as well as a photo she'd taken that day. She wouldn't tell them about her adventure tomorrow until she decided if she was ready for freedom on the road.

She chose a typical tourist photo she'd taken from a lookout. It showed the beach, with striped umbrellas and people, the white hotels and red rooftop houses stepping up the side of the town to meet the perfectly blue sky. She included her new number and hugs and kisses emoticons.

Stacy and Nathan would eventually be concerned if she wasn't in contact, but she had told them she needed a rest from everything. She wanted to choose what was best for her and the business. Stacy and Nathan assured her that they were ready to go forward with support from Miranda. Subtle guidance was a new concept for Miranda.

Miranda had always been in charge, interested in quality rather than quantity. If something was slapped dashed together but looked pretty, she wasn't afraid to poke at corners and inside cupboards and at support beams to learn the truth.

Was she doing that right now? Was she attempting to peel back the corners, investigate the cupboards, and learn about her support beams? She'd worked for more than thirty-five plus years, nose to the grindstone. But it wasn't a chore. She loved helping people find their houses, which became homes. She had built up her business with hard work and joy, and had repeat customers and even her customers' children and sometimes grandkids. These referrals had made her the happiest.

When Stacy and Nathan were young, they went with her to view houses for clients who had children. They noticed things at their eye level. When the clients with children went through a home, they too found the positives that Stacy and Nathan loved, whether it was a cubby hole or the sink at a specific height or a room with the right dimensions for child play while remaining connected with their parents.

As they grew older, she took them for the teenagers' opinions about privacy issues.

She was as honest with her children as a parent could be, so why didn't she want to share her insecurity about who she might be without her work? She glanced over at the oranges on the bedside table, a lovely reminder of her afternoon. Time enough to dwell on her insecurities later. She was in a beautiful country with an adventure on the way tomorrow. Eduardo had left a message with Maria that a driver would pick her up, and she would meet his cousin at the fairground empty parking lot.

She paged through the scooter brochure for the available colors and decided that red was it. At home, she would have chosen conservatively, but where no one knew her, she'd be a red woman.

Now to decide what to have for dinner. With the sea in view, fresh fish seemed appropriate. It was early by local standards, but she was hungry and from the sound drifting up through her open window, there were many people out and about. She would walk until she discovered an outdoor café where she could view the beach and the ocean waves.

She remembered seeing blankets on the backs of most chairs at the outdoor cafes when she wandered the narrow streets that afternoon but added a sweater and tied a shawl around her waist just in case. The tourist books warned that the temperature cooled drastically at sunset. Before she closed the door, she stepped back into the room and lifted her oranges off the table and tucked them into her pocket. She tapped the fastener on her purse. It was secure.

Listening for a minute in the front hallway, she couldn't hear Maria and, as instructed, signed out of her room. She doubted the wisdom of this practice, but when in Rome. Her key was safely inside her purse.

The narrow streets held the warmth from the daytime sun, but there was a nip in the air. She buttoned her sweater to her neck, thankful she had remembered her shawl. As she got closer to the fisherman's beach, the wind picked up. She may have to abandon her plans to dine outdoors.

Couples holding hands or stopping to admire a store window seemed to be everywhere. With her head held high, she walked determinedly past. Their twoness was like visiting an art gallery. She could appreciate the sentiment, but it didn't mean that she would like to own the piece and have it in her living room to gaze at every day. She chuckled to herself with this analogy. She hadn't complicated her wish for children with a relationship. Going solo had always been her plan. When Miranda had an idea, she worked methodically toward obtaining it. She'd scoured the profiles of the sperm donors and purchased semen. With the help of a family planning clinic, Stacy arrived, and eighteen months later, Nathan was born from the same donor. They became the family she'd intended with the help of daycare providers who were open for professionals working odd hours. As she wandered past cafes, she slowed her pace and accepted a menu from a young woman standing in front of a restaurant. A tantalizing aroma of onions, garlic, tomatoes, and peppers floated from a copper pot when the server lifted the lid on a pot simmering just inside the restaurant with a flourish. The server explained that it was a traditional seafood stew, Cataplana. She couldn't resist a meal that teamed with clams, mussels, and prawns covered by the earthy aromatic coriander spice.

The restaurant had a row of tables next to the windows. Miranda indicated she would enjoy an outdoor seat.

The server brought a basket of bread and a tray with three small bowls. In understandable English, the server explained that one bowl held tuna paste, another marinated feta cheese and the third, olives. *Coverts*, which Miranda translated in her head to starters.

"Obrigada." She popped a salty, oily olive into her mouth. She bit down on the meaty texture and realized that she was hungry. For the past months, she had only eaten to keep up her strength while they transferred the business, but today she was famished.

She was counting the swells crashing against the giant rock formation. When she sensed a person approach her. She glanced down, hoping it was the server's black trousers, dreading if it was the satin striped trouser of the singer who was wandering through the cafe. She was somewhat relieved to see thick, hairy legs standing beside her table.

"Miranda, hello."

Her eyes traveled the length of his never-ending legs, over his broad chest and thick neck, to his round face, his full lips and finally his brown eyes. "*Ohlá.*"

"*Como está?*" His lips twitched.

She rubbed her palm across her belly. "Hungry." The coverts were almost gone. "Hungrier than I realized. I'm waiting for my Cataplana. Are you out for dinner?"

"I am out looking for somewhere to eat, yes."

"Would you like to join me?" Her hand flew to her mouth. She didn't usually invite strangers to join her.

"Yes, thank you." He drew a chair from the other end of the table. With her ocean view blocked, she observed the man in front of her while he signaled the server and indicated he'd have the main course, too. "Would you mind if I ordered some wine?"

"Please, and I'll join you for a glass. I wasn't sure which type would complement my dinner."

After studying the wine list and a rapid conversation with the server, he ordered a carafe of the house white with two glasses. "Their white wine is made from grapes from a good vineyard. I hope you'll enjoy it."

When the server returned, Renato indicated that Miranda should sample the wine. She brought the glass to her nose and inhaled the sweet, fruity tang. "Very nice. Obrigada." After a sip, she said, "It's a light, almost champagne wine."

The server poured Renato's glass and then left the table to attend to other customers just arriving.

He lifted his glass toward her. "*Saude,*" he said.

"What does that mean?"

"To good health."

She lifted her glass. "And long life."

The server arrived with the most aromatic dish she had ever inhaled. "Any suggestions on how to begin to eat this picturesque dish?"

"The Portuguese are proud of their cuisine, but they prefer you to eat with gusto and savor the attention the chefs gave to the meal they have served you." He plucked bread from the basket, dipped it into the sauce, and brought it to his mouth.

Miranda was mesmerized by the skill with which he slipped the bread, dripping with sauce, into his mouth without losing a drop onto his dark blue golf shirt.

"Your turn," he said.

She followed his example but tore only a small corner of the bread and dipped it into the sauce. Her tongue and mouth savored the subtle lobster flavor. She felt like the dog in the cartoon that swooned and floated above his dish. It had been a long time since she tasted such a meal.

In between morsels of shellfish and white fish, Renato recommended things she might do while visiting the area. He suggested a walking tour through a reputable group, and she wrote it in her notepad. She was surprisingly disappointed that he didn't recommend himself as a tour guide.

More and more customers arrived at the restaurant as dusk gave way to darkness.

"I see the Portuguese, like other Europeans, eat late," she said.

"Yes, many of them wait until after their shops close for the day. They eat a later lunch when their shops are closed in the afternoon." He sipped his wine.

Miranda couldn't stop watching his lips. They seemed soft and kissable. She shook her head. It must be the time change or the weather or the wine. Or the fact that she was in the last stage of her life to experience things that she had missed. She didn't even know if he was married. He didn't wear a wedding band, but nowadays, that didn't mean that he didn't have a partner waiting somewhere, here or wherever he was visiting from. Right now, she didn't need to know his past, but he was certainly old enough to have children. She may as well get right to the point. "Do you have children?"

He shook his head. "No, but I'm a professional uncle." His eyes glinted in the candlelight. "I'm that cool guy who is away and sends money and brings the things they dream about."

"You're the guy kids love, but the parents wonder about."

"Yes, that describes me pretty well. I'll be the man in their lives who helps them come to Canada if they wish to leave home. But so far, none of them have taken me up on it. You?"

She coughed into her serviette. Renato was from Canada. She wouldn't be asking where in Canada. Nor, what do you do? She didn't want any complications. She just wanted to enjoy this meal. Reaching for her water, she drank before she spoke. "Two. Stacy and Nathan. They're my business partners."

"Is your husband coming to join you?"

Miranda could make up some tale, but she wasn't going to play games. "I'm a single parent, by choice."

"Would you mind spending time together while you're here?" Renato asked.

"I don't want to take up a lot of your time. You must have friends and family here." Miranda raised her hand. "I take that back. I'd love to spend time with you when you're free."

Renato signaled for the check by motioning to write on his palm.

She reached for her purse. "If we are going to spend time together, I plan to pay my way."

"My countrymen would not understand, but I do."

"Thank you. I'm glad you joined me for dinner."

"Perhaps one day, we could go to Loulé, another city, not too far from here."

"I'm tied up tomorrow. But any other day, I'd love to." She covered her mouth with her palm. "I'm still adjusting to the time change."

He stood and offered his arm. "May I walk you back to your hotel?"

She had to ask. "Before you do, do you have a partner?"

"No. I'm not in a relationship. You?"

"No. I'm not committed to anyone."

"Then let's walk." He motioned for her to proceed him out of the restaurant and onto the street.

Miranda drew her pashmina around her shoulders. They walked side by side except when they met other pedestrians, and then Renato dropped back and followed her. They greeted others with smiles, and at times, Renato spoke Portuguese to those he knew. When they reached Maria's, she wished they could have spent more time together. But they would soon.

"Here I am."

They stopped and Renato turned to face her, his brow furrowed. "You may think this is a strange question, but are you going to try out a scooter tomorrow, arranged by Eduardo?"

"Yes. He's sending a car at one o'clock."

"I believe that I will be your instructor."

It was her turn to furrow her brow. "You?"

"Eduardo's my cousin. He tried to arrange for our other cousin, Katia, however, she's busy. And because we are cousins, he asked me. Do you mind?"

The way the butterflies in her tummy woke up in a swarm of excitement, she had to tell him the truth.

"I like the idea a great deal. Thank you."

"Until tomorrow then. I'll bring the scooter to the fairgrounds, and we'll determine if you are adept at riding safely." He lifted his hand, "*Boa noite* goodnight."

"Boa noite."

"Wait." He turned back toward her. "Did you ask for a pink scooter?"

"No, red."

He shook his head, "Eduardo." Then he offered his hand. "For you, Miranda, I would have ridden a pink scooter through the town of my youth, where most of my classmates still live. Within minutes it would be on Facebook, Instagram, and Snapchat."

She laughed. "You forgot the very short hashtag story on Twitter."

Chapter 6

Renato took his time returning home. He strolled through tiny streets where your arms touched walls on either side, the roads the tourists would never find or would think were too spooky to go down. Strangers who didn't grow up racing through the streets playing hide and seek, or Ninja Turtles, wouldn't know where the narrow lanes ended. He reached and plucked an olive from an overhanging branch and rolled it between his thumb and forefinger, testing the texture for ripeness.

Glancing up, he smiled at the filigree chimney tops. He wondered if he should carve a chimney top to announce his riches for the available women to see, as was the long-ago custom in Albufeira. He could afford to cut down a tree, and he had a good job and savings to support a wife and family. If he were searching for that life, it would be a helpful advertisement.

Some men were just born to be single. He had all the love and support he needed from his large extended family. But if he were honest with himself, he felt alone on certain holidays in Canada. Not lonely, never lonely, but alone. He participated in friends' family dinners, but it was different. If he wasn't at his aunt and uncle's, he didn't hear the language of his youth or eat his family's traditional dishes. Once the celebratory day was over and he was back at work, he was fine.

However, when he was in a mall or happened down a street when someone spoke Portuguese, he smiled to himself. With new industry growth, many of his countrymen were coming to Regina and the surrounding area to work. He spoke his language more frequently, usually to explain a technical term or perhaps a particular food item and, most of all, the weather and clothing or housing requirements to make it through the harsh climate. And he found himself explaining the difference in women's reactions to certain advances. Some newly arrived workers could get into trouble quickly and easily without malicious intentions. He was glad Eduardo asked him to show Miranda how to ride a scooter, rather than some of the other cousins whose charm could offend a tourist without meaning to.

But why was he thinking about Saskatchewan when he had a day to look forward to with a beautiful woman? And for planning payback for Eduardo for his little pink joke. Ren climbed the stairs to the front door and clicked the lock. He longed to hear his avó's chair rocking on the tiled floor, waiting for his return.

Digging around in the front closet, he found his old helmet and riding gloves. He would wear his jeans, a long-sleeved T-shirt, and runners tomorrow. Even though the temperature would be quite warm at noon, he didn't want to chance road rash. He wondered why Miranda wanted to ride a scooter. He didn't want to know where she was from, yet. He wasn't ready for comparing geographical history. They shared the most relevant information, both unattached and not hurting anyone by spending time together.

~ ~ ~

At noon the following day, Ren walked down the paved streets with his helmet swinging at his side. He felt like his thirteen, fourteen, fifteen, and even sixteen-year-old self. Cool, grownup. He chuckled to himself. So mature! Like those questions that float around now and again, what would you tell your younger self? He wouldn't change anything. That younger self had been all swagger and confidence.

Now, however, his pants were snug around his hips instead of showing off the brand of boxers he wore.

"Just on time, Ren," Eduardo called from the doorway. "Come around the back. The pink lady is all shined up just for you."

Ren coughed into his hand, hiding his smile. "And really, pink? But for you . . ." Ren said as he reached for the scooter. "What kind of woman would want to ride a pink scooter, except a girl too young to ride?"

"No, she's sophisticated." Eduardo lifted a pink jacket off a hanger. "Take this with you. It's a new product. It looks like mesh, but it will protect her during any fall."

Ren studied the pink scooter in front of him. "I haven't ridden in a long time, but it's all coming back to me, especially weaving in and out of traffic, and the car drivers playing chicken with scooter riders. I don't know, Eduardo, I have to go back to work. I've made commitments. I need all four of my limbs." He held up his hands. "And all of my fingers. Not to mention my dignity. And, really, pink?" He grimaced.

"Got you." Eduardo slapped Ren on his back. "That's the one over there." He pointed toward a cherry red scooter. "It's an automatic and has a little more power than the last bike you rode. It should be able to pull you out of any difficulties. There's a jacket and helmet in the storage compartment."

"Now I want to meet the woman whose considering this fine ride," Ren said, strapping on his helmet.

"Remember, she thinks Katia's coming to show her how to ride. Don't scare her with your charm."

"How will I know her?"

"Georgeo will be bringing her in the car. He'll introduce you. If you miss each other, look for a classy woman who looks as if she is waiting for someone."

"Open those garage doors, and I'll be on the open road," Ren pushed the bike out of the shop and, once outside, he turned the ignition and tested the brakes. He wasn't kidding. He needed to get back to Canada in one piece.

He drove onto the quiet street, keeping to the speed limit, remembered how rough the ride could be on a scooter. He had mapped out the route in his head so that he wouldn't have to go on any bypasses, but he hadn't counted on construction. He followed the detour signs, and soon found himself zipping along with traffic at highway speeds.

Fear of being killed by heavier and faster vehicles, he turned onto the side streets as soon as possible and was happy to see the fairgrounds sign come into view. He slowed and wiped the sweat from his upper lip. He'd become soft. Maybe he should move back to his home country where people took chances.

The fairgrounds sign rotated on the top of a giant pole. He was almost there. He had to gather his wits. He didn't want Miranda to think he was a chicken. He needed to be the best instructor she could have.

When he drove through the gates, he spied Miranda sitting on a bench under a lone tree cradling an orange again. Was he late? Where was Georgeo? And what was with the orange? Perhaps she had diabetes and had to carry snacks. But she held it as if it were a precious object rather than something that could be purchased in a stall on most roads or even plucked from an overhanging branch.

Dodging the potholes and cracks, more than he remembered there being, he drove up to the bench. As he eased the throttle, the motor hummed and Miranda lifted her head. With the scooter stabilized on its stand, he removed his helmet and slid onto the bench beside her. "A quarter for your thoughts."

"The price has gone up?"

"We did away with the penny in Canada, and you appear to be deep in thought."

She cupped her orange. "I miss me."

That was deep. "Want to tell me one of the things you miss?"

"I miss checking my twitter account." She half-smiled.

"Then why don't you #scooterride with #mysteriousguy?"

"That could work." She looked up at him. "But I promised myself this time away from my previous life, and that includes social media accounts."

His heart pounded. He had changes to think about, himself. "And is one of your other thoughts whether or not to ride this beauty?" He placed his hand on the cherry-red fender. "Or"—he dug into his pocket—"wait, all I have is a euro."

She stood and ran her hand over the seat. "This scooter is exactly what I asked for. Eduardo got it right." Tipping her head toward his hand, she said, "Keep your euro for now."

"Ok, if you're sure." He dropped the coin back into his pocket.

She nodded.

"He sent you some gear." He opened the side compartment and brought out a red jacket, gloves, and helmet.

"But I thought I could ride with only a helmet. The woman I saw the other day had on a lovely business suit and seemed to add only a matching helmet."

"Of course you can dress as you wish, but while you're practicing, we strongly suggest the gear. If you should happen to slide to the pavement or a bug hits your hand while you are driving, it hurts."

"I guess that makes sense." She slipped on the jacket and dropped her orange in her slacks pocket. "What else do I need to know?"

"We'll go over the basics. The scooter is a twist and go technology."

"Yes, Eduardo and the infomercial went over that."

"Come closer. I'll show you the handlebars and the speedometer and the kill switch."

She slipped her leg over the seat.

"With this bike, the handlebars must be unlocked like this. If you forget, you'll be trying to ride, and the steering won't go in the direction you need."

"Makes sense."

"Then you turn on the ignition. These are your brakes. You've probably ridden a bicycle, so you know all about them and how to use them."

"I have and do."

"This seat makes it easy, like sitting on your easy chair in your living room, but with a lot more life going on around you. These huge wings protect your feet while they are positioned on this platform unless you have one foot on the pavement providing stability for you and your scooter."

He handed Miranda the gloves and finally the helmet.

"Now it's time to move off the stand. When you adjust the mirrors to your height, you can see behind you." Had he told her everything necessary? He wanted her to be safe. "I know you're anxious to get started, however, two more tips. One. Always scan the road for obstacles and hazards. Two. Watch up the road toward where you're going." He took a deep breath. He could tell she was anxious to try it out. He had to let her go on her own. "Are you ready?"

Miranda turned the key in the ignition, and the motor purred to life.

"Keep one foot on the ground until you get going."

She twisted the accelerator, and the scooter jumped. His heart leapt into his throat. He reached for the scooter. He'd forgotten to explain the kill switch. "Miranda, this is the kill switch. If you ever feel as if you are going to lose control, hit it like this." Why was he so nervous? She was a woman who doubtless had many experiences.

She gingerly twisted the accelerator this time and the scooter inched forward. She lifted her foot onto the platform and drove the length of the parking lot, made a full, wide turn and came back to him. Ren didn't realize he had been breathing quick, shallow breaths until he gulped a big breath of relief.

Her eyes sparkled and her smile was dazzling. "I love this. I'm going again. Relax on the bench. I'm fine." She looked exhilarated.

There went his hope that she would decide on a vehicle with a steel frame for protection. And he knew he'd have to join her if he wanted to be with her. The rider logic motto he had on his wall when he was a teenager came back: *It's not what you're riding but where you're going.*

The scooter drew up beside him. "I can't thank you enough." Miranda glanced at her watch, her elation turning to disappointment. "The car should be here soon to take me back to the shop."

"I noticed Georgeo wasn't here when I came. Eduardo said he'd introduce us."

"His wife called. A baby was crying in the background. I said I'd be fine." She continued to straddle the scooter.

He'd talk to Eduardo about leaving a woman stranded. What would have happened if he had been delayed for any number of reasons? "Why don't I call Eduardo and cancel the car. We can go for a ride. I'll drive, and you ride."

"Really? In traffic?"

"Yes." He searched her face for signs of fear of him as a stranger, but only saw excitement shining from her blue eyes. "You do want to drive around the city and not just in an empty parking lot?"

"Yes, of course." She turned to look at what now appeared to be a limited piece of white leather. "But two of us on this?"

He held up his phone. "Eduardo's asking if you're sure. He wants to speak with you."

Ren listened to her side of the conversation. "Yes, he has. No, he hasn't. Quite sure." She did what everyone seems to do while on the phone, nodded in affirmation and shook her head to the negative. "Yes, that would be lovely. Same time tomorrow."

"What have you agreed to?" he asked.

"Your cousin Katia's going to meet me tomorrow. He's hoping you will drive the scooter to meet us. But I can understand if you have plans."

"Why Katia?"

"He said women drive differently than men, and she's used to driving here."

"Trust Eduardo to put his water in my gas," Ren muttered.

"Pardon."

"Nothing important." He tugged the strap on his helmet and zipped his jacket. "Are you ready?"

She scooted until her back was straight against the bar. If she went any further, she'd be riding on the fender. "Are you sure you're okay with this?"

"Yes, please. But I don't want to be in your way." She squirmed. "What can I do to help? Do I lean into the corners with you?"

"Place your feet on the guest pedals, and you can hold onto the handles on the side. Or if you wish, you can hold onto me." She grasped the handles and sat perfectly straight. He cheated and slid closer between her legs. There were more ways to eat a pizza than with a knife and fork.

"Signal with your flat palm on my back for stop and squeeze your thighs if you want me to slow down." He was glad she was behind him and couldn't see his lips because he felt them twitch into a smile.

Ren drove toward the entrance, stopped, and then sped up into the flow of traffic. When necessary, he lane-split and slipped between the rows of cars and past a stalled vehicle that snarled the way home for many commuters.

By the way the bike handled, he knew when she relaxed

and when she tensed and her hand either gripped his waist or lightly held on. He still had it, whatever *it* was. He relished the feel of the wind on his face and the tentative pressure of her inner thighs against his. Perhaps he would enjoy reliving his youth again. He'd convince Eduardo to lend him a scooter. He began planning excursions in his mind.

Perhaps he'd call Katia later and convince her to give tomorrow a miss.

Chapter 7

Miranda had been sitting on the bench, staring at her orange as if it would reveal her future. Of course, it couldn't. It was a citrus fruit. She'd probably have to eat them soon. Her uncertain future was like her oranges'. This indecision wasn't like her previous self, she missed that woman. But she didn't miss the uncertainty if a buyer's finances were all in order so they could afford the house they wanted. And she didn't miss trudging through the snow to shovel walks and turn on lights to create a welcoming home.

Before her mind could conjure more heavy thoughts, the air changed and the sound of a motor purred next to her. Renato. Of course. She'd been waiting for him. Waiting to attempt something daring, riding on two wheels with a motor. It wasn't a Harley. It was a scooter. A challenge for her to overcome and leave the redundancy she felt behind. Delivered by a lovely man.

She had remembered how to balance, and there wasn't any shifting but merely a twist and go. She squeezed the brakes in the wrong order once and remembered how easily she could go ass over teakettle, as her mom used to say. It was so much fun that she circled the parking lot more times than she should have. She was thrilled when Renato had suggested they go for a drive.

Now she was seated behind Renato, who wove in and out of traffic with practiced skill. When a car cut them off, Renato swerved, and Miranda gripped his jacket. After that, she kept her hands firmly around his waist. She enjoyed his thighs between her legs. She wondered how long he was staying before returning to Canada. She still hadn't told him that she too lived in Canada, and a little voice whispered, *No games.*

Before she could dwell on that, she recognized the square near Eduardo's shop. The ride, as well as someone caring for her, was over. She tried to recall when another adult had taken responsibility for her. Not since she was a preteen.

Renato stabilized the scooter with both feet. She analyzed how to dismount gracefully. She put one foot on the ground and slid to a standing position while the other leg followed her across the seat.

Eduardo steadied her, a hopeful look on his face. Was she going to make his day and give him a sale?

"Miss Miranda, how was your lesson?"

"Invigorating, a little frightening, and a big feeling of freedom," she said. She felt Renato standing behind her, and Eduardo's eyes flicked between them. She felt as if Renato had her back. She smiled to herself, then cleared her throat. "I'm still unsure if this is what I want. It's the reality of it, rather than the romantic idea to be like the beautiful, self-assured woman I saw yesterday."

Renato stepped forward. "Katia, our cousin. You must understand that she has been riding a scooter since she was a child, and she knows every nook and cranny of this town." He moved closer to her. "I'm sorry if I frightened you."

"I had forgotten about the motor scooters I've seen on vacations when they sneak up between cars and around bus bumpers." She was reluctant to remove the jacket she'd had on for protection. It felt like a shield between her and the intimate contact she'd just shared with Renato.

Eduardo took the decision out of her hands as he lifted the jacket from her shoulders. "I can understand your concerns. Ren, why don't you borrow a bigger motorcycle tomorrow and take Miranda to the next town, show her all the back roads she can discover while on one of these." He patted the fender. "I'll cancel Katia until you tell me if you want to try again."

"Obrigada, Eduardo." Miranda's shoulders loosened. Then she rolled around the shorten form of Renato. Ren.

"My pleasure."

Two women in their twenties walked toward Eduardo. "We're back. We're going to take the yellow and the pink scooter."

"Please forgive me." He bowed toward Miranda. "Right this way, I have the papers ready for you."

Renato rolled his eyes. "Always a salesman. When we were kids, he'd go up and down the streets before the sanitation workers came. If there was something worth selling, he always picked it up and then in a week, he'd have a sale. Soon, all of the neighbors were coming to his front yard and buying things their neighbors tossed."

"I understand. I've been in sales all of my life. I enjoy finding something a customer would like." She sighed. "He recognized my reluctance. I'm not offended."

"Would you like to go for a ride tomorrow? I promise not to lane-split in traffic unless absolutely necessary while we are in the city."

"I felt safe with you." She pushed her hand into the pocket of her slacks and touched the dimpled orange peel. "I just don't think I want to be the driver in those circumstances. And yes, I'd enjoy a ride into the country."

He checked his watch. "Are you walking back to Casa O Mar?"

"Yes, and then I must find another place to stay. I know there are many hotels, but I'd rather be somewhere with an atmosphere."

"May I ask, why?"

"When I booked with Maria, she told me that I could only stay for a few days. I like the feeling of home she provides her guests, and I would like to find something similar for the remainder of my stay."

"Mind if I walk with you?"

Miranda smiled. She wanted him to walk with her back to Casa O Mar. It was a pleasure speaking to someone who knew the area and spoke English so well. She didn't have to struggle to understand what said. And right now she could do with a little help from a friend. He had been there to bolster her when she felt unsettled before the scooter lesson. She could trust him that he was looking after her rather than helping his cousin make a sale. "I'm used to making my own decisions, but I'm hesitating about purchasing a scooter."

"They are slightly more complicated than their colored fenders, but with practice, I'm sure you could master it."

"My gut is telling me to consider this purchase." She felt the weight of unknowing across her shoulders.

"Let's take that gut of yours to a coffee shop."

"Renato."

"Ren, to my friends."

"Thank you." She rested her hand on his arm. "Ren, I don't think I'm hungry. I'm indecisive. I'm never indecisive."

"Albufeira has that effect on people. It says, *slow down*. Come on."

He turned them into the first café they came to and led her to a table with deep-cushioned chairs. She sank gratefully into its enveloping softness. She ordered a café latte while he ordered the famed espresso.

The sound of the sea, the smell of fish, and the calls of children drew their attention toward the expanse of sand, occasionally dotted with towels and blankets.

"It isn't always like this," Ren said. "In the summer, there is hardly space to move between towels, umbrellas, and sandcastles."

Miranda plucked a napkin from the holder and folded it over and over again. "I suppose the traffic is heavier as well."

"Of course. And we Portuguese curse the foreign drivers. We yell at them when they go round and round in the traffic circles. We shake our fists when they stop for pedestrians."

"You're not helping me make a decision."

"Sorry. But must you make it today? I thought you needed to find a place to stay first."

"A permanent place for a while, yes. Where I can cook meals, invite friends over."

He tapped his chest. "Me?"

Miranda tipped her head and examined him. Was he her friend? She placed her hand over his. "Yes." He seemed to be nudging her to accepting where she was now, who she was now.

"Could it possibly be because I'm so very handsome?"

"Perhaps." Butterflies danced on the coffee in her tummy.

"Could it be because I'm going to take you on a trip around the country tomorrow?"

"Perhaps." She couldn't help but smile.

"Or could it be because I speak English, and you can understand me?"

She laughed. "That's it. You guessed."

The people around them were a blur of colors and accents through her peripheral vision because she focused on Ren. Yes, Ren to his friends and now her as well. She marveled at the depth of his brown eyes, the lines fanning out from the corners, a testament that he enjoyed life's moments and showed it. The lines around his mouth proof he used his mega smile often. Miranda tipped the last drops out of her cup.

"Ready?"

Although she nodded and accepted his hand, she reminded herself that this was a vacation friendship.

After handing cash to the server and waving away change, Ren escorted her back onto the street. As they walked, he told her the histories behind the tiles on the side of houses, on stairways, and in gardens. All too soon, they were at the corner of the Casa under an almond tree.

"One day, I will tell you the story of the almond trees in this area, but for now, I would like to kiss you."

It had been a long time since she had been held and kissed. If not now, when?

She searched his eyes. Just the fact he had asked should have been enough to know he would not hurt her or push past her boundaries. His eyes reflected his sincerity and gentleness. The fluttering was back in her belly. Hopefulness. She leaned toward him.

He opened his arms, and she stepped into them. He closed his arms loosely around her back. This was an open and two-way body dialogue. She leaned forward, keeping inches between them. He brought one hand up behind her head. Their lips touched. His lips were soft and moist and tasted like coffee. She languished in his arms. Participated in the positioning for a better fit. When the moment of contact had passed, they leaned their foreheads against each other.

He reached for both her hands. "Tomorrow at ten?"

"Sim." She squeezed his hands. "Obrigada."

"*Seja bem-vindo*-you're welcome." His lips rose slightly at the corners, and their hands slid apart. "*Amanhã.*"

She watched him saunter down the street. Right now, decisions about scooters and life options didn't matter. She basked in the loving touch and emotional closeness she had just shared with Ren.

The scent of paprika and tomatoes filled the air, and a woman's soulful song floated from the kitchen. Miranda stood in the foyer of the guest house and savored the feeling of home. She tried to recall when she last felt this, and the memory was deep. Analyn, a woman her parents had hired to cook and clean for the summer when Miranda was nine. Her last summer as a little girl.

During that year, Miranda learned how to make simple meals and bake cookies. And she read to Analyn, who immigrated from the Philippines. She loved Analyn like the grandmothers she'd read about in her books. She hadn't thought of Analyn for many years. She supposed she'd be almost a hundred years old now.

The soulful melancholy of Maria's unmistakable voice wrapped its melody around Miranda and brought her back to the present. And the scooter decision. Who was she kidding? She was a mother. She wanted to be with her children and, eventually, hopefully, grandchildren. She couldn't invest in a freedom machine. She wanted the protection from a cage of steel and fibreglass. She'd rent a car and ask Ren to drive it and explain the rules of the Portuguese roads. Perhaps it could have a sunroof so she could feel the warmth of the sun while she explored the country.

The music stopped, and Maria called out, "Miss Miranda, is that you?"

"Yes, I'm back all in one piece." Miranda stood in the kitchen doorway.

Maria placed a hand on her hip and waved her wooden spoon at Miranda.

"Was that Renato Monteiro with you? Kissing you?"

"Yes," she said quietly, winding her arms around herself. Wait a minute. She didn't need to be embarrassed. He wasn't married and neither was she. She straightened. "Yes."

Maria fanned herself with her spoon and then turned and stirred the pot on the stove. "He's a good man. He came home to visit his grandmother every year. He wanted her to go to Canada to visit him, but she couldn't."

"He said he's home for a while." Miranda stepped further into the kitchen and pulled out a chair. She was curious.

"When he came home to bury his grandmother, he discovered he had inherited her home. The safest home he knew growing up." Maria wiped her hands on her apron.

Miranda covered her quick intake of breath with her fingers. Ren hadn't said anything about his grandmother. Suddenly, she understood why he wanted to be with a stranger. He didn't have to discuss his innermost thoughts.

"I've said too much." Maria pressed her lips together.

Miranda shook her head. "No. Thank you. He's going to take me to visit the countryside tomorrow." Miranda swallowed. "I'm grateful."

"You're not going on one of Eduardo's scooters again?" Maria spoke as she stirred.

"No. I decided even though I want to try new experiences in your country, this isn't one of them."

"Visit, yes. Taste, yes. But tempt the fates with the other cars on the road, no." Maria nodded. "Good decision."

"Eduardo offered to lend us a motorcycle. I don't want to disappoint Ren now that I know he is grieving."

"Believe me. Ren doesn't want to ride one either if he can sit protected in a car." Maria dipped a clean spoon into the sauce and tasted. "Call him. I've seen him driving his grandmother's car since he arrived."

"I don't have his number."

"I'll tell you where he lives. Drop over and if he's not there, leave him a note." Maria added a pinch of oregano into the pot.

"If you don't mind, I'll take a bottle of cold water up to my room and think about what you've said."

"Yes, yes, go and rest. You're on vacation."

With leaden legs, she climbed the stairs and passed the bathroom with the luxuriously deep bathtub. The etiquette at a B&B was different than a hotel. Could she indulge herself and soak, allowing her indecisions to float away and burst as the bubbles in a bath would? She didn't want to walk back down the stairs.

"Maria? Maria," she called from the top of the stairs.

"Is everything all right?" Maria asked.

"Yes, I'm sorry, but I was wondering if it would be okay if I took a bath?"

"Of course, Miss Miranda. There is only you here today. I have another guest arriving tomorrow afternoon, but just for one night."

"Thank you. I'll clean up after myself."

"Sim. Obrigada."

Miranda stripped off her clothes and slipped into the fleece bathrobe. She padded into the bathroom and sat on the edge of the deep tub. As the water rushed out of the taps, she shook in scented bath salts. Soon, citrus filled the air. She reached into the robe pocket and cupped the orange. It had become a sign of longing. She wasn't exactly sure what the longing entailed. A different life? Someone special in this next chapter? A definite plan? A romance? She could not return home without a plan.

And like that, she knew she would return home. Just as she wasn't the stylish woman on a scooter, she wasn't a vagabond. She had a loving family back home. She didn't need to find a permanent place to live.

She stepped into the tub and submerged her body up to her chin. Her plane ticket was open-ended. She could decide when she returned home. Not tomorrow, but sooner than she had thought. Tomorrow she would be exploring with a handsome man. Something good had come from her venture with the scooter.

After her soak, she would ask Maria for directions to Ren's home. If he was home, she would share her concerns about the motorcycle. If not, she would write a note and share her decision that she'd rather travel in a car and if his wasn't available, she would rent one. She would bring a picnic.

She recalled the pastelaria around the corner with their flakey croissants and then the cheese shop, and finally the wine. Everyone drank wine with their picnics, or at least they did in the movies. She would ask for Maria's advice about the wine. Then she remembered Maria's brochure stated she supplied picnic lunches. Presto, when the fog lifted, the mind woke up.

Chapter 8

Ren answered his cell phone on the third ring, his voice husky from sleep.

"*Olá.*"

"Ren, Will Cleaver, here. Did I catch you at a bad time?"

Ren shook the sleep from his brain and glanced at the bedside clock. He had meant to put his feet up for a nap but fallen into a deep sleep. "Hello, Will."

"Sorry to call you at this time, but I was wondering if you know when you might be returning?"

"I haven't made any plans. What's up?" Ren rolled and slipped his legs over the side of the bed.

"Marco's wife had her child early, and he wants to spend more time with them. He was hoping you'd come back soon so he wouldn't have to work such long hours."

Ren didn't recall much on the workload that would cause the long hours. "Has something changed in the schedule?"

"One of the seniors homes in the city has some structural issues, and they need to place ten seniors in our residence. We need bathrooms and kitchens. I hate to ask. I know how important family is to you."

Ren scrubbed his hand over his chin. He needed a shave. He had a date to show an intriguing woman around the countryside, and he hadn't made any progress with his avó's gift to him—their home.

"Are you still there, Ren?"

He pictured Will sitting with his feet up on his desk and his crutches close at hand. "Yes, I'm here. I'm thinking."

"I'll give you extra time off and pay for a return ticket home when we have these residents settled," Will promised.

"Let me think, Will." Did he want to leave his family and his avó's wishes in the lurch? He had been avoiding sorting anything except the few things the family had taken. He couldn't go yet. But he also owed his talents to his boss. His uncle? Maybe. "My uncle is retired, and he's having trouble being at home with my aunt all day every day. Perhaps they could stay in my place for a week, and he can help out Marco? He's excellent, he taught me the finer points of tile setting. I'd like to ask him, and if he does, that gives me a few days grace here."

"He may not be as fast as you, but we could get bathrooms done. Kitchens can be last. It could work. Ask him and email me his answer or your arrival details."

"I'm going to tell your fiancé that you're working too hard."

"Someone has to. We can't all fly to Europe and enjoy sunshine and ocean breezes."

"I'll let you know tomorrow. Goodnight, Will."

"Thank you, Ren. You understand that this situation is critical, or I wouldn't ask?"

"Yeah, I'll email or phone you depending on time."

Ren thought about his uncle and aunt. Did he want them in his space for a week? His aunt would move everything around, and she would scrub every inch of the walls and floors. His uncle would work slowly but methodically, with pride. It might work.

Ren changed his T-shirt and headed down to the kitchen. His mouth was as dry as a Saskatchewan summer day. The container that had always been full of his favorite cookie when his avó was alive caught his eye. Of course, it was empty. He glanced around the kitchen that held so many memories. He wasn't ready to sell. Truthfully, he wasn't even sure he wanted anyone else living in it.

Tugging his jacket from the hook by the door, he ran down the front steps, toward the ocean. He needed fresh air and the sea to soothe his tumbled memories and thoughts.

"Boa noite, Senhor Jorge," Ren called to the glow at the end of a cigarette. Ever since he was a small child, he had received lollipops from the grocer, Senhor Jorge, who sat in his chair every night until midnight. When Ren was a teenager, he couldn't sneak home late because Jorge was sure to mention to Avó on her way to the market the next day what time he saw him. When he had his motorcycle, he would rev the engine, and Senhor Jorge would check the time on his pocket watch.

But now Avó wasn't here.

The man raised his hand, and the cigarette glowed high. It was as if he could read Ren's mood.

Ren continued on past dead houses that belonged to families no longer in the country. The surviving children who inherited their family homes didn't take the responsibility of having someone whitewash the outside and keep the yards free of weeds. They should just sell it. But he heard the stories where one sibling wanted to sell while others did not, so it stayed empty, dead. Then the widower, or old bachelor fisherman who could still climb steps, walked through the yards and peeked in the windows and witnessed the slow death as walls crumbled and roof trusses collapsed. Is this what he wanted for his home?

The last thing his avó would want was for their home to stand empty. Or an old neighbor who decided to be the keeper of dead houses visit as the plaster gradually peeled away, and the walls inside turned black, and the curtains tattered. No, that was not the fate he would want for his home.

He had reached the beach. He kicked off his sandals and the waves lapped across his toes and circled his ankles. His footprints gradually disappeared with each successive pass of the saltwater. The thumbnail curve of the moon hung in the sky and reflected on the ocean surface.

What would become of the memories tucked away in the drawers and closets? He must discuss this with his aunts and cousins. They knew the neighborhood, especially cousin Katia. With that decision made, he skipped a few pebbles across the ocean surface and then stepped into his sandals and strolled home.

The shouts from Manuel's Bar meant that someone had scored a football goal. It seemed as if there was a game every hour of the day and night. A dog barked from a balcony above the street. It probably wanted to be down on the ground, chasing whatever moved, sniffing out other dog's calling cards on the sides of buildings. When he first arrived in Canada, he couldn't get used to the idea of the street signs being on a pole instead of on the buildings. But now, he looked for the sign pole. Had he been away too long?

He walked under a scaffold on the street with a portable cement mixer. In Canada, they call for a cement truck, but the roads here were too narrow for such activity. A baby cried, and the mother answered with a song. He missed this the most, the sense of community. Most buildings in Canada were constructed to keep out the severe cold and the extreme heat with insulation and soundproofing. Here, the buildings were built close together to shade each other from the sun. It was like comparing almonds and oranges.

A porch light lit up a green doorway with a knocker in the shape of a lady's slim hand waiting to be lifted and tapped against the wood. The sound would echo up the tiled stairs to the occupants to announce their visitor. In his childhood, of course, they played knock and run. There were many hiding places, but because the houses were so close together someone always saw them. Everyone kept watch. Did he miss that?

Ren took the steps two at a time and closed the door quietly. He needed to phone his uncle. He would ask if he could help out for a week. By then, he should return to Apex. He padded to the kitchen and poured himself a large glass of cold water. He sat on the hard kitchen chair and dialed his uncle. The phone rang, once, twice, three, four, five times before he heard a distracted, "Bom dia."

"Uncle Tomas, it's Renato calling from Albufeira."

"I don't have any money to rescue my nephew. I know a scam when I hear it. I'm going to hang up now."

"No, Tomas, it's me," he said in Portuguese.

"What are you doing calling me?"

"I have a favor to ask you."

"This doesn't sound good. Are you sure you don't need money to bail you out of jail?"

"No, Uncle. I want you to go to work for me."

"I'm seventy years old."

"I'm fifty-five."

"Yes, you're old too. Quick tell me. Isabell is in the garden."

"You know I've been doing the tile work on the new residence building next to the medical complex in Apex."

"Sim."

"They need someone to take my place right away, and I want to stay here for a while longer."

"Have you found a good Portuguese woman?"

"No, Uncle. I'm trying to settle Avó's house."

"I'm too old to commute to a job, and your aunt would not like it."

"I'll arrange for a place for you to stay. Possibly my place."

"Would it be long days?"

"There's a rush as I understand it. You probably heard about the senior home that has to close due to dangerous conditions."

"Sim. I was just reading about it."

"The boss has accepted ten new residents, and the bathrooms and kitchens need to be tiled."

"Here comes Isabell. You convince her, and I'm your man."

Ren heard Uncle Tomas telling his aunt that her favorite nephew was on the phone and wanted to talk with her. Her reply, "Eduardo wants to talk to me?" came through loud and clear. He heard the love in her voice.

"Non, not Eduardo. Your other favorite."

Ren could imagine Uncle Tomas planting a palm on his forehead.

He could hear rustling, as if they were fighting over the receiver.

"Non, Renato." Tomas's frustration was audible.

"Ah, yes, he is a favorite but not my favorite because I see him all the time. Those others we only see when we go home. Hello. Hello?"

"Tia Isabell. It's Renato. I'm calling from Albufeira, so perhaps I can be a favorite for a few minutes?"

"Of course. Of course. What can I do?"

"My boss, Mr. Cleaver, has to hurry and make room for ten seniors in his new facility, but I'm here. And my partner's wife had her baby early, so we need help to get the suites ready. He needs someone who can clean like a goddess, and he needs a few tiles laid to finish off some of the space. We thought if you would consent to go and help out and supervise the cleaners, maybe Uncle Tomas could go along and help with a bit of tiling."

"Ah-ha! Now the truth comes out. You want to stay in Albufeira and enjoy the warm weather and fresh seafood, and you want your old uncle to do your work. No wonder you are not my first favorite nephew."

"Tia, it's true that I would like to stay here for a while

longer, but only to settle Avó's house. I don't know what to do."

"I have an idea. You pay for me to come there, and your uncle can go to Apex and tile until his heart is content." She sighed. "I would enjoy being in my mother's house and seeing our family and friends. The doctor wouldn't allow me to miss the test for anything so I couldn't say goodbye to my mother."

"Would you come?" His heartbeat doubled.

"In a blink of an eye. But who would look after your uncle?"

"My boss will set him up in an apartment or he can stay in my place, and he can eat with the other residents." Ren crossed his fingers. She would have him sorted out in no time.

"Then buy me the ticket and tell your boss to pick up this old guy and his tools. He's been moping around ever since lawn bowling was over. I can't take his sad face much longer."

"One quick question, Tia."

"Hurry, already. I have to pack."

"Is your passport up to date?"

"Of course, it is. I'm seventy and not forgetful."

"When can you leave?"

"You get the ticket and tell me when to get on the plane, that's when I can leave."

"I may not be your favorite nephew, but you are my favorite aunt." Ren pumped the air with his fist. "I will email you the particulars. And I will arrange for Uncle Tomas to go to Apex."

"Here, you talk to the guy. He's pacing like a caged tiger."

His uncle came on the line. "I'll gather my tools. You tell me when to be ready."

"I will email you as soon as I have arranged the time and a driver."

"Thank you, Renato. You're my special nephew. Always were."

Tears welled up and Ren swiped his hand across his face. "Thank you. I'll begin the arrangements. No time for sleep tonight."

The time difference worked to his advantage. First, he phoned his boss. Will was agreeable. He'd arrange Uncle Tomas's ride and a key to Ren's townhouse on condition that Ren was back as soon as possible. Ren promised.

Then, the airline. The line wasn't busy, and he reached a Portuguese speaking customer service person. She found a direct flight for Isabell from Toronto to Faro leaving the following evening. He just had to get her from Regina to Toronto. Dipping into his savings, he paid for a first-class ticket. She deserved it. Uncle Tomas would be as happy as a pig in the proverbial mud, and knowing Tia Isabell and her sister, Tia Ester, they would have his avó's house sorted out and even someone to live in it within days. And he would be able to stay for another week and get to know Miranda better.

At dawn, he finally fell into a deep sleep only to be woken by his alarm. Moaning, he hit the snooze button until he was woken again by a motorcycle revving its engine outside his window reminding him of the day. He had a date, and he didn't want to be late.

Rushing through his shower, dressed and headed for the door, he slipped the keys to his avó's compact car into his jeans. He would apologize to Miranda and hoped she would still accept a tour of the countryside in a car. When he reached for the door, a piece of paper out of place under the door demanded his attention. He wondered how he missed it last night. Curious, he picked it up. He skipped to the signature. Miranda. He took a deep breath, hoping she wasn't cancelling, and then smiled at her request to have their adventure in a car today. She would explain when she saw him at ten. He pumped his fist in the air. His stars were aligning.

The little red car bounced up the curb outside Casa O Mar and Ren checked his watch. On time. Thankfully, there had been no road construction to delay him. He looked up to see Maria waving to him from the open kitchen window.

"Come, come," she called.

He pocketed the key and walked up the stairs to the blue door, rapped once and entered the kitchen. Kissing Maria on both cheeks, he said, "Bom dia."

"I'm glad you and Miranda will be in a car, so much safer. I made lunch for you. There is a good red wine to go with the other goodies. A surprise for when you stop to eat."

"You are a queen. Obrigado."

"Don't be silly. I look after my guests. I hear her coming toward the stairs. That one seems to have some heavy thoughts."

He didn't want to discuss Miranda's thoughts. He wanted her to tell him if she wished. "Tia Isabell is arriving Friday night. She will help me with Avó's house and then stay on and visit."

Maria covered both her cheeks. "I don't believe it. I'm leaving and she's coming."

"But you will have some time for a visit."

He heard Miranda call, "Renato. Bom dia. I'm sorry if I've kept you waiting. The time always gets away from me here."

He met her at the kitchen door, set the lunch bag on the floor and bent and kissed her on both cheeks. "I ran late as well. I'm happy you suggested using a car to drive around today." Her face lit up like a candle.

He reached for her hand, and they walked out the door and onto the street.

Chapter 9

Ren directed her to the red car parked halfway up the curb. "My avó's, grandmother's, car." He held the door open for her.

Ren's grandmother had been a red compact car woman. That told Miranda a little about her. Should she offer him comfort? He hadn't told her. She knew from experience that some sorrows should be protected for a while.

"Nice and comfy." Miranda settled into the seat as Ren folded his body into the driver's seat.

"Small." He winked at her as he shifted into gear. "Maria made us a picnic lunch."

"Yes, she's kind." She liked the looks of his hands on the steering wheel. Confident, in control, ready to guide her through the day.

"I think Lorenzo would like her to move to Canada, but she's most comfortable here."

Miranda didn't want to think about Canada. "So, where are we going?"

The car bumped off the curb and Ren drove with familiarity to the open highway. They had not gone far when he turned onto a secondary road and reduced his speed. He named the orange orchards and almond groves they passed. Then he pulled into an access road in front of rows and rows of trees with bare, pruned branches.

"When Portugal was ruled by the Moors many years ago, a young king married a young Nordic princess." His voice softened. "He loved her very much and watched her get sadder and sadder as time went on. He discovered she missed the snow-covered landscape of her homeland. The king ordered thousands of almond trees planted as far as the eye could see around the palace. And when the trees blossomed at the end of winter, the landscape resembled the freshly fallen snow."

He glanced over at her. "They lived happily ever after."

Miranda gazed at the trees waiting for spring to give them another year of white blossoms, another chance to grow the nuts for another season. "It's hard to imagine these fields resembling snow. But I'm glad the king loved his wife and gave Portugal a future crop for life. There is hope in all seasons."

"That's true." Ren shifted gears and pulled back onto the road. They passed a pottery business advertising their wares on every space of the outer wall. Garden statues of lions, angels, birdbaths, and fountains covered the front driveway. Past a copse of trees, a steeple would appear and then the notice of a small town around the bend. The villages were a majority of whitewashed houses with the either bright or faded red tile roof. Often there would be a few tables and chairs set outside of a café, with customers enjoying a coffee or glass of wine.

"These towns are charming," Miranda said.

"To the tourist's eye," Ren answered. "But to us, these are home. We hate to see some of them abandoned and go into disrepair, or the younger generation leave and only the parents and grandparents are left to carry on."

"No, we shouldn't judge a house by the door, just like a book by its cover." A sense of calm confirmation in her decision to return to her children sooner than she planned settled over her.

"There's a park with some Eduardo trees for shade on the other side of the square. Are you ready to stop for lunch?"

"Absolutely."

Once he had parked the car, Ren opened the trunk and brought out a car blanket, which he handed to Miranda before reaching for the cooler. She followed him to a shady area, spread out the blanket, and he placed the cooler in the middle.

"I'm starved."

"I'm not used to a big breakfast. Maria understands just plenty of coffee and a croissant or toast is all I like. But then I enjoy lunch a lot." She greedily helped unpack the cooler. But instead of the cold sandwiches she expected, hot packs had been placed surrounding the delicacies wrapped in foil. Spicy fragrances wafted and mixed with the air.

Ren closed his eyes and hummed. "*Salgadinhos*." He picked up another package and sniffed. "*Rissois de Camarã*."

Miranda accepted each package and sniffed before setting them on the blanket.

"Ahh, *coquettes*. I'm in love with Maria," Ren said as he passed her the last packet.

He drew out a bottle of rosé wine and two glasses.

Miranda tipped over the picnic cooler to peek inside. "No cut carrots and celery?"

"When you have food made for kings, then who needs food to feed to the rabbits?" He drew the cork out of the bottle and poured two glasses. "A toast to a new friendship."

"To friendship." She drank deeply. Had she had many male friends? Colleagues, yes. But friends, no. Another interesting experience.

They ate their fill of breaded fried finger food, bread filled with creamed shrimp, and coquettes of minced beef.

She lay back and groaned. "I'm so full."

He did the same, the cooler between them filled with only warm packs and empty foil. "There is one packet left to open. I'm hoping it's our specialty, egg custard tart."

"I couldn't. Not yet."

"There are many things I miss when I'm in Canada, but to tell the truth, it is the food, most of all."

"I can see why." There it was again. He was in Canada. She should just open up and tell him they lived in the same country, but something held her tongue.

"I left here and went to Saskatchewan, Canada, for work, and now I work in Apex."

Did she hear him correctly? There might be more communities in Canada called Apex, but he'd said Saskatchewan. Could it be that it was the community outside of Regina? That they lived closer than she ever imagined.

"Miranda, where did you go?" A furrow formed between his brows. "Why did you come to my home country?"

The leaves cast shadows across her arms chilling her. She wrapped her arms around herself. "I've passed my business to my children, so I need time to discover who I am without my career." She straightened and dropped her arms. "I know me. I'd want to interfere. The best way for me was . . ." She gulped down her indecision about sharing something so personal. "It sounds so new age, but it's true. I don't know who I am without my business and my clients. I'm superfluous."

Now she would discover if his toast had been sincere. Friendship. A friend doesn't judge but accepts. Or at least that is what her confident, business self would have said. Her heart wanted him to understand. She smoothed the blanket. As her mother used to sing, "Que sera, sera, what will be will be." She closed her eyes and wished for a sign.

Tingling sensations ran from her shoulder down to her hand. The contact was light but positive. She reached up and covered Ren's hand while they sat with the cooler between them listening to the passersby's chatter, the roar of motorcycle engines, the squeal of brakes, and the breeze rustling the leaves. She was willing to believe that everything would be all right. She felt selfish, recalling the resentment she had felt at the platitudes that had been on so many friends' and acquaintances' lips. Granted, they may not have known any other words to use, but if she heard one more time that she was lucky to be able to sleep all day, or take art classes or even dance lessons, she'd tear out someone's larynx.

She patted his hand twice and straightened her shoulders. She could share that they lived within an easy drive of each other. "You said you are working in Apex. Is that Apex, Saskatchewan?"

"Yes, it is." His surprise at her knowing where Apex was evident. "I'm working on a large project there."

"With Will Cleaver, or the mine?"

"Will." He turned to face her. "I'm part of the building team for the inclusive community. Do you know about it?"

"I have heard about it. The concept of a neighborhood where everyone, physically challenged or fit, could access all buildings was big news about him putting Apex on the map. I'm from Regina."

Ren's eyes flew open. "Really? We're neighbors. We'll be able to see each other when we're back in Saskatchewan." His full smile reached his brown eyes.

Her immediate instinct was to scoot away from Ren. But why should she? This could be more than a vacation thing. Ren's touch was solid. She relished the warmth from his contact. They had it right here in the countries that greeted each other with kisses or handshakes. These forms of touching were becoming increasingly rare at home.

As if sensing her unease with his declaration of seeing each other back home, he removed his hand and said, "It's a good concept. Will's neighborhood. Here, the older adults gather outdoors but if you look carefully, some elderly people can no longer come out of their homes. There are so many outdoor steps, and it's slippery when it rains. The neighbors try to purchase their groceries and visit, especially if their children have moved away, but it can be very lonely. Some should be getting more care than they do. Perhaps there will be a Will Cleaver come to my city one day soon."

A silence seemed to slip over them. Miranda needed to change the subject. She wanted to be here with him again. "Tell me another legend." She brushed a flower petal from his shoulder.

"My stomach's full and my mind is empty. Let me think a minute or two." He extended his legs and lowered himself down until his head was on the blanket. Without a moment's thought, Miranda followed suit, pleased when he reached for her hand and intertwined her fingers with his. She basked in the warmth of the sun and the pleasure of touch. Soon, her eyelids grew heavy, and she slipped away into sleep.

A murmur awakened her. By the sound of Ren's voice, he had turned toward her.

"The story of the Rose Queen. Once long ago, there was a queen who couldn't bear to see anyone in need when she had so much."

Miranda shifted her hips and turned toward his melodic voice but kept her eyes closed. She didn't want to break the spell.

"She would go out every day and give alms and food to the poor. One day, the king's accountant went to the king and said, 'The queen goes out every day and spends a lot of your money. Your money is running low. You should stop her. The poor can fend for themselves.' The king was angry, thinking that his subjects might think he was a fool. The next morning, he went to the queen's rooms as she was getting ready to go out.

"'Where are you going, my queen?

"'To the convent to visit the sisters.

"'And what have you in your lap?

"'Roses.

"'Roses in the winter? Ha, you are lying to me.

"'The queen does not lie.' She stood up, and rose petals fell from her lap where the bread had been.

"And she is forever known as the Rose Queen for that miracle."

Miranda smiled sleepily. "Thank you, Ren, for a lovely story."

"One day, I will ask you to tell me stories about your history."

"Although Canada is a tapestry of many cultures, I'm sure I'll be able to think of one or two."

He gave her hand a final squeeze before he released her. "And now, I'm afraid we must return. My aunt arrives the day after tomorrow, and I have some people to see and some housekeeping to take care of."

"And I need to find a place for the rest of my stay. However, it will not be as long as I first thought when I came."

"I'll have to return a lot sooner than I thought, as well. I hope we can spend more time together before we each have to go our separate ways."

"I'd like that." She'd enjoy every moment here and not think about home.

They packed up and returned to the car. Miranda leaned over and kissed Ren on the cheek. "Thank you for a lovely day. I'll treasure this memory."

"It was my pleasure. My country and its people are friendly."

"I can attest to that. I haven't met anyone rude or insensitive, even when my pronunciation is awkward."

"But you try, and we appreciate the effort."

They drove in comfortable silence until the road signs told of the approach to Albufeira. "Why does the return drive seem so much quicker than the road away?"

"Because good times are precious," Ren said with a sigh.

"Are you not happy to return?"

"Home usually has more responsibilities than away. We've learned that with our life experience."

"That's true." She reached over and put her hand on his thigh. "Remember when we were young? We didn't think much of those we left behind, we only thought of the adventures ahead."

"But we have the next week before I leave this behind and you return to what you have left, so we must enjoy these times."

"I liked the legend of the Rose Queen. While we are away, our laps will have rose petals, and when we return home, we will have bread."

"But I'm the opposite of you. I'm home and must deal with bread, and when I'm in Apex, my lap's full of rose petals."

"Then we must see each other in Saskatchewan, too," she said. "I will share my bread as you are doing here, and you can share your roses."

His smile told her that he had been waiting for her to suggest their future again. "If by bread you mean food, then yes. My aunt, while she's here, will enjoy cooking for all of the family she doesn't see very often. I'll invite you."

"I'd like that, and I'll return the favor in Canada."

"Here we are. I'll come in and compliment Maria on the fine lunch."

Miranda wanted to spend more time with Ren, but did she even know how to be with a man? She was a colleague, an acquaintance, a mother, but she had not been a lover. No, that was too high a stake. She wanted a friend and would learn how to become one. A lover was a definite maybe, but not after only a week. A friend in a week, that was something she could aspire to.

The metallic taste in her mouth pulled her from her thoughts. She hadn't worried the inside of her lip in years.

And she wasn't about to bleed from dreams now. She led Ren into the guest house.

Ren spoke to Maria in Portuguese and Miranda watched her landlady's face brighten and Miranda spied the gleam in her eye when she hugged him to her.

"Miranda, your country has shown this man some manners. When he was a younger man, he would have eaten and run."

Miranda caught the veiled innuendo but chose to ignore it. "The lunch was delicious. Just what we needed."

Chapter 10

Ren spent the rest of the day and the next doing dishes and tidying. He recalled how his aunt liked to complain and tidy at the same time. It was her way of showing her love. He bought groceries and stopped in with many relatives and neighbors to mention that Isabell was coming on Friday. He would have to be careful, though, that she didn't do too much work around the house and not leave time to visit with friends and family. She was devastated to miss the funeral, and Uncle Tomas would not come without her. He understood how important that was.

It felt good knowing Miranda was here. It was a mix of his old life and his new. There weren't many of his friends and family who understood the cold, the flat country, or the food. He always missed his home *frites*, but now he had cravings from his new home. A large double, double, for instance, or perogies and sauerkraut would be a welcome addition to his day.

Will emailed back to say he was going to Regina on Friday morning and picking up Uncle Tomas. Ren had spent time again on the phone checking that Tomas knew to be ready. Then he napped like a child.

Now, glancing at his watch, he had time to change into his trunks for his post siesta swim before a quick shower. He ran down the steps and across the road with his towel around his neck and his flip-flops slapping against his heels. Once on the beach, he dropped his towel, his T-shirt, and kicked off his sandals before he dove into the waves.

The cold January water shocked his system awake, and the saltwater sloshed over his head. He rubbed it out of his eyes and down the furrows caused by sun and age.

Age was just a number to some people but to him, it was a sign that time was running out to find the love of a special person. He dove underwater again to clear his thoughts. His acceptance that he was single would be scrutinized when the aunts and cousins got together and passed judgement on why he didn't have what it took to find and keep a woman. His best approach would be what he had always done, laugh it off. Accept their criticism no matter how much it hurt.

Avó, he thought. *See what I'm doing for you.*

He could almost imagine her reply. *I left you this house so you would come home and marry a good Portuguese woman—younger, of course, to give you sons. If a seventy-year-old man can do your work, then you can stay here.*

Could he ever return to Albufeira again full-time? Perhaps when he retired from work, he could spend more time. But after years of being away, he had less in common with his old classmates and cousins. His close friends had moved on.

He climbed the steps back to his avó's home, no, his house, and he decided to allow what would happen to play itself out. He could control his reactions but not the hopes and schemes of his aunts, uncles, and cousins. They had their beliefs in family and responsibility. It was hard for them to realize that while he was in Canada, he had learned a different way of life, another option for a fulfilled life and family made up of friends. And he hoped that Miranda would be one of those.

After he showered, he dressed carefully in clean jeans and a long-sleeve shirt and walked to the corner bar for a quick bite. Tourists who came to use the free Wi-Fi clustered together, drinking Cerveja and speaking in many different languages. His city was a destination, a place that brought

ORANGES FOR MIRANDA | 75

happiness to many travelers. Tomorrow his aunt would arrive and she would bring her memories and the feelings for her old home.

~ ~ ~

As he watched the tourists and locals come and go, cheer and jeer at the TV soccer game, he'd leave early and not have to rush. Tia Isabell wouldn't pay much attention after the greeting kisses. She would instruct him on how to handle her luggage. Then later, traveling through the landscape of her birth, she would breathe in the air and absorb the familiar sites, all the while commenting on the changes since her last visit. Somewhere through the commentary, she would worry about Uncle Tomas for a moment.

~ ~ ~

He drove slowly through the old town. At the corner near the café where he and Miranda shared a meal; he spied her leaning against a wall, glancing up toward the sky. He slowed to a stop and rolled down the passenger window, "Miranda, would you like to go for a drive to Faro airport with me?" The moment the words left his mouth, he felt they were inspired. Miranda's presence would keep Tia Isabell's questions to a minimum and all the while, she would be watching them and dreaming of a wedding.

Miranda seemed to waken from a daydream. "Hi, Ren. What did you say?"

He jumped out of the car and approached her on the sidewalk. "I'm going to pick up my aunt from the airport, and I hope you might want to come for a ride."

"Oh, but you probably want to visit with your aunt."

"I'll have lots of time for that."

"If you're sure?" She looked up into his eyes and must have found approval because she said, "I'd love to."

He helped her into the passenger seat and closed the door. When he was behind the wheel, she said, "Have you noticed that this blue sky is the same as our blue sky above Saskatchewan?" She opened her phone app and showed him two photos side by side. "I have a photo of a Saskatchewan sky and when I compare them, they are the same. Of course, it's warmer here."

"That must be why we feel comfortable in both places. We recognize our sky." He tuned the radio to a station playing fado music.

After a few kilometers, Miranda relaxed. "Maria was playing this music and singing along with it. Are they Portuguese folk songs?"

"Yes, you could compare it to some folk songs."

"Are they about love lost?"

"They are about loss, some lovers, some country, some ways of life."

"They seem sad."

"They are."

"Would you change the channel then? I would rather listen to something upbeat, even old rock and roll."

"I don't want to be a distracted driver. Will you search, please? Try turning the knob left, English songs are on a channel at that end of the dial."

She turned the dial slowly until an old song filled the inside of the car. Soon, she sang along with a song about waking up with a big smile on her face.

"That was fun. My mom used to play rock and roll when she needed to clean the house or any house in a hurry. It reminded me of her and of all the times we rushed to a house, tucking personal photos and ornaments under sofas and in drawers, even freezers. Anywhere a potential home buyer may not look."

"It sounds as if you and your mom spent a lot of time together."

ORANGES FOR MIRANDA | 77

"Yes. After Dad passed away. Before that, they both taught me everything I know about sales and marketing. Mom set up the real estate business, and then it was up to me to grow it. Now I'm passing that same business to Stacy and Nathan."

"But surely they won't need to run the business for many years to come."

"They are ready." Her voice was frosty.

He could kick himself for speaking out of turn. After her disclosure yesterday, he knew she was retiring, moving on, trying to decide who she was without her career. Sometimes *estupido* was his middle name.

"Should I tune the station back to Fado for your aunt?" she asked.

"Not necessary. Tia Isabell will chat." He glanced over at her. He had to come clean. "I'm using you, Miranda."

She turned toward him, away and then back again. "What do you mean?"

"How old do you think I am?"

He could feel her eyes assessing salt and pepper hair at his temples, the lines that ran from his nose to his mouth, his jawline, his neck and his hands.

"We're probably this same age or close enough. I'd guess, fiftyish."

"Add a couple of years onto the ish. I'll be fifty-five on my next birthday. I haven't married a good Portuguese woman, nor have I had children to carry on our name." He scrubbed a hand over his eyes. "The women in my family . . . Well, perhaps you know."

"Oh. Since you haven't accomplished these on your own, they will want to fix things and make them right."

He glanced over to see her trying to suppress a giggle. He groaned. "You got it in one. Family and passing on family names are important to our culture."

"May I ask why you didn't marry?"

"I was twenty when I immigrated to Canada. I worked hard, so there wasn't any time while I was young and handsome," He winked at her. "I wasn't confident making English small talk and women reacted differently than they did back home." Ren slowed as he approached the roundabout that would take him to the airport. "There were women, of course, but none that stuck with me."

"It sounds as if you didn't stick with any of the women you dated either. You just haven't found the right one."

"You know that, and I know that, but here in the old country, they do things differently. They will put their heads together and find me a wife. Their hope is a younger one so that she can still give me children. Really, would you like to be with an old guy like me if you were young?"

"My question to you is, would you like to be with a woman young enough to have children?" He heard the concern in her voice. "Twenty plus years is a big difference, a generation or more. They've listened to different music than we have; they remember different world events, they have different friends and needs. It's a huge decision."

"Excellent points and I've thought of them all. I'd be like a grandfather to any child rather than a dad. Besides, I don't know if I'll return to Portugal to live permanently. Whoever I married might have to leave her family. And that is difficult to ask of a new mom."

"You've given this a great deal of consideration."

"I have. I'm not saying I don't want someone to be with the rest of my life. And it would be amazing to see a little person carry my name forward. Or at least my nose." He laughed as he placed a finger on the end of his nose.

She laughed. "I'm fortunate I have my daughter and son, but it takes a while until they truly begin to look like their parents."

"I recognize my male relatives when I look in the mirror now, in the pattern of wrinkles on my cheeks and forehead, even though they were fishers and the majority of my work is indoors."

Ren negotiated the parking garage and once parked, moved around to the passenger side to help Miranda out.

"Thank you for asking me to come along, and you may introduce me as a friend. We'll allow your aunt to draw her conclusions."

"Thank you, my Canadian friend." He reached out and clasped her hand. He had a lifeline. He just hoped she was up to the barrage of interrogations that were sure to be coming at them.

They walked hand in hand from the parking area to the arrivals section to stand with the many others waiting to pick up family and friends. The door to the international arrivals remained firmly closed and obscured by frosted glass.

Finally, the doors slid open, and Isabell was the first to exit. Ren dropped Miranda's hand. Tia Isabell charged toward him. After dropping her bag and purse, she reached out with both hands and framed his face. "Renato, my boy." She kissed each cheek.

"Tia Isabell, *bem-vindo a casa*," Ren pulled his aunt to his chest. He heard her sniffle, and she reached up and wiped a tear from her eye.

"Obrigada, Ren." She straightened in his arms and stepped away with the pride of all Portuguese who return to their homeland. "Come, I will show you which is my bag. Then I'm ready to drive with you to my mother's house. Forgive me, your home, dear boy."

"I, too, think of it as her home. It's hard for me to believe she will not walk through the door and tell me to wash my hands and sit down to a plate of sardines." Ren kept his arm around her while turning her toward Miranda.

He gestured for Miranda to come forward. "Tia Isabell, I'd like you to meet my friend from Canada, Miranda."

Tia Isabell raised her eyebrows at him and smiled while she said, "Hello."

"Bem-vindo a casa," Miranda replied.

Tia Isabell linked her arms through Miranda's and then Ren's. "Look, my bags are there. Time to go home."

Chapter 11

Isabell's touch brought a smile to Miranda and warmth spread throughout her chest. Hers had been a family of three until her dad died. From the time she could walk and fold napkins to help stage a house, they had worked side by side. More play than work, she would straighten children's rooms, color coordinate the closets, and line up books and stuffed animals. If she had time, she would build Lego for a boy's room and set miniature cars up around the building. She carried the tradition on in her family. Just the three of them, her, Stacy and Nathan. They didn't need anyone else.

But perhaps they had needed more than just the three of them. She watched Ren as he helped Isabell into the car, as she once again caressed his cheek. Maybe a parent can't be everything to a child.

She couldn't go back and change the past. There wasn't any way to add siblings and, therefore, no aunts or uncles or cousins for Stacy and Nathan. Her children were as independent as she had been. They built their families from their friends. She wondered how Ren adapted to his life without his family? Perhaps he made his family of friends as well.

Did she have anyone like Aunt Isabell? There were always adult women in her life when she was a child, and a few of them were special to her. Then there were her parents' friends and associates. But no one life-long special. Why were these deficits climbing into her brain right now?

"Are you all right, Miranda?"

She heard the concern in his voice. She glanced up and met his worried eyes in the rear-view mirror. "Yes, fine. I was thinking about families."

Isabell turned in her seat to face Miranda. "Are you moving to Albufeira, Miranda?"

"I had considered it. However, I've decided I'm only here for a vacation."

"You will return to . . .?"

"I live in Regina with my two children."

"Oh, we live in Regina, too. It is a small city but a large one where you don't meet everyone. Tomas is filling in for Ren, so I can help him tidy up his home here."

"You came from Canada to help Ren clean?"

"No, it isn't like that."

"Tia." Ren's voice held a warning.

She turned and babbled in Portuguese to Ren. Then she swatted his arm before she turned again. "He has asked me to let him tell you his story."

She muttered more Portuguese and settled in her seat. Miranda laid her head against the back seat and wondered when Ren would share his story with her. Soon, the hum of the tires on the road lulled her to sleep.

"Miranda, we're here." Ren had opened the back door and was leaning over her. "We're at Casa O Mar."

Isabell screeched, "You're staying at my best friend's? You must be a good woman. She doesn't lend her rooms out to just anyone."

Ren held out his hand and Miranda accepted it gratefully. She popped her head back into the car. "Isabell, boa noite. I wish you many happy moments."

"Obrigada, Miranda."

The pressure of Ren's hand on her back guided her until they reached the front porch. "You look done in," he said.

"I was taking in some sights today and the motion of the car lulled me to sleep."

His breath was warm on her neck as he bent to place his lips on one cheek and then the other. However, she wished he'd kiss her properly, yet, with Isabell, and most likely, Maria watching if she happened to hear the car, it wouldn't be very wise.

"Thank you for coming with me. It will give Isabell and Maria something to begin their conversation with tomorrow before they slip back into the memories of days when they were younger and looking for husbands."

"I suppose I won't see you very much. You'll be busy with your aunt and other families." She blinked rapidly, surprised at the feeling of loss she felt, similar to losing someone's dream house, but this was closer to her heart, a deeper meaning for her.

"Please don't even suggest that. I will need moments of respite. I hope you'll promise to be that for me. And you will be coming to dinner."

"I'll look forward to all the time you can share, Ren." She placed her hand on his cheek. "Boa noite."

He took the key from her and twisted it in the lock. The door swung open.

"Will you be all right?" Ren handed her the key.

"Yes, thank you." She turned and looked him in the eyes, wondering if she dared kiss him. She wanted to cherish the closeness until they met again.

"Renato?"

Isabell's voice interrupted her thoughts. "Your aunt is calling you."

"See what I mean. I'll need a safe corner to be my Portuguese/Canadian self."

She watched him go. She should have kissed him. Where had these longings come from? Kissing Ren, wishing for an extended family.

The music from the open window suggested a walk. While she wandered, she would watch for the perfect place to stay. The scent of the sea and the birdsong interspersed with the sound of the breeze swishing through the flat, green leaves of the plane trees eased her restlessness. In the lights from the restaurants and streetlights, she felt safe walking alone.

She instinctively headed toward the sea next to a large hotel that cast light to ease the shadows' uncertainty. She caught sight of a fisher on the shore with a rod twice his height and a fish dangling from the line. Someone would have fresh fish for dinner. With that thought, she realized she was hungry.

Turning back from the sea, she walked toward the square. There were always well lit, inviting restaurants with a small table for two in front of the window or on the outdoor dining area's edge. Watching people strolling by was entertaining and she realized she wasn't lonely. Yes, she was alone but an independent streak from her former self surfaced.

~ ~ ~

"Miss Miranda, Miss Miranda, breakfast is almost ready."

The sun glared through the open window and across Miranda's face. She had overslept. This vacation was breaking her of lifelong habits, including going to breakfast fully dressed for the day. She quickly brushed her teeth and her hair, drew the belt of her dressing gown tight, and slipped on a pair of fluffy slippers. She was Maria's last guest, and therefore no other guests would see her.

With her hand on the swinging door that led to the kitchen, Miranda came to a complete stop when she heard other voices. It couldn't be, not so early. Ren and his aunt.

She was about to turn around and slink back upstairs when the door opened from the other side. "Oh, there you are. Please come and join us before everything becomes too cold to enjoy."

"Maria, I didn't know you had company. I'll run up and change."

"Isabell and Ren are like family. And you are too. Come. You look just fine."

What do you do when you attend a party dressed inappropriately? She heard her mother's voice. You hold your head up high, square your shoulders and walk into the room as if they were the ones who read the wrong memo. She lifted her head, squared her shoulders, and stepped through the door behind Maria.

"Sit, sit."

Miranda took her place beside Ren, across from his aunt. "Boa dia."

His aunt observed her openly before she nodded her head.

Ren plucked her sleeve. "You might be a little warm in this today."

"I don't plan to wear it all day, only for my first meal, and then I intend to dress for the weather. Your golden biceps and calves have soaked up the sun." She felt her face flush at her boldness. Had she ever commented on a man's physique before? And in front of his aunt and Maria. She glanced over.

His aunt raised her eyebrows and cleared her throat. "I trust you slept well at Maria's?"

"Of course. It's a beautiful room, and I open the window to the sounds of the night, which lulled me to sleep." Miranda smiled. "Obviously, a much-needed sleep."

"Coffee?" Maria asked.

"Yes, please." Miranda watched the dark brown liquid flow from the pot. She lifted the mug to her face and inhaled. "Is there a better scent in the whole world than the first cup of coffee of the day?"

Ren watched her over the rim of his cup. Did he really wink at her?

Isabell said something in Portuguese.

"Tia Isabell appreciates your reverence of the fine coffee her friend Maria goes through the trouble to make. She selects her coffee beans at the market, and then she grinds just enough for fresh coffee."

"What will she do when she's visiting Lorenzo?" Miranda asked.

"She may fill her suitcase with coffee beans," Ren said.

"Can she take them to Canada? Will it make it through customs?"

Ren spoke rapidly to Maria, who answered him back just as fast with rapid-fire speed. "She can. But she has so many other things to take this time, and she's not sure what she will do. She doesn't want to pay for more than one suitcase." Ren leaned over to whisper in her ear. "And poor Lorenzo needs his special pasta and olives and sardines."

Miranda hid her smile behind her mug.

Maria placed a fresh croissant in front of Miranda. "You must find somewhere to stay soon. Miss Miranda, so I know you are safe."

She never thought that fate or the universe or whatever took care of things, but here she was hoping that it would do just that. She should have found a place to stay by now if she had been more determined. "Maria, you have been lovely, and I will find something today. I promise."

Isabell tapped her spoon toward Ren. He set down his croissant. "I'll help you. I can read the advertisements and check the leases to make sure you understand."

"Thank you, Ren. But I don't want to take you away from your family. Your aunt just arrived and if I understand correctly, you have work to attend to."

"But there are so very many rules and regulations for the people who rent their houses, or even sell them," Maria said. "Ren must help you. A new language and a new country are always difficult, and Portugal is hard. We've had so many changes of governments that there are such strange things still on the books, as they say."

"You've all been so kind, but I must insist. I am a businesswoman in Canada. I will find a way."

Ren was watching. She put her hands onto her lap, so he wouldn't notice if they shook just a bit. "I admit that Tia Isabell came here to help me deal with something important. But may I ask you to at least share the name of the person and area before you sign anything?"

"That's a good arrangement," Isabell said. "Tomas and I always compromise."

Both Maria and Ren laughed at this pronouncement.

"Tia Isabell, we must go." Ren stood. "Thank you, Maria, for a lovely breakfast. I may just come and stay here when I come back for visits."

Isabell swatted his arm as he reached to help her up. "You will do no such thing. You will stay in the house my mother bequeathed to you."

Then, both women were speaking rapidly in their first language and pointing and shaking fingers at him. He put his hands over his head and made for the door.

Miranda followed him onto the porch. "What's that all about?"

"I didn't tell you why I am back. Thumbnail sketch. I spent a lot of my time as a child and a teenager with my grandmother. She thought I was special and wanted me to come back and marry a nice Portuguese woman, so her house became mine in her will. Sadly, I didn't fulfill her dream before she passed away. I'm having a hard time believing she is gone." He glanced down. When he looked back at her, tears welled in the corner of his eyes.

She wrapped her arm around his waist. "I'm so sorry, Ren."

"Thank you. I need to find ways to make the house mine." He pulled her close.

"Ah, yes," she whispered. She had seen this situation during her career as well.

Wrapping her arms around him tighter, she said, "I'm sorry for your loss, dear Ren."

The women stepped onto the porch and stopped talking. Both of them stared at Miranda standing in Ren's arms.

"Ren, is there something you would like to tell us?"

"No. You, Miranda?"

"I tripped on the stone. Ren caught me." She pushed her foot firmly into her slipper. She didn't want the moment Ren had chosen to share with her scrutinized.

Isabell and Maria glanced at each other. Neither of them looked like they believed Miranda's tale.

"Tia Isabell, shall we go?" Ren asked.

Miranda felt his hand slip from her back. She turned to Isabell. "Thank you for allowing me to join you for breakfast. I know you and Maria must have many things to catch up on."

"Yes, we do. And perhaps you are right. Ren has responsibilities at home." Isabell's voice was frosty.

Miranda shivered. Straightening her shoulders, she said, "Maria, please don't be concerned. Your Lorenzo will not have to wait a single minute longer for his sister to visit him."

"Here is my number if you need some help. Just call, and I'll talk to whoever and translate," Ren said for her ears only and placed a slip of paper in her hand.

She gripped his palm. "Thank you, but I'm sure I'll be fine."

He squeezed her palm. "Keep it."

"Ren, I'm ready," Isabell called from the street.

Chapter 12

"You cannot be interested in that Canadian woman, Renato. She's much too old to give you children."

"Perhaps I'm too old to have children myself," he answered as they walked around the square, past the church and up the stairs to the door that had always been opened with love.

Again, he wondered why his avó had done this. She could have given it to any of her other grandchildren, and they would have been less conflicted, happy, in fact, to have a family home. He shook his head and reminded himself of the gift he had been given rather than looking at it as a chore. He was the child who had spent the most time with her. He helped her with the handy work she could no longer do while she baked and cooked for him. His cousins had always thought he was spoiled, but he had toted and carried and hammered and screwed anything she had wanted to be repaired or taken apart.

And she had rewarded him with meals he hadn't tasted since the last time he was back, before she had passed. He didn't know how ill she had been. And he claimed to be a man who observed those he loved. His mind skipped to Miranda. Now, why would it do that?

In his mind's eye, he reviewed the unguarded moments when she looked as if she carried the world instead of the lightness of being a new retiree. She was trying to find out who she was without work in a new challenging environment. He understood how comforting home could be when newness was too much. When he'd come home in those early days, he reveled in speaking his language, eating familiar food and taking part in the community. But if he'd stayed too long, he would never have learned to love Canada.

"Do not say that. A man is never too old to be a father," Aunt Isabell said. "Look how much pleasure you have brought to your family as a son and grandson and uncle."

"To father a child is a whole lot different than being a dad, someone who is there for their child every step of the way," Ren said, surprised at the sadness that had replaced the hope he had held on to for so very many years.

"I once listened to a famous author on CBC radio who said, it isn't so bad if a son's father dies early, it gives that son a chance to choose many different role models, dear Renato."

"I agree. But when I was young, I only missed my dad. The man who took me to soccer matches, and who sat on the stoop after a long day and told me stories about his younger days."

"He loved you and your mother, don't ever doubt that."

Ren was tired of the same old explanations. "My father chose to put himself in danger."

"*Querido*, that is how he made extra money. They were hard times in our country." She patted his cheek. "He loved you and your mama."

"You weren't there, Tia Isabell, to watch Mama twist her handkerchief when she thought I wasn't looking, worried when he was on a boat. She worried all the time."

"That's the way it's for wives, we worry. Why do you think they built the walks on the roofs of houses close to the coast?"

"They call them widow's walks."

"First, they were the captain's watches so he could look out over his vast treasure opportunities," she said. "Then, they became a widow's place."

"Only after the man didn't come home from the sea." He remembered the many nights he sat at his bedroom window at the top of their house listening for the roar of his father's motorcycle engine long before the headlights rounded the corner. But it never did again after the last fishing trip.

"Being a doctor didn't pay much, and he fished for food for his family."

"Tia Isabell, he wasn't experienced. He should have taken Mother. She had fished more than both he and his brother."

"She wanted to go, but she wasn't well. She thought she might be with child again." She moved closer and he stepped away. "The stress changed that."

"We didn't say goodbye to my papa." He swiped at his eyes. Being in this house was bringing back his childhood anguish. He rarely thought about the tragedy of his father's death when he was away from here. He had trained himself to recall the good times, the family picnics, the birthday parties with all of the cousins, not his mother waiting until she could move away from her memories. Nor his moving his few possessions to his grandmother's house, this house. And now she was gone, too.

"If you never become a parent, Renato, you will never understand. You will always be that child."

"I won't believe that to be true, Tia Isabell. I have learned so many things. I can and must come to terms with my past."

"Then let us begin, Ren. What will be the easiest room for you to start?"

"Her room."

"You bring the boxes, and we will start there. I will be glad to have room in the closet to hang up my few things."

"Are you always so practical?"

"No, but sometimes it is necessary. If I were not practical, I would have gone with Tomas to Apex and not come and put my nose into your business."

He loved the wise women of his family.

"Tia Isabell, we are family, and I welcome your nose most of the time." He followed her to his grandmother's bedroom. "How many boxes should I put together?"

"We will start with three. One to keep for memories, one to donate and one, of course, to throw away. Sorry, Mama." His aunt addressed the closet. "But somethings we have to discard."

Ren returned with three boxes and adhesive tape. When the tape secured the bottom flaps, the stretching sound added to the sound of hangers shifting on the closet rod.

Tia Isabell examined each dress before placing it in one of the boxes. But Ren sat on the side of the bed and gazed around the room. Her sanctuary. He knocked on her door, called through her door, but she had not invited him in. As an almost teen, he wasn't interested in his avó's room. He sneaked by many nights, much later than she told him to be home. He never saw the shrine she had to the Blessed Mother or the hanging rosaries. The Bible on her bedside table. The photos of the family.

The tablet he'd given her on his last visit still lay on the table beside her bed. He had shown her how to send emails and text messages and increase the font size when she read. The data service was his gift to her. She amazed him in her desire to stay up-to-date and communicate with her children, grandchildren and, more recently, great-grandchildren.

Avó printed and filed emails from her grandchildren. Her printer light flashed, ready to be used. He stood and, with a lump in his throat, opened her filing cabinet. The files with the children's names in alphabetical order stood at attention, some stuffed with more letters than others. He scooped them up and placed them in his to-keep box. He wasn't sure why or what he'd do with them, but he couldn't put them in the recycle bin. Not yet. They weren't his to read, but they had been her treasures.

He made his way through other papers, old bills, tax receipts, and tax forms. Some he saved and others he put aside for shredding.

Isabell's heavy sigh brought his attention back to the closet. "The closet is empty. I've put aside a few items that are important to me. Is there anything you wish to keep?"

He had memories of the shawls she wore when they hugged good night. He remembered her apron's rustle when she lifted a pot from the stove instead of using a hot cloth. He knew the scent her Sunday best dresses bore. He didn't need her clothes but, "I'd like to keep the house exactly as it was, but that isn't realistic. When you find her handkerchiefs, I'd like one of her fancy ones she always kept in her purse but never used."

"Yes, she carried them for an emergency, but I don't remember her ever using the dainty pieces." Isabell opened one of the bureau drawers. "Found them." She opened a box, and the familiar lavender scent filled the room. "Choose away. These can be mementos for the other grandchildren, too."

Ren tucked a lavender lace handkerchief into the shirt pocket over his heart.

His cell phone rang. He swiped to answer.

"Ren, I need your help." The sound of Miranda's hushed voice. Her distress made his heart jump.

"Who is it?"

He cupped his hand over the speaker. "Miranda, she needs help."

"Answer the lady friend," Tia Isabell said.

"Tell me."

"It's difficult to explain," Miranda said breathlessly.

"I'm listening." He heard a loud male and female voice in the background speaking Portuguese. They seemed to be arguing.

"I found a lovely house with a view of the ocean, a private patio, green lawn, but I can't seem to get the proprietors to understand that I need the space in two days. I'm willing to pay extra."

The voices grew louder as if Miranda had held the phone out toward the couple. Then, she was back. "I think the gentleman understands, but the woman appears to think I've made an improper proposition to the man." He could hear the frustration in her voice.

"Where are you?"

"I'm not quite sure. I was walking along the beach and looked up and saw the sign that said for rent. Can I please pass you to one of these two people, and you can find out what the problem is?" she whispered. "It looks perfect, Ren, but I don't want to cause any difficulties. I don't know what I could have said or done to cause this fuss."

"Pass me to the woman, please, and I will ask her."

"Olá."

~ ~ ~

"Olá," Ren said. "I'm a friend of the English lady. Can I help?"

The woman spoke quickly and loudly. He could visualize her gesturing with her hands because her voice cut in and out at times. He only picked up what she said because of the volume. He could feel himself giving into laughter, but for everyone's sake, he had to remain professional. "What is your address, please?"

She told him, and he said, "I will be right over to help settle this. But while you wait, may I please tell you she is a very nice Canadian lady. She would not offend you or your husband."

The line went dead. Ren pocketed the phone. "Tia, I have to help Miranda."

"Go, I will take a break while you are gone and check in on my sister. She should have been over here with her nose in everything. She either has her nose out of joint, or she is very sick."

Ren kissed her cheek, aware that this had to be hard for her, too. He had lost a grandmother, and his aunts had lost their mother. "Thank you, Tia."

Ren ran down steps, past the square and up the street to the address. The man and woman were sitting with their backs to each other at the house, while Miranda paced nearby.

For all he wanted to rush to Miranda's side, he had to respect his elders as his avó had taught him. He approached the couple. "*Desculpe*, excuse me. I'm a friend of the lady." He pointed to Miranda. "May I ask how I may help?"

The woman crossed her arms over her stomach. The man stubbed out his cigarette and gestured to the woman to begin.

She asked, "Who are you?"

Ren bowed. "Renato Tiago Monteiro. I spoke to you on the phone."

"Are you Ana's grandson who was away in Canada and now has come home to live in her house?" The woman's lips stretched into a smile.

"Sim." Ren's shoulders slumped. It seemed everyone knew of Avó's bequest. He pulled himself upright and looked into her eyes.

"Ana and I were good friends these last few years. I used to help her down the stairs to the church."

"Obrigado." Ren winced at the pinch in his heart.

"I'm so happy to meet you finally. Ana loved you so much. I am Lusiana." The woman threw her arms around him and kissed him on both cheeks. She turned to the man. "The lady is a friend of Ana's grandson. We must make it possible for her to stay."

"I always said it was possible," the man replied. "It was you who wanted to repaint the rooms, and it was you who thought I was making eyes at the guest." He muttered under his breath.

"I'm sorry, Jack." She reached out and patted his cheek. "Call the lady, and we will make a deal."

Ren asked for the details so that he might explain them to Miranda. The situation reminded him of renting his first apartment in Regina. He had thought specific items were included but ended up paying more to the landlord and the power company and for a parking space than he imagined.

Lusiana brought out the standard rental agreement.

Ren quickly scanned the document and then called, "Miranda, would you come here, please? I believe we have everything worked out."

She approached with measured steps as if she was contemplating her decision. She stood farther away from everyone than Ren expected.

He liked that she would be within jogging distance, even though he wouldn't be here for long. But he would be back. Perhaps she would still be there. "It was just a misunderstanding. Lusiana has shown me the rental agreement, and it seems reasonable. You want to rent month to month, correct?"

"Yes, that was my hope, but I may leave and return during the four months I would rent. I would like their assurance that they would not rent it out to anyone else after I've paid the rent."

Ren spoke to the proprietors and explained. Lusiana nodded and her husband shuffled his feet before he nodded.

"It appears as if you have an agreement."

"Ren, would you ask where they live and how often they think they would need to enter my space, please?" Her arms crossed protectively around her stomach.

Her unease was palpable. Ren translated for Miranda, "She will come to clean once a week, and her husband will do the routine repairs."

"I would like to think about it until tomorrow if that's okay?"

The husband lit another cigarette and mumbled something to Lusiana. She waved her arms around and spoke so fast Ren had a hard time keeping up. Finally, she turned to him with an answer.

~ ~ ~

"They agreed, unless someone else comes along and signs the agreement, then you will have lost out."

"That seems fair." Miranda reached for Lusiana's hand and shook it, but she only nodded to the husband. Then she reached for Ren's hand and gripped his fingers tight. "I'm ready to leave now."

They walked down the flights of stairs and onto the square before he spoke. "Would you like to tell me what's wrong?"

"I'm not sure I can trust the man. I've dealt with his type in my sales career before. The situation feels unsafe, but I do like the house."

Ren wove his fingers with hers. They walked silently across the square to an outdoor café. "Stop for coffee?"

"Add brandy and I'm your woman."

He felt her reluctance to release his hand when he pulled a chair out for her. "Brandy, it will be."

"I'm sorry I've taken you away from your grandmother's house, but I'm glad you came. I was wrong. I couldn't do it on my own."

He ordered from the server, reached across the table and clasped both her hands. "Want to tell me why you're hesitant about the rental?"

"I can't put my finger on it, truly, but I think he beats his wife."

"I didn't see any bruises."

"She's wearing a long sleeve top and a great deal of makeup around her eye."

"That's a big stretch to beating." He murmured his appreciation when the server placed two espresso coffees and two brandies on their table. Reluctantly he released one hand but held the other when she looked longingly at the coffee.

"The landlord gives off a meanness vibe. I have an antenna for meanness. I worked alone a great deal of the time in houses where men would come on their own to either view a house before they brought their spouse or sometimes to harass me. I learned to read people pretty fast."

"Were you ever in danger?" He swirled the contents in his glass.

She looked into his eyes. "Yes."

"Did someone hurt you?"

"Yes."

"What happened?" His body tensed.

"I called the police, had the man charged, and hired an assistant. And I never again met a man alone." She lifted the brandy glass to her lips.

He imagined grabbing a jerk like that by his collar and throwing him onto the street. "I'm sorry."

"Me, too. That man stole something from me that I won't let anyone, ever again, take." She looked directly into his eyes and shrugged. "But that's water under the bridge."

"You can't stay there." He shuffled the cream pitcher.

"But what will I tell them? I think Lusiana was protecting me." She stared into her brandy.

"You did say to them that you'd like to think about it. I'll call Lusiana in the morning and tell her you've had a change in plans. They can keep their for-rent sign in their window. You keep looking." He wasn't sure how she'd take this direction. But there was no way she was going to rent that house.

"Obrigada, amigo." She smiled at him. Her eyes bright, and her shoulders relaxed while she slipped a little further into her chair. "If all else fails, I'll move into a hotel with a pool and the amenities that go with it."

"Hotels aren't so bad. They have security."

"Thank you, Ren. Imagine coming halfway around the world and meeting someone who works within miles from me and becoming friends." She lifted her near-empty glass toward him.

He raised his glass. "I'm glad I could help. To meeting friends."

Chapter 13

Miranda straightened her purse and turned to see Ren standing beside the table with their empty cups. Her thinking had become muddled. She ran away from home looking for a home, but she had one and beautiful children. Her first plan was to purchase a property, but that changed because she witnessed family life as it was with its love and challenges. Meeting this man gave her another reason to stay. A month. She'd return in a month.

Exhaustion hung on her shoulders like a cloak. She had read that major life changes could cause unexplained fatigue. When she passed a stall selling tourist items, she decided to buy a beach towel and hang out near the ocean. She spread her towel on the sand, laid on her back, and closed her eyes. After she rested, she would book a hotel and move tomorrow. The moist air and salt scent, along with the gentle lapping of the ocean waves, lulled her into a deep sleep.

The screeching of children woke Miranda. Shielding her eyes from the bright sun, she turned onto her side and covered her face with her arm until a lifeguard shook her awake. "Lady, are you okay?"

"Sim. Obrigada." She sat up, brushing the sand off her cheek and out of her hair. Then she pulled out her phone and entered her hotel requirements into the search engine—time to become efficient again.

A family of four built a castle with a moat. They bailed water away from the foundation and dug channels diverting the water, but the tide was coming in, and they would soon lose the battle. The youngest child, the daughter, stomped her foot through the middle of the elaborate structure ending the need to fight a lost battle. Miranda could relate. But she was not a physical fighter, more of a strategist. In business, she knew when to cut her losses and begin something new. Now, her search was for a new way of living in this next chapter.

She laughed to herself. Retirement? The scooter? And now, thoughts of experiencing love? Had she subconsciously come away thinking she'd have a fling? Away from her children's eyes? That, of course, took Ren out of the picture. Not only because she believed he wasn't that sort of man but also, he was going back to Saskatchewan, back to her area. With the business and the growth of Apex, Stacy and Nathan would quite possibly meet him. She wasn't ready for that kind of new experience.

After a quick phone call to secure her accommodation, Miranda tugged off her shoes and socks. She brushed the sand off her butt when she stood and strode toward the water's edge. The waves lapped across her toes, then up to her ankles, and soon the foam touched her pant legs rolled up to her calves. It was cold, she wanted to run from it, but her body adjusted with each pass of the wave. Soon it was pleasurable to feel the water lap while it advanced and then sucked the sand from under her feet when it slipped back into the ocean. If she could get used to this, she could get used to anything. With time, she would adjust.

And to do that, she was going to live. Not think of retiring as an ending. Tomorrow, she'd buy a bathing suit. She'd skype the kids, share her hotel view, and begin again. She might not be a stylish woman on a scooter weaving through the traffic on her way to an exciting job, but she could be Miranda, discovering what life had to offer, opening a new chapter in her life. Tomorrow she would be like her mother, the woman who gave her strength and the ability to be independent and stand on her own two feet. She was going back home healthy and tanned. She laughed out loud.

Miranda stepped out of the water and dropped onto the sand to build a castle. She chose cracked and broken shells and gave them a new life as decoration. Then she dug a trench, allowing the water access to her creation. It would go back to its earlier form, and the shells would drop again into the sand.

She slung her towel across her shoulder, tied her shoes together, and walked to the street above the beach. Tomorrow, she was coming back to herself. She missed her. Tonight, she would enjoy her last night at Maria's.

"Maria? Maria, where are you?" Miranda pushed open the main door.

"Miss Miranda, are you hurt?" Maria came running from the kitchen, wiping her hands on her apron.

"No, I'm happy. I've found a place to stay in the old town with a view of the ocean."

"Is it a home? Perhaps I know the people." Maria looked expectantly.

"No, The Plaza Del Sol with a pool and dining room. Thank you for your welcoming presence." It meant more to her than she would ever be able to tell this woman. "When I'm back in Canada, I hope you will come and visit me and meet my children."

"You have children?" Maria squinted over her reading glasses. "And I've been thinking of you as a miss all this time."

"I am a miss, but I'm a mother to two wonderful children. My daughter, Stacy, and son, Nathan."

"And you left them alone?" Maria's eyes widened.

She laughed, "I did, but they are young adults. They are busy taking care of our business."

"Miss Miranda, you do not look old enough to have working children."

"Thank you." Miranda followed Maria back into the kitchen and pulled out a chair at the table. "I've decided tomorrow, besides moving out and letting you get ready for your trip, I'm going to purchase a bathing suit. Do you have a recommendation?"

"For a woman such as you, I would suggest you get a taxi and go to the big mall. That is where the movie stars shop when they come."

"Do you go?"

"Only to watch for celebrities. I purchase many of my clothes in the markets. I know all of the sellers, and they give me good prices when I pretend to barter."

"I know how to negotiate prices. Perhaps I should try the market before the mall for the stars."

"Of course." Maria studied Miranda. "But you should wear a suit to show off your success and maturity."

"You think so? I don't mind something like the local women wear."

"Ah, but don't you want Ren to see you as someone different than the usual Portuguese woman?"

Miranda clasped her hands under her chin. "Not yet. But perhaps one day." Then she dropped them quickly when she realized they were pressed together in a prayer gesture.

"It's better men know fairly quickly and then you'll know the good from the not so good. And believe me, many men in my country are not so good. They see you from the back and whistle their heads off. Then they see your wrinkles, and rude remarks take the place of winks and kisses."

"Everyone I've met so far has been kind," Miranda said with her shoulders back. The landlord, Jack, was the exception, but she didn't need to share that with Maria.

"May I ask if you've had petite breasts all your life?" Maria seemed genuinely curious.

"Yes." Miranda had no idea where the conversation was going. She crossed her arms over her chest.

"Oh, my poor dear." She scrutinized Miranda. "It is tough to buy clothing for a woman with tiny breasts."

"I'm not advertising my position, Maria. I'm just going to buy a bathing suit. I'm going to wear clothes and enjoy the sun, even though I'm a mature woman with tiny breasts."

"I'm sorry, my dear," Maria said. "I am a nosy old woman. It is a good thing I'm going on a vacation soon."

"Would you like me to leave now? I can move into the hotel, and you can get on with your packing?"

"No, no Miranda. I would like to make you one more breakfast."

"I'd love to have one more breakfast with you, Maria." Miranda wrapped her arms around Maria.

A timer rang. "Oh, I almost forgot my cake."

"I'll go up and pack before I go out for dinner and tomorrow I'll have my last bath in your beautiful tub," Miranda said.

Home wasn't so much a place as a feeling and here had the feeling of home, but it wasn't her home. Swimming would give her upper body strength and a suntan. The sun on her skin would help her relax. She couldn't remember the last vacation she took without a tour itinerary. She was glad for the anonymity of the hotel. Maria's care was exactly what she needed when she first came, however, she was ready to take that next independent step.

She put on one of her flared dresses for dinner and wound an infinity scarf around her neck. She slipped on a pair of dress sandals she'd packed just in case an occasion called for elegance. She couldn't remember the last time she felt so alive and looking forward to the future.

With a shawl slung over one shoulder and her purse securely in place, she locked the front door behind her. Walking toward the square in the warm dusk, she hummed to herself and nodded and smiled to passersby. Those with children brought a glow of delight. She missed Stacy and Nathan. The time they were children, exploring the world. She wondered if they missed not having a male figure in their lives. They had plenty of male influences they could choose from, but no permanent man. They'd have to deal with it if it became a problem. Hopefully, they wouldn't need to spend dollars and time on a psychiatrist couch somewhere. But if they did, then they did.

She stopped to pluck a hibiscus flower and tucked it behind her ear.

"Ola, Miranda." She turned at the familiar deep voice and there he was, Renato.

"Ola, senhor. Fancy meeting you in a place like this." She laughed when he looked around at the white houses with flower boxes in the shadows and the high walls with mailboxes beside the ornate gates.

"May I ask where you are off to this evening?" He bowed from his waist.

Miranda laughed. "I'm on my way to discover a *restaurante*. I believe that is what you call an excellent restaurant?"

"It is indeed, and I know just the place. May I join you?"

"I don't want to take you away from your aunt and your duties," Miranda said, wishing secretly he would join her for dinner.

"Not at all. Tia Isabel told me to get out of her way, and that I was crazy if I thought she was going to cook dinner after such a busy day."

"Do you think she'd like to join us?"

"Oh, no, she wouldn't. She's had enough of me for one day. Besides, she is going to visit Tia Ester."

"Why don't you call her and make certain. Tell her I'm with you."

"Why should that make a difference?"

"I have a feeling the older women are trying to matchmake, and you're not making it easy. Especially if you hang out with a woman who isn't Portuguese or fertile, she might come just to protect you from me."

"You're very perceptive. What the women in my family want is not what I want. I could like the life I could have here." He tucked her arm through his. "I like my life in Canada. I'm going back."

"Hmm, loyal, and a good nephew and grandson." She put her finger to her chin. "You would be a good catch."

"Are you fishing?"

"Me, I'm fifty-five years old and have two grown children. I might fish, but it would be catch and release."

He reached for her hand. "I've never heard that term. Would you explain the concept to me?"

"Over dinner. Lead the way," she said, swinging their hands in an arc as they walked.

Ren led her to a short, rock wall with an opening that led to a beautiful oak door. A man in a tuxedo opened it. "Senhor and Senhora, welcome."

Chapter 14

Ren reluctantly released Miranda's hand when the server held her chair and gestured to the chair across. It seemed far from the warmth of her skin and the gentle fragrance from the hibiscus in her hair. The scent reminded him of riding his bicycle down the streets and brushing against the flowers hanging over fence edges.

He couldn't take his eyes off her. She was beautiful. Tonight he wanted to know her more, hear her laugh and see the laugh lines crinkle around her eyes.

They ordered their wine to accompany their tempting nibbles of smoked ham and cheeses, followed by the traditional Cataplana again, and possibly a dessert.

Ren waited for the server to pour their wine and then leaned forward. "Well."

"A hole in the ground, usually filled with water," she said with a straight face but a twinkle in her eye.

"Pardon?" He shook his head.

"A well is usually a hole in the ground." This time she smiled widely. "I used to tell that joke to my son, Nathan when he was growing up, and the word had a permanent place in his storytelling."

He lifted his glass toward her and raised his eyebrows. "Catch and release?"

While she layered ham and cheese on her bread, she said, "You must have fished in Saskatchewan?"

"Yes."

"Then you know that in many of our lakes, we have fishers who want to help conserve the fish stock, but they enjoy the sport. Therefore, they catch the fish but remove the hook and drop them back into the water." She popped the morsel into her mouth.

"Of course, but what does this have to do with a man and a woman getting to know each other?" Ren twirled his wine, watching Miranda's delicate hands as she tore a piece of bread and reached for the knife to cut a wedge of cheese.

"Sometimes, couples like the sport of getting to know another person in a special way, but they aren't looking for a permanent relationship." She tipped her head and studied him. He wondered what she saw besides a man with a dark complexion and salt and pepper hair.

Miranda cleared her throat. "I didn't mean to suggest that we would be that type of friends." She looked down at her hands.

"I was considering the possibility. I'd like to show you around my country while I'm here for another week and, of course, we can meet up in Saskatchewan when you go back."

A slow blush worked its way up over her jawline and stained her cheeks a lovely red. He wanted to reach across the table and touch her, but the server appeared with their soup.

"I'm moving into the hotel tomorrow and then I'm going shopping for a bathing suit," she announced.

The subject had obviously changed. "Will this take all day, or will you have time to go for a drive to the community the tourist brochures declare as the quintessential Portuguese town?"

"Oh, Ren, I'd love to, but your aunt and the work she needs you to do. You said you only have a week."

"We'll work together in the morning, and then I'll encourage her to visit friends. She can't work all the time."

"If you're sure, then it's a date," she said with the sweetest smile on her lips.

The server brought the copper pan shaped like a clam and set it in the middle of the table and, with one hand behind his back, he scooped Cataplana into two bowls. The aroma of onion, sweet pepper, tomatoes, and seafood wafted across the table. Ren leaned forward and waved the steam toward his face.

"Let's see if it measures up to the first time you savored this traditional stew, the first time we dined together." Again, her blush pleased him.

Miranda dipped her spoon into the broth and brought it to her lips. "Heavenly."

Ren passed her the basket of crusty bread. "I really must find a woman who can make this when I return to Saskatchewan."

"A woman?" Her head jerked up. "Why wouldn't you learn to make it? You have the history, you know the flavors you would expect to taste. If you make it, I'll come to your house for dinner."

"And now it is my turn to say it's a date." Why hadn't he learned how to make the dishes he loved? Because his avó made everything special whenever he returned home.

"Is it always made with fish?"

"There are varieties," he said between spoonfuls. "Sometimes, there is smoked sausage and chicken along with the clams and prawns."

"You can usually find prawns in Saskatchewan, always chicken, and probably the Italian deli would have the smoked sausage."

"You're right. There isn't a legitimate reason why I haven't learned to make this. I'll ask my aunt for hints, and I'll take a pan back with me." He dipped bread into the remaining broth in his bowl and then piled rice and bits of clams and shrimp onto it before popping it into his mouth.

Miranda reached across the table. Ren tried to drop his fork, his bread, and pick up his cloth napkin before she made it halfway so that he could meet her. But she stopped at the gleaming copper dish. "What can you tell me about this beautiful pot?"

He cleared his throat and took a deep breath to slow down his heart. Had he thought Miranda was coming toward him for a kiss, in the middle of a restaurant? He must not be getting enough sleep. She was too reserved, mature for that. And so should he be. He dabbed his mouth with his napkin. "If you notice, it has a lock. When sealed, the steam creates rich flavors because none of the juices evaporate, they flow back into the food and create this tasty broth at the bottom." He broke another morsel of bread and dipped it into his bowl.

"Is this a recent invention?" She ran her index finger over the dimples on the outer surface of the pan.

"Early twentieth century for sure. But I'd have to contact Wikipedia for more info." He winked at her. "It's one of those things that have always been in our houses. What's a kitchen appliance that has been in your family forever?"

"A takeout menu." A wistful smile appeared on her face. "My mom and her mother worked outside the home. I come from a long line of career women." She sat straighter and tipped her chin forward.

"I understand. In Canada, especially in urban centers, women could work outside of the home." He recalled the times his mother was away when he came home from school and then later, his grandmother, and it hadn't been often. It was an event when he was in the house alone or with his cousins, without adult supervision. But every day? "How did that make you feel?"

"Feel? It was normal. I went to daycare, school, or went to my mom's office and stayed there until we went home. Except when I was nine, Mom hired Analyn. She was special." She ran her finger around the rim of her wine glass. "She was like the grandmothers I had read about or saw in movies. I would run home from school and stayed home on weekends just to be with her."

The sparkle in her eyes said more than words how valuable that year was for Miranda.

The server appeared at their table. "May I offer you coffee and a liqueur with your dessert?"

"What is the house specialty tonight?" Ren asked.

"Sweet rice pudding, Senhor." He stacked the bowls and bread plates on his tray.

"Had I known, I wouldn't have eaten so much." Miranda rubbed her tummy.

Ren whispered, "It's our traditional upsell."

Miranda nodded with a small smile. She was a businesswoman who understood sales tactics.

"The pudding will clean your palette for our traditional liqueur and coffee," he explained.

"Sounds wonderful." Contentment flooded her face as she leaned back against the chair and closed her eyes momentarily.

Ren glanced around the restaurant for the first time since they arrived. Tourists were leaving as the locals came to take over the tables. He wanted the evening to go on and on.

The pudding came, and as promised, it was the perfect dessert. The liqueur was complimentary. The coffee was thick and dark for him and white for her.

"I don't suppose you ever played knock and run when you were young?"

She smiled. "Sorry. But I take it you did."

He placed his empty cup on the table. "I remembered those carefree times recently when I walk the streets. However, most everyone knew every child and if we got out of hand, our parents soon heard about it."

"You're lucky you had a free-range childhood."

"Is free-range something like catch and release?"

"Hmm, no. I just meant that you had freedom when you were a child." She covered her mouth to hide her yawn.

He didn't want the night to end, but he signalled for the bill. "Even though we were part of a city, the adults knew the children in their neighborhood, so we were safe to roam within limits."

Ren covered Miranda's hand as she reached for the bill when the waiter placed it on the table. "I asked to join you. Please, allow me."

"As you wish, but I will leave a tip."

"Agreed." He passed his card to the server while Miranda reached into her purse, drew out cash and tucked it next to her saucer.

When they left the restaurant, they turned instinctively toward the sound of the evening's ocean call. Ren reached for her hand and intertwined her fingers with his.

"This is the catch part," she said.

"I'm glad."

While they sat on a bench watching the moon's light reflected in the sea, he said, "Instead of going to the typical village tomorrow, would you like to go to the end of the earth?"

"Pardon?"

"To Cape St. Vincent, the farthest tip of Portugal. It was where Henry the Navigator founded his navigation school and set off to discover if the world was flat or round."

"The end of the earth? Sounds exciting."

He could hear the smile in her voice. "It's a different landscape than you see here. There is a vast expanse of undeveloped coast because of the strong Atlantic winds, but the rugged cliffs and the birds are worth battling the wind."

"I suppose strappy sandals would not be appropriate footwear."

He glanced down at her feet. "Although those sandals show off your beautiful feet, your walking shoes would be best. If the lighthouse keeper is in the mood, he may even give us a tour of the tower. If we go in the afternoon, it will be warmer. The downside is there may be busloads of tourists."

"I'm okay with that if you are. Remember, I'm a tourist. Also, I'm moving to the hotel, and I need to shop for a few things. And you need to be with your aunt."

They both agreed it was time to move along. Again, he held her hand as they walked. Miranda was slowing with every step. "Are we walking too quickly?" Ren stopped in the yellow circle of the streetlight at the edge of the square.

"No." She turned to face him. "I'm trying to find the courage to tell you something, and I'm dithering because, in many aspects, we are strangers, but in others, you are my best friend here."

"Is this part of the catch and release you were talking about?" He winked.

"Perhaps."

"We're not far from Maria's Casa. Would you like to wait and chat there? I know Maria has a porch swing, and it is a warm evening."

"No, let's stop here."

He led her into the square, to the village fountain, and they sat on the stone steps surrounding it. Miranda reached into her purse and pulled out a coin. With her eyes closed, she hesitated and then dropped it into the water. Ren wondered what she had wished. Then she straightened her shoulders and took a deep breath. "Before you spend more of your valuable time with me, you should know that I came here for the third act of my life. A place where I didn't know the language and away from family and friends." She twisted her infinity scarf.

Ren's mind scrambled for comprehension. What was she telling him?

"Thank you for not offering any platitudes." She ran her hands down the bodice of her dress while she held his gaze.

"I've worked all my life, and now I must do something else, be someone else. I know I've told you this before. I miss Stacy and Nathan. I miss my house. I'm not sure here is where I'll stay."

He blew out a breath. Was she saying that he wasn't what she wanted? "I'm sorry."

"No, please don't be. I left home because I was tired. I came here to find a new way to live my life."

"Okay?"

"When we first met, you asked if I would like you to email me a copy of some of your photos. I thought it was a unique pickup line. But I didn't believe I was worthy of attention. Today, I decided that I'm embracing the here and now and the weather. I'm going to buy a bathing suit, and I'm going to be who I am with my white hair and less than toned body."

"Okay." Ren liked her hair, the way it shone in the streetlights and accentuated her defined jawline.

"I'm new to this male friendship situation. I've had associates and clients, but I haven't made a lot of time to have a special man in my life. I'm not sure how to go forward. I just wanted you to know."

His heart sped up. She said special. He tried to remain calm. He didn't want to frighten her away with declarations he wasn't sure he would be able to keep.

"Okay. I appreciate you telling me. So, where should I pick you up tomorrow? I'll come around two when the shops close for their afternoon break?"

Her smile challenged the streetlamp. She reached for his hand and curled her fingers into his. "I'll be in the Plaza Del Sol lobby waiting for you."

They strolled hand in hand back to the Casa O Mar. He watched while she unlocked the door. Should he kiss her? Would she want him to after she revealed her reason for arriving in his home city? What a strange coincidence that they would spend time together here when they could have met in Apex or even Regina.

She turned to face him. "When I get inside, I'm going to wish you kissed me. So rather than wish, would you?" She cocked her head to one side.

"Great minds think alike. I was warring with that very question in my brain."

"And?"

"I didn't know how you'd feel about it after being so open with me. I thought you might feel awkward."

"I might, but I'd rather have the memory of awkward than of a missed opportunity. In my line of business, we catch when we can." She reached for him.

He wrapped his arms around her waist and drew her close. He bent his head and touched her lips with his.

She wrapped her arms around his neck and her body melded with his.

When the kiss ended, she said, "I wondered if I'd become aroused at this late stage in life." She shook her head in wonder. "The body is a mysterious thing."

He ran his finger along her jaw. "Yes, it is."

"See you tomorrow." She opened the door and the hall light cast shadows against the wall. "And Ren?"

"Yes?"

"Thank you."

He made a motion of casting a fishing line. "'Til Tomorrow."

Chapter 15

Miranda leaned against the wall and wanted to sing out loud, but the lights were out and Maria was possibly asleep. Miranda wrapped her arms around herself and sighed with relief and joy. She'd asked for what she needed, and Ren hadn't run away or attached himself to her hip. And she didn't die from embarrassment.

She wouldn't worry about tomorrow. Right now, she allowed the surge of joy. Carrying her shoes in her hand, she tiptoed up the stairs. She laid on her bed and kicked her heels and pulled a pillow over her face while she laughed.

Tomorrow she would go to the end of the earth with Ren and witness the place where people thought the world was flat. Henry the Navigator didn't believe it and he dared to discover the truth. Perhaps that's what she was doing. Daring to discover the true Miranda. Not the businesswoman, not the mother, but a woman entering the third act of life.

With her hands behind her head, she wondered what it must have been like to find crew members who were ready to sail with you, possibly off the edge of the earth? Was this what she was asking Ren to do? No, she was asking him to help her stock her boat with strength and courage while she embarked on the journey.

She got up and packed everything but what she planned to wear the next day. She changed into her soft cotton nightie and crawled into bed. A quick smiley and hug emoticon to both Stacy and Nathan before she turned off the light and slept, knowing her alarm would waken her for another day of adventures.

She woke to a light tap on the door and the sun slipping around the curtains' edges. "Miss Miranda, are you awake?"

Rubbing the sleep from her eyes, she blinked rapidly at the clock. She had overslept. "Yes."

"I brought you coffee and a croissant. May I come in?"

Miranda pushed herself up, flattened the sheet across her waist, and called, "Come in."

Maria held the tray in front of her. "I hope you don't mind. I heard the alarm ring and then it stopped and then it rang and stopped and again."

"That's what happened. I hadn't meant to sleep in." Her heart swelled at this generous woman. "Thank you, Maria."

"No trouble, Miranda." She arranged the settings on the bedside tray. "I wish I wasn't going so you could stay and not have to move into a hotel, but the world works in mysterious ways."

"It does. But we will see each other again." Miranda lifted the steaming espresso to her lips. The deep flavor slid across her tongue. "I will come back as often as I can and perhaps one day, you will ask Lorenzo to drive you to Regina."

"I heard from my friend this morning that a certain man is going to show you to the place where we discovered the world was round." A tiny smile slid across her lips.

"He's a kind man."

Maria nodded. "He always helps many women."

Miranda reached for her hand. "And I appreciate the time he spends with me sharing his Portugal."

"Ah, a woman who needs him."

"No such thing." Miranda straightened her shoulders.

"I meant no harm. Just that sometimes a man likes a woman who needs him." She pulled back the curtains.

"I'm sorry. I'm touchy when it comes to asking for assistance."

"You've been on your own for a long time. It's hard to change."

"I came here."

"But perhaps you must ask yourself why?"

Miranda knew the answer, but was that still the reason she stayed? She was trying to cope with learning a new way of life. Her thinking was less confused then it had been in months. A sign that her mental health was indeed improving. And the tension in her stomach had decreased.

"Maria, come, please." Miranda patted the mattress.

Maria sat gingerly on the edge of the bed.

"How long have you been a single woman?" Miranda asked.

"I have never been married."

"Then you understand what it's like to think about changing your life."

"True. Lorenzo has asked me to come and live in Canada, but I don't want to leave everything I know. But it does get lonely."

"That's one of the reasons I came away. My children and I have done everything together from the moment they were born. It's not good. They need to find their way. I know they will, but not if I'm in their pocket."

"And the other is to learn to be who you are now with what remains of your life," Maria said quietly.

"Exactly. It's time for me. Isn't it strange? We get so busy and all of a sudden middle age has passed."

"But we do for others, and that has its rewards, too."

"Sometimes it's a habit, Maria. Somewhere we are comfortable." She glanced at her bedside clock. "Oh no, I have to get going. I need to finish packing, purchase a bathing suit, go to the hotel and be ready for Ren to take me to the end of the earth."

"If you let him hold you and kiss you, you may not have to drive to the end of the earth to see stars." Maria struck her palm to her forehead. "Forget I said that. His aunt will try to tell him he needs a woman who can give him children. But he knows what he needs more than those of us who give all sorts of advice." Maria patted Miranda's hand, gathered up the tray and closed the door behind her.

Miranda quickly dressed in a T-shirt and capris, no time for a leisurely bath in Maria's old clawfoot tub since she had slept in. She carried her laptop and luggage down the stairs and set them in the front entrance. Miranda walked toward the kitchen to find Maria. She heard voices and someone was crying. She heard Renato's name. But Ren had said it was a common name.

Miranda didn't want to interrupt, but her taxi would be there shortly and she needed to say goodbye. She tapped tentatively on the door.

Maria called, "Come in."

Miranda pushed the door open just enough to ask, "I'm sorry to disturb you, Maria, but could you come here for a minute?"

Maria looked toward the end of the table where her visitor sat. "Um momento."

Miranda backed into the hall and turned away from the sobbing. She couldn't listen. It wrenched at her soul. She slipped quietly out the door and stood in the foyer, waiting for Maria. She turned when she heard the door squeak. "I'm sorry to disturb you. I wanted to settle my bill and thank you for welcoming me into your home."

"I'm sorry. My friend came and, as you heard, is having some trouble with her husband." She handed Miranda a written invoice.

Miranda paid the bill. "May I give you a hug?"

"You don't need to ask." Maria opened her arms. "You take care. You're strong. You're beautiful. You will find your way."

Miranda swallowed a lump and nodded. A horn blared on the street. She looked up and saw a taxi waiting. "You look after Lorenzo and enjoy your visit. Obrigada, *a minha amiga.*" Yes, Maria was her friend.

The taxi driver placed her cases in the trunk and then opened the passenger door for her.

"To the Plaza Del Sol, por favor."

Miranda discovered that her room had a patio at the apartment-style hotel, a patch of grass, and two lounge chairs that faced the sea. It was even better than she had imagined and the perfect place to continue her quest to find herself. She hung up her few clothes and then walked back out to the main street toward the Modelo Continente. Maria had assured her the grocery and everything-else-you'd-need store would also have bathing suits. Miranda would go to the market and barter another day.

The fresh fruits and vegetables tempted her, but she purposefully dragged her wheeled basket and hopped the flat escalator to the second floor to stand in front of the bathing suit display. She decided to be daring and buy a two-piece. She found one with a floral pattern on the top and a navy-blue bottom. She measured them against herself and tossed them in the basket for her reveal in the privacy of her room.

As she headed back down to the first floor to stock up on vegetables, fruits, bread, wine, and brandy, a cherry-red bathing suit caught her eye. She had to have it. She snagged it from the hanger, dropped it on top of the two-piece and rode the escalator back down to the first floor.

In her room, she lay the bathing suits on the bed and then put the groceries away. As she walked back and forth along the hall, finding places to store things, her eyes would stray to the bed. Finally, she stopped the time-wasting nonsense and decided the blue floral would be her first foray into the world of bathing suits again. She slipped off her clothes and pulled on the high-rise bottoms and the smocked bandeau. With a deep breath, she turned toward the full-length mirror on the closet door.

Miranda smiled. Her legs were slim, her bottom had a curve, and she had a defined waist with a flat stomach. The top design masked her less-than-endowed bust. She twisted to see all of herself, pleased with her purchase. She walked purposefully through the apartment and out the patio doors to a lounge chair. The sun warmed her. It was heavenly.

Her stomach growled for the first time in months. She was hungry, actually hungry. A glance at her watch indicated she had enough time for a snack before Ren picked her up. In the kitchen, she made up a plate of cheese and fruit, which she snacked from while she dressed for her trip to the end of the world.

She decided on blue jean capris, a pink V-neck T-shirt and walking shoes. Ren had told her it would be rocky and windy. She put an extra sweater in her backpack. When her phone signalled an incoming text, she glanced at the name. He was here.

She ran to the security gate. Ren jumped out of his grandmother's car and held out both hands to her. He leaned in to kiss her on each cheek. The warmth of his skin against hers gave her a tingling pleasure. He released her and opened the passenger door.

Miranda slid into the seat and buckled up while Ren rounded the hood and settled behind the steering wheel. He was a striking man in his teal shirt, the long sleeves rolled up his forearms, and his jeans rolled at the cuffs.

"I think we should drive straight to Cape St. Vincent, Europe's southwestern tip where the land ends and the sea begins. It's just over an hour's drive. We can spend some time at the Fortress in Sagres where Henry the Navigator's school was established and perhaps tour the lighthouse. On our way back, we can stop at some of the villages along the way."

"You're my guide, and I'm your follower. Lead the way."

Ren merged onto the freeway. Miranda watched the landscape change from agricultural to ragged rock. They passed cyclists peddling through the windswept landscape, and hikers bent into the wind using walking sticks for support.

They parked on an open piece of land where drivers parked other cars and buses. "If you have a sweater, you might want to bring it. I'll get my jacket from the trunk. The wind is relentless up here."

Walking along the rocks, they passed stalls selling knitted sweaters, shawls, hats, mittens, and Portuguese flags. There were even souvenir T-shirts claiming that grandma and grandpa made it to the end of the earth and all they brought back was this T-shirt.

Miranda paused to admire the knitting's artistry, but Ren, with his hand under her elbow, encouraged her toward the entrance. He guided her through a dark cave and out to the other end toward a gate.

When Ren reached into his pocket to purchase tickets, Miranda placed her hand on his. "Please, allow me."

After she handed over Euros and received her change, they stepped through the gate. The awe of the land meets the sea stopped her heart momentarily before it pounded again at the magnificent view. This stunning and terrifying landscape would have been where the Portuguese sailors lived before they sailed into the unknown.

When they entered the expanse surrounded by portions of walls, Ren pointed out a circle of stones. "There are differing opinions. It is either a compass to tell which way the wind's blowing or a sundial."

"Was it from the time of Henry the Navigator?"

"They can't tell for certain. Archaeologists discovered it in 1921, but it is near a chapel which dates back to the fifteenth century."

Miranda strolled to the edge, closest to the wall, and saw fishers perched precariously on bits of rock with huge fishing rods and lines dropped down hundreds of feet into the Atlantic. She felt Ren beside her. "Has anyone fallen off while fishing?"

"Of course. And the fishers understand that there is no way to save them. But the ledges are larger than they appear from here."

"What are they hoping to catch?"

"Dinner."

She turned and smacked his arm.

"I'm not sure what types of fish. I do know that I'd rather go to the fish market than take this risk," he said.

She looked out at the vast Atlantic Ocean. "I can't imagine the sailors risking everything to sail into the unknown."

"Remember, even though it was the end of the world as they knew it, it was also a new beginning."

New beginnings she understood. "Where to now, guide?"

"I was hoping that we could see the lighthouse, but there are too many tourists, I'm afraid he won't select anyone." Miranda glanced over at the lighthouse, "That's too bad, perhaps next time."

"Okay, do you like figs? We could purchase some from the vendor and nibble while driving through the small towns on our way back to Albufeira. And if we see a place and we'd like to stop for a coffee and perhaps a brandy, we will."

"Figs. Hmm, can't say that they've been a staple in my diet before, but if you recommend them, by all means. But you must let me treat you."

They studied the figs at the stall. A grizzled vendor wore a thick sweater and a broad smile with a few missing teeth. Lines, more like crevices, fanned out from his eyes, as if he'd squinted too long into the sun. His leather skin spoke volumes of the wind he had battled through his years. She couldn't tell his chronological age, but it may be the universal age of a seafaring man.

"Which would you choose, Ren?"

"Miranda, you choose, they will be good."

She turned to whisper in his ear, "I don't want to barter."

"Then don't."

Comforted by the hand he placed lightly on the small of her back, she chose a disposable tray with glistening figs covered in cling wrap. Then she handed over a ten euro and waited for the change. When the vendor didn't, she glanced back at Ren.

"He's expecting you to ask to pay less."

"How do I tell him that this is a fair price, and I will pay what he asks?"

Ren spoke to the man in their language, and the merchant bowed slightly toward Miranda. He patted her hand when he passed her the change. Miranda's heart flooded with joy.

Ren reached for her hand and intertwined their fingers. "He appreciated your respect. It isn't often a tourist pays the price written on the item. For that matter, neither will the locals. The vendors usually mark a higher price for a little bargaining room."

"For anyone to stand out here all day, they deserve respect. And fair prices for their wares. Thank you for translating for me."

When she slipped into the passenger seat, he reached in and pulled the belt across her chest and clicked it into place. She drew in her breath, trying to sink into the upholstery.

He smiled at her. "All safe now."

Yes, she was safe.

They drove through the fishing village, which clung to the harsh landscape. People with backpacks were hiking along the ridges, and they passed cars with surfboards secured to their roofs.

"I know we're not all the same, but I wouldn't want to surf in these waves. Have you ever tried it?"

"Of course. What true Portuguese teenager wouldn't think he was invincible and fling himself into nature sure he was going to win?"

She laughed. "Well, I'm glad you did win."

"How can you be so sure?"

"You're here with me."

"And we have figs." Ren tipped his chin toward her bag.

"Oh, wait." She tugged open her backpack. "I'm sure I have wipes in my bag."

Miranda handed him a wipe and cleaned her hands before opening the see-through wrap. They both drew a deep breath, inhaling the sweet aroma. She chose a soft, moist fruit and offered it to Ren. He turned slightly, his mouth open like a bird. She lifted it to his lips, and he bit through the glistening flesh sending waves of sweetness through the air. Sticky juice ran down her fingers. She popped the rest of the fig into her mouth and bit into the sweet, chewy fruit. Her eyelids fluttered closed at the exquisite experience.

The car slowed while Ren pulled over onto the side of the road.

"I'm not safe to drive glancing at your enchanted face and sweet lips." He leaned across the console and kissed her with lips flavored from the fruit they had shared. He drew back slightly and ran his thumb across her bottom lip.

"How was your first fig?"

"It could become a steady part of my diet when you're here to share with me," she sighed.

"I will never take a fig for granted again." He settled into his seat and steered the car back onto the road. She reached over and placed her hand on his thigh.

When they drove into Lagos, Ren asked, "Would you care to walk and perhaps have a coffee break?"

"Sure, you're the guide." Miranda hadn't given up the lead in her life very often. She sought advice and relied on trusted mentors, but she forged her path. Her mom had encouraged her thoughts and decisions rather than accepting someone else's. But this felt different. When Ren offered his hand to assist her out of the car, she took it.

They walked hand in hand, down pavements inlaid with the tile to resemble sea-creatures. They walked past craft shops and outdoor cafes until they stopped at a marker that designated the spot of the slave market.

"This was the village from which the sailors set out on their expeditions and where they returned with their bounty. Sadly, it wasn't all spices and gold."

While standing and reading the inscription, she said, "In Canada, we like to pretend that we don't have this history, but we do."

Ren waited for her to finish reading the information and then they walked in silence until they came to the market square. "I think we should find somewhere that will give you a flavor of home-style meals."

"Is it true that we should always search out where the locals eat?"

"As long as it isn't their relative." He smiled and guided her to an outdoor table with an apparent local clientele, many of whom acknowledged Ren with a wave or polite nod. "When I'm home and close to the sea, I want to have seafood. I've been told they serve the best-grilled fish."

"Are you related?"

"Distant."

"Ah, explains no air kisses from anyone."

Ren ordered wine to accompany their grilled fish. After sampling the wine, he told her more about the area. In the bright sunlight, Ren wore sunglasses, and she missed seeing his expressive eyes as he regaled her with local stories.

Their meal arrived sooner than Miranda had anticipated. She ate enthusiastically.

"Your source was correct. This fish is light and tasty. I don't know how to cook fish, so I don't very often."

"Cooking fish fresh versus thawed as we have in Saskatchewan takes more skill."

After their meal, Ren ordered coffee. While they sipped, they watched the people strolling along.

The seagulls soared overhead and then scrambled for scraps of food under and around the tables. Miranda was surprised at the number of dogs. "The pets' owners must train their dogs from the time they were born. They appear not to notice the birds scavenging for food."

"I didn't understand when I arrived in Canada why owners tied dogs up outside of restaurants or grocery stores." He nodded toward a fluffy white dog curled up at his mistress's feet.

"Do they treat cats the same as some owners in Saskatchewan?"

"I know there are cat rescue organizations that build cat houses and put out food and water for feral cats, but they also spay or neuter them to keep down the population. But treat them like they're furbabies? I'm not sure."

"I wasn't allowed to have a pet. And then I didn't encourage my children to have them either." Her breathing slowed as she remembered begging for a puppy to keep her company. Her practical mom drew up a cost-effective sheet, and the expenses seemed to outweigh the emotional satisfaction she would receive.

"Why?" His brow furrowed.

"When I was young, I wanted to please my parents and their colleagues. When my children were young, I suppose they wanted to please me." She suddenly recalled writing in her diary that she'd never deny her children. They could have twelve dogs and twelve kittens if they wanted.

"A fleeting sadness just crossed over your face," he said.

"I remembered that I had promised myself I wouldn't refuse my children if they asked for pets. But I did. Of course, my reasons were different and made sense, but the outcome was the same."

"What were your reasons?"

"I took my children on trips to experience as much of the world as we could. I said it wouldn't be fair for a pet to be left behind so often. I realize now that we were home most of the time. I guess I just didn't want to add one more thing to my responsibilities. Being a single mom and the sole provider was enough."

"That sounds reasonable."

"But it wasn't fair. Did you ever hear the story about a woman who used to cut off the end of her roast before she put it in the pan to cook?"

He shook his head.

"One day, her daughter asked her why she did it. She said because her mother had."

"Then she asked her mother why, didn't she?"

"Her mother cut the end of the roast because her pan was too small. All these years, the daughter copied her mother but didn't know why. We do so many things because we learned them, but we don't truly understand why."

"I agree. When I came to Canada, I wanted all of the equipment and the materials to be the same as here at home. But they weren't, so I thought the Canadian ways were inferior. I have since learned differently."

"Maybe when I go home, I'll get a fluffy, white dog that will sit on my lap and look wistfully at me."

"Until you give it a treat." He laughed.

"I wonder, is that all it would take for wistful gazes?" She raised an eyebrow at him. "I have more figs."

Chapter 16

Ren shook his head. "I'm afraid I'm missing your innuendo."

She blushed a pretty shade of pink. "I was trying for coy and humorous."

"I would never take you as a coy sort of woman. To have had a successful career, I think you would've had to be honest and straightforward." He smiled at her serious expression. "And perhaps humorous on occasion."

"I'm attracted to you, Ren. And I've been serious most of my life." She shook her head. "I never was good at flirting."

"Neither was I, even as a young man here, speaking my first language."

"I didn't learn the dating rules, either. Owning my own business and being successful were my goals. I also wanted children, and I managed that all on my own."

Ren's heart jumped to his throat. This conversation had taken a serious swerve, one he wasn't sure he wanted to continue. He cleared his throat, "Would you like to walk around the old town?"

"How do you define old from new?"

The way she looked at him, he wasn't sure if she was attempting more flirting. Or if she was looking for an answer to more than he had asked. "The old section's surrounded by a medieval wall."

"Many old things have their walls," she said. "I'm ready to explore."

Aha, she was trying to tell him something. Ren folded money and slid it under his cup even though the bill included a gratuity. They had stayed and chatted longer than most patrons.

Outside of the restaurant, she tucked her hand into the crook of his elbow. He pulled his arm tight to his side. She fit perfectly next to him. Her soft skin and the scent from her hair comforted him as he guided her across the street.

In his country, people walked close to one another. When he first immigrated to Canada, he watched how men and women walked and sat together. Unless they were in the first stage of love, they didn't touch openly. They might graze fingers or peck a cheek before they left or in greeting, but none of the open affection his country folks display. Men didn't touch with tenderness unless they were related or in a gay relationship. There seemed to be a disconnect between friendly touching and touching for sexual gratification. But Miranda was different.

She stopped and pointed to a light post.

The pole looked like it was wearing a large straw hat. "It's a stork's nest," he said.

"Storks?"

"Yes, they're used to nesting in high places and in the urban centers, it ends up being light poles, or even church steeples."

She tipped her head back and scanned the area. "Amazing how these birds adapt to find a place to call home while they waited to deliver babies to couples around the world."

He did a double-take. Of course, she was joking. She said she raised two children. "Did you place your order for one of each?"

"Of course. The million-dollar family."

"I knew I should have saved more money." He was pleased when she snuggled closer.

"How did you adapt without the sea and the moist air, Ren?"

"I won't pretend that it was easy. For many months, and even a few years, I ached to return home. I'd save all of my spare cash for return tickets. Then, I'd come here and the jobs were scarce and the slower technology development, so I'd ache to be in Canada. I may be more like the stork than I ever considered. Except I haven't brought anyone a baby." He smiled down at her. "But this country is catching up, and I'm slowing down, and home seems to have a bigger pull."

"I get that. When I first planned this trip, as you know, I was intent on purchasing a property and staying here. But I do long for home."

"Are you ready to continue our drive?" He pointed to the car. They had strolled through the streets, along the marina, and had ended up back at the car. Reluctantly, he released her and opened the car door.

His arm felt heavier without hers linked through the crook of his elbow and her hand resting on his forearm. He was glad they would both be back in Canada with an opportunity to continue their friendship. But he cautioned himself not to get in front of himself. Intentions after a holiday friendship sometimes go south, especially when both of them were involved in their own lives. Wasn't the wisdom of the day to enjoy the moments and allow the days to take care of themselves?

She reached over the stick shift and laid her hand on his arm. "Thank you for sharing your knowledge and expertise."

"Thank you. There are many things I do not know, but because you don't know them either, I appear to be the bright bulb. When we meet up in Regina, you will astound me with your experiences."

"I do know a great deal about Regina and many of the surrounding districts, including Apex."

"There's a pretty park just around the bend. We have a blanket, and we could rest below a tree. You can tell me a story."

Miranda gave a small laugh and then nodded her acceptance to his proposal. Ren drove down the narrow path that led to the park bordering the sea. Once parked, he opened the trunk and took out the blanket and a pillow his grandmother always packed for just this kind of experience.

Choosing a tree so they could rest with their feet toward the sea, he shook out the blanket and tossed the cushion. Miranda instinctively zeroed in on the pillow and put her head down, curling onto her side. He pointed the key fob at the car, watched the lights flash, then stretched out beside her. He envied her pillow for a few minutes while he watched the clouds bob along the horizon.

When he woke, his head was on the pillow, his arm was curled around her waist, and her head rested on his shoulder. It was as if a magnetic pull of their needs helped them determine in their sleep what they wouldn't admit to when they were awake. But perhaps Miranda would. She had been forthright with him. He wondered about the father of her children, where he fit in the picture.

Even though darkness had descended, in the light cast from the park lights, he studied the style of her shirt and capris, the texture, the crispness even after being out all day. He had noticed before, without realizing it, that her clothes were expensive. Ordinary, but fine quality. Just like her.

She reached up and brushed something from her face. Ren hadn't noticed a bug or web. Perhaps she was dreaming. Her eyes fluttered and gradually opened. She didn't jump up embarrassed instead, she grinned at him. "I hope I didn't drool on your shoulder."

"If you did, I'd keep the shirt just as it is rather than wash it," he kidded her. The strange thing was that he did feel that way. He would have a speck of her. "But you didn't, so you don't have anything to worry about."

"Did your arm fall asleep?"

"I don't need this arm for anything important."

"I've haven't heard about any one-armed tile setter."

"Then you haven't heard about many of the Portuguese men's talents." He laughed. Never before had he been this comfortable with a woman.

She yawned. "I forgot about my story."

He had to ask. "Is the father of your children in your picture frame?"

"He's in Stacy's and Nathan's genetics, but other than that, I don't even know who he is."

Ren's surprise must have registered on his face, for she quickly said, "Here's my story. I didn't sleep around. I went to a sperm bank and after I was pregnant, I paid to hold the sperm for my second child. So technically," she said with a laugh, "I'm a fifty-five-year-old virgin."

"You may be a virgin in the basic definition of the word but in reality, a woman who doesn't know much about life you are not."

"I don't know anything about having a relationship with a man," she said wistfully.

"There's therapy for that."

"I'll consider that when there is a man in my life who would like to be with me for as long as we live."

He propped up on one elbow and looked into her eyes. "Is there longevity in your family?"

"My maternal side, yes."

"Is that why you came away, knowing you will have a long, what did you call it, third act?"

She smiled. "Mostly. I honestly think that it's best for my children if I am away, while they take over the business without my interference from the back office. But now I know that's not the real reason. You've helped with that. And Maria and your aunt, too."

"Me, I can understand, but Maria and Tia Isabell?"

"Lorenza and your grandmother, too." She drew a circle in the air. "Family who are willing to fly halfway across the world to do what is right for love."

Was it always love, or was it also the feeling of responsibility? Ren loved his grandmother, and he tried to give back equally as much as he received. Perhaps it was time to step back and wonder why he felt that equal and similar giving and receiving was enough for him. His heart sped up. For the love of himself and perhaps his future, could he, should he sell the house his family still thought of belonging to the family as a whole?

He felt her shiver. "The breeze is coming up. Are you ready to drive back to Albufeira?"

"Yes."

He helped her up and passed her the pillow, which she hugged to her chest. She pushed her hand through her hair. "It can't be bedhead if the wind is blowing."

"And if it was?" He lifted the blanket and folded it.

"I'm worried about your reputation." She looked around the park. "Isabell wants you to stay in the family with a wife and children."

"I'm not sure I've ever done what the matriarchs in my family have wanted."

"From what I've experienced, you're a kind man. You probably wouldn't hurt them unnecessarily."

His tongue stuck to the roof of his mouth. "I might." He turned toward the horizon where the sea met the sky, "Hey, would you like to come over for dinner tomorrow evening? I'll help Tia Isabell cook, and you can have an authentic Portuguese meal."

"Could I come over and help?"

"Are you always this forward? No disrespect meant."

"None taken. I've learned to ask for things I want, and now it's even more important."

"Good. I'll text you when we're going to shop and begin cooking."

"When does your aunt return to Canada?"

"After I do. Isabell's husband, Tomas, is taking over for me in an emergency, but I'm needed. I have to purchase a ticket. I'm planning for the weekend or early next week."

"Are you sure you want me to interrupt your family dinner?"

"I, too, have learned some things. I try not to set up a situation that I don't think will work. Eduardo, the motorcycle salesman and our cousin, Katia, will be there as well. And who knows who else Tia Isabell has invited."

"I would like to help then. And I'll be able to take home the experience of a family dinner."

"And when will you return?"

"Right now I've decided on a month."

Ren wished he could stay. He popped the trunk, and they stowed the pillow and blanket. Miranda buckled up, and he drove the familiar highway back to Albufeira.

Once in the city, Miranda pointed out the window. "Ah, here are the globes, and then the watches and then we turn toward my hotel."

"The city planners wanted the tourists to find their way along the main street and the traffic circles, so they created these landmarks."

"Smart designers."

"What are you going to do this evening?"

"I'm going to have a swim and then have a drink in the hotel dining room. There's a Fado singer performing tonight."

When he stopped the car, she leaned over and kissed him on his surprised lips. "Thank you."

"You're welcome, Miranda. I'll text you in the morning about times."

"I look forward to it."

He watched her stride toward the entrance. Her sweater tied around her waist. If anyone looked closely, would they notice the lovely woman they just passed?

And now he had to decide how much he was going to tell his aunt.

He was still undecided even as he opened the door. The usual slight scrape along the tiled floor announced his arrival. He had asked his avó over and over if he could plane the door and stop the catch against the slight rise. She refused, explaining that it was better than a doorbell. And just as his avó had said, he heard, "Ren, is that you?"

He walked toward the kitchen. "Yes, I'm back."

"Thank heaven. I've been worried about you."

She was sitting with a custard tart and coffee at the table.

"Why?" He pulled out a chair and sat.

"Out with a tourist all day, you never know what they will ask you to do and the money you'll spend."

"Where does this come from?" He snagged the plate with the tart and forked up a mouthful.

"Well, I just know. I wanted you to meet Luscinda, the granddaughter of the head librarian. She walked me home from the library. She's a lovely woman here visiting her grandfather. She lives in Faro."

"That was kind of her to carry your books home for you."

"She is a lovely woman. Not too young that she is silly but not too old that she likes to be single. She grew up in Faro and spent all of her summers here swimming in the sea with her grandfather and grandmother."

"She was fortunate, indeed."

"I've invited Luscinda and her grandparents to join us for dinner tomorrow, along with Eduardo and Katia. Remember, you promised to help me cook."

If he were a teenager, he'd roll his eyes. He knew a matchmaking attempt when he heard one. "I remember. I also invited Miranda, and she would like to help with the dinner preparations. She would like to help prepare and share a Portuguese family dinner." Miranda would be his winger as if this was a soccer match. Someone who could protect both his right and left side.

Isabell spread her hands and rubbed them down the front of her skirt. "Does this woman have children?"

"Yes, they work in Regina."

"Oh. And I suppose you mean to see her when you are both back in Canada?"

"Maybe. But you know how holiday friendships are, and I'll be swamped in Apex." He had a sudden urge to place his hand over his heart as if to protect it.

"That is true. In that case, I'm delighted to show Miranda how to make my sauce handed down from my mother's mother to my mother and then to me."

He kissed her on her cheek. "Thank you. I knew that you would find it in your heart to make her feel welcome."

She jammed her hands into her apron pockets. "Are you sure she isn't after you? After all, you have a house."

"Tia Isabell, she has a house, too. Besides, she's a friend. And a man can never have too many friends."

"You're such an innocent."

"I'm fifty-five years old. I know a few things."

"Then I hope you know how to shop at the market tomorrow. We will have to make a big batch of sauce and, I hate to say it, we will have to buy the noodles from the market. They'll be fresh but not mine."

"The family will be happy to be together. Did you visit with Maria today?"

"She and I had a long chat while you were out with that floozy."

"Tia, where do you get your ideas? Miranda's not a floozy. She's an accomplished businesswoman. If anything, I should be scouting her for my old age."

"Since when does a Portuguese man look for financial comfort in a woman?"

"Since we get tired of crawling on our knees, and our permanently scarred knuckles ache, and because we spend all of our retirement money coming home to the old country."

She gave him a playful push.

"Can I take you out to dinner tonight? You've been working hard helping me, and I've left you alone too much."

"I would love a good plate of sardines. I hate to cook them in the house because they smell for days, and we have company coming."

"Where is your favorite place?"

"Let's go to Pequena Peixe. I always enjoy eating outdoors even if they have to have the plastic walls up to protect us from the wind."

"I'll change my clothes and meet you at the door in fifteen minutes."

"I knew there was a reason you are my favorite nephew."

"I count myself lucky when I am. Tomorrow, I may not be."

Chapter 17

On her way through the lobby, Miranda walked past a German-speaking couple, a couple with a British accent, and a toddler who kicked the wheel on his stroller with his heel. No one paid much attention to her. They missed seeing the joy on her face, the smile on her lips, and the just been kissed look on her lived-life face.

When she approached the front desk on her way to the stairs, the porter called her over and handed her a message.

Once in her room, the moist breeze carried floral scents riding on the tinge of salt air. Again, she reminded herself to breathe, then she opened the flap and removed the single folded notepaper. She closed her eyes, then opened them and unfolded it to reveal a neat script with a message to call this number as soon as possible. Her eyes watered. Stacy's number. It's just after seven in the evening. She did a quick calculation minus eight hours, just before lunch. What could be wrong?

Miranda pushed out of her chair, found her Canadian phone in the bedside table, plugged it in, and dialled the office.

"Hello, Mom," Stacy answered on the first ring.

Hearing her daughter's voice amped up her heart rate. "Stacy, honey. Hello."

"I'm so sorry to call, but we have a problem."

Miranda sighed with relief. A problem was work-related, not a tragedy. She collapsed against the cushions on the bed. "Tell me."

"Our client, Mr. Keene."

"Of Keene Commercial Buildings, yes."

"He's decided that Nathan and I are not experienced enough to close this next deal. It's important, Mom. It's a big commission."

Miranda heard the fright crawl into her little girl's voice. "Tell me what we have."

It felt good to be in the wheelhouse again as Stacy listed off the steps and counteroffers that had been received and accepted. "You see, Mom, we need you even if it is just for a few days. Can you come back?"

"You said they have four days for the conditions to be met, but you think there will be more complications?"

"Yes."

"I'll check the flights and call you back."

"I have flights lined up if you'll come. The first option leaves tomorrow at two-thirty in the afternoon and with the stopovers and transfers, you'll be here the next day. A day to rest and the next to come to the office and work your magic. If it was anyone else I wouldn't ask."

Miranda closed her eyes and saw Ren's face, his hands. She remembered the feel of his protective arm around her waist as they lay in the park that afternoon. Her breath caught in her chest.

"Mom, are you all right?"

"Yes, honey. Confirm the seats. I'll be there. Love you."

"You, too. And Mom? Thank you."

Her swim and then a drink while listening to the fado singer were soon forgotten. Her children needed her. Tomorrow, she'd be on the plane going back to them. Her organized brain kicked in. She called the desk and cancelled her apartment for her planned extended stay. She asked for the hotel transport to the Faro airport and then she sank further down onto the bed. The bathing suit on the other chair drew her attention. She wouldn't discover if the new Miranda were comfortable exposing so much of her body.

She wouldn't have time to practice getting used to her new self. She was going to have to do what she'd always done, jump in with both feet.

She poured herself a glass of wine and walked out onto the patio. She needed to call Ren. This change required more than a text message. Disappointment bubbled up and she slumped in the chair. She wasn't going to learn to cook a traditional meal or sit down with a Portuguese family. Nor was she going to be able to say, perhaps see you in Canada because she didn't want him to think he owed her any more than he had given her. Holiday friendships might continue with good intentions and perhaps a few emails, but the desire to fulfill promises dwindled as time went by. She wouldn't put that responsibility on this special man. She knew where he worked, and she could initiate communication. Had she told him the real estate company name? She couldn't recall. They hadn't spoken of mundane details when they were talking about life choices and holiday adventures.

Her finger shook when she pressed the contact icon and his name. Taking a deep breath, she almost hoped he wouldn't answer. Perhaps there was a soccer game he couldn't miss. Or maybe he was spending time with his old buddies. The phone rang, once, twice, three times. Would she leave a voicemail? Could she?

"Hello," a tentative female voice answered, anxious and heavily accented.

Miranda's heart thudded against her rib cage. "I'm sorry I must have the wrong number."

"Sim, sim. Ren away."

"Obrigada."

"Okay. Goodbye."

Miranda dropped the phone and didn't care if it shattered. He was probably out with someone his family thought was more appropriate. Stacy had called at the perfect time. The retirement preparation courses suggested that the adjustment would be difficult and to be careful that she didn't put her emotions in places that couldn't be returned. And sometimes those emotions pretended to be one thing but were something else entirely. Had she done what was recommended not to do?

Tears welled up, and her throat closed. She didn't want to go through another loss, no matter how small. But she needed to say thank you and goodbye. Ren had been so generous with his time. She may even give him her number in Saskatchewan, perhaps suggest that she drive out to Apex and check on the construction's progress. They could remain acquaintances. She needed positive thoughts.

Raking her fingers through her hair gave her time to think of positive ways to rescue this situation. Protect her heart. After all, it was nothing more than friendship. Stepping back into the living room, she poured herself a glass of brandy instead of another wine. Thank goodness for a grocery store that sold bathing suits, fruits and vegetables, and spirits. She stepped out onto the balcony and stared over the rooftops to the ocean.

Her phone signalled a text.

Hi, Miranda. I took Tia Isabell for dinner. Did you call?

Should she pretend she was asleep and deal with this in the morning? Her fingers hovered over the keyboard. She checked the time, 9:30 p.m. Many locals were only eating their dinner.

Can you come over for a nightcap? I need to tell you something.

Before she hit send, she counted to ten. Did she want to go through *we'll meet again*? No, that wouldn't be her favorite part, but she owed Ren honesty.

She pressed send, then closed her eyes. If she didn't look, she wouldn't have to see if Ren replied, sorry I have plans.

Her eyes flashed open with the notification *bing* and vibration in her palm. A dancing emoticon appeared with a thumbs-up and smiley face and then another *bing* with the words *twenty minutes*.

She sent the clapping hands back to him. Twenty minutes to plan what to say. Twenty minutes to wonder if he would stay the night. Nineteen minutes to wonder if she wanted him to. Eighteen minutes to contemplate the idea. Fifteen minutes to wait, knowing she couldn't. She wasn't ready yet.

Miranda brushed her teeth then found a second brandy snifter in the cupboard and set them with the bottle on a tray. She fluffed pillows and swiped her hand across the surfaces that hadn't had time to get dusty. She stared at the floor and wondered why tiles were such a hard sell back home. She and other realtors moaned when they saw tiles in houses because potential owners would ask how to remove them and replace them with another flooring type. There was no way to remove tiles other than a jackhammer and a lot of hard work.

But did she care what potential buyers thought, now? Did she need to at this time of her life? Tiles would be lovely in her home in Regina. And she could always dream about having Ren create the magic of this place.

Her phone buzzed again. She gave security permission to allow Ren to visit. There wasn't time to consider other life options. Ren had arrived. While she walked to the door to answer the light tap, the image of him with his sleeves rolled up, and his salt and pepper hair slicked back with sweat doing something he loved in her home brought gleefulness to her soul. After peering through the security lens, she opened both the door and her hope wide.

She stepped aside. "Ren, come in."

He handed her a bouquet. She pressed them to her chest. "Where did you find a flower seller at this time of night?"

He hung his head and mumbled, "My grandmother's garden."

She tapped his chest with a rose before she lifted the bouquet and shook away dirt from a few root threads. "I'll put these in water, but first, I'll use a very sharp knife to trim the stems."

She smiled to herself. Ren had brought her flowers. Meeting this man and having this type of attention and fun was the best that had happened to her in a long time. She hadn't worried about the business or her children since she had met him, but that time was over. Her children needed her, and the business needed her, especially if it meant financial security to move forward. Now she had to tell Ren she was leaving.

She placed the flowers on the cutting board to trim them. A clean cut on the angle would allow the blooms to flourish for days, but who would enjoy them? "Ren, would you pour the brandy, please? I'll press the button on the coffee maker."

She heard the pop of the cork, the slight gurgle from the bottle as it flowed into the glasses. Then he stepped into the kitchen with a snifter in each hand.

"Filtered coffee?"

"The Continente has everything. It's the things that bring us comfort in a strange environment that we need at special times."

"Is this a special time, Miranda?" He placed a glass on the counter next to the flowers and stepped away, giving her space.

After turning on the tap and running water into a jar, she arranged the flowers and stood back to admire their beauty.

She took a deep breath, picked up her glass, and turned to face him. "I had a message from Stacy, my daughter, when I got home. The business needs me. She needs me. She's booked my flight for tomorrow out of Faro." Her eyes watered as she swallowed a slick of brandy. "I can't come with you tomorrow to help you shop or cook, or eat dinner with you and your guests. I'm so sorry."

He took two long strides toward her and then lifted her glass from her hand and placed it on the counter with his. "Is that all?"

"Yes. No. I mean, I'm like these flowers. I yanked myself out of the place I belong, and I've been living on water in a jar." Her spine tingled and straightened. Yes, her business life was a big part of her and that was okay. She was good at it. It was who she had been and still was. It felt so good to admit it. "I need to go back to where I belong."

"Okay. What time do we need to leave for the airport?"

"No, Ren. I can't have you do this. It's too much. I've arranged for transport."

"Then why did you call me over?"

She looked up at him, puzzled. "Because I didn't want to text you. I wanted to tell you personally."

"But we'll see each other in Apex or Regina or Regina Beach."

"Okay." She would go along with the fantasy, but it was highly unlikely they would. "Would you carry the flowers to the sitting area, and I'll bring coffee and our glasses?"

Miranda envied the ease and comfort he had in any situation, as he sat in the too-small tub chair. She would miss him. She looked out toward the ocean, and the half-moon illuminated the surf as waves crested.

"What do you take in your filtered coffee?"

"The way it comes out of the pot."

"At least you never have to worry if there's milk in your fridge."

She sat in the matching tub chair with a small table between them.

Suddenly the lights flickered and went out. Ren sat calmly in the deep quiet without the refrigerator humming or the radio she had turned on for background. So she did the same.

"I've appreciated your friendship and the time you've spent with me, Ren. My vacation would have been so very different without you." It was easier to say in the dark without being able to see his eyes or the smile he may have on his lips. She heard the rustle of his sleeve as he sipped his brandy.

"You make it sound as if we won't ever see each other again."

"You've traveled. You know what vacation friendships are like."

"But we live within an hour of each other. You'll be someone who knows a little about me and where I come from."

"I'm willing to try. But I don't think I can sit by the phone and wait for you to call like a lovesick teenager."

"Lovesick? Sometimes you Canadians have such a weird pairing of words. Love-happy. Love-inspired. Just plain love-friend, but not lovesick."

"You must have some of those sayings in your language that don't make sense to people from away." She could see his hand outlined against the chair.

"Of course, but it's more fun to make fun of someone else's language than our own." A slip of light bounced off the glass as he lifted it to his lips.

Why was she fascinated by his lips? She hadn't had these thoughts in years. It was time for her to go back to where she belonged, where her feelings were collegial, friendly, and familial, not talking about lovesickness to Ren.

In the darkness, Miranda found it was easier to talk.

"I feel like a cliché, Ren." She snorted. "Like everything else in my life, I took the right courses and planned down to the last detail but suddenly, there was this big question, who are you, Miranda Porter?"

"Who do you want to be?"

She turned toward him. "I'm not sure. Stacy and Nathan need me for this deal, and there may be more. I'm a businesswoman. I've always been a businesswoman. I should be back home."

"And you don't think there is a place for me in your life when you return?"

"Ren, I've enjoyed every moment with you from when we bumped heads, and you asked to take my photo, also sharing our first dinner and teaching me how to ride a scooter. Not to mention how many places I've discovered because of you. I'll take back so many memories of the cliffs overhanging the beaches, the walkthrough cliff front yards, cataplana, gigantic ice cream sundaes and oranges. And best of all, relaxing with you in the beautiful sun next to the sea."

"But?"

He couldn't see her chin drop toward her chest.

She heard the rustle of his shirt and the shuffle of his feet. Her heart raced. He was either going to come closer or leave. She wasn't sure which she wanted most. What chance was she willing to take? She reached for him when she felt his presence. They stood together.

"Yes, we will both be busy when we return. But I'll enjoy meeting you and reminiscing of our time here in Albufeira. Even if it is only one or two times, please don't deny us that. You'll be one of the few people who have experienced my roots and understand my family. Sometimes I need a place that reminds me of home."

She leaned forward and put her forehead against his. With his hand behind her head, he guided her to him until their lips touched. She went from friend to hungry and hot within minutes. If this had been a race, she would have beaten all the cars off the starting mark.

Chapter 18

When his neighbor, Senhora Vargas, told Ren that he had a call from an English lady, he was sorry he missed it. He'd accidentally left his phone on the step when he helped Tia Isabell into the car. Miranda hadn't texted, so the reason must have been important. After dinner, he made sure Tia was safely in the house and then texted Miranda. His skin tingled when she wanted to see him for a nightcap.

He couldn't show up empty-handed. That was when he had the bright idea of bringing flowers from the garden. He should have used his flashlight app on his phone. But Miranda was charmed and had laughed. He enjoyed being someone who brought her laughter. But now she was telling him she had to go back to where she belonged. Like most travelers, she needed to return home. He understood this. No matter how far one went, home called to the heart.

Could his home be somewhere else? He was becoming more and more comfortable in Apex, a community that gradually opened its heart to the other. Those people who appeared different on the outside and perhaps the inside but were simply humans with needs.

Her pessimistic view of vacation friends troubled him, but they would be living so close to each other how could they not continue to see each other? Not so close where he could grab flowers from a garden and the earth would still be moist on the root by the time he arrived, but with his truck and he was sure she had a vehicle, close enough. His extended family was pushing for a younger woman who would give him children. But this decision was his to make.

And, if he were honest with himself, he didn't want to be a man continually travelling and returning between two countries with allegiances in both but always alone.

Miranda wouldn't be with him tomorrow, learning how to prepare one of his favorite meals. Nor would she meet his family and those Tia had invited. He couldn't fault his aunt because she was only here for a short time and wanted to catch up with as many family and friends as she could. Ren had attended too many big reunions with less and less to talk about except the past because he no longer shared their present. He could almost repeat the stories they'd tell around the table. He was looking forward to those stories this time because they would be new to Miranda.

Their kisses had gone from light to pretty hot within a short time. His hunger wanted to go deeper, get closer. But in his heart, he knew this wasn't where this evening should go. He pulled away but held Miranda close. He could relish the feel of her without pressing issues. He wasn't young and needy. "Come." He offered his hand and tipped his head toward the patio where the stars shone. "We'll see each other if we make an effort. I know I want to. Don't you?"

She hesitated. "Okay, let's not decide now. Why do we say the things we do to people we don't know very well?" She cupped his hand between her palms. "Why do we put stress on strangers to sort out things they don't have enough information to work with?"

He wasn't sure how to interpret her questions. Their steamy kisses had robbed him of their conversation. Sometimes he had to change the words he heard in English into his native language, but the intonation and the meaning might differ. The intensity with which her gaze flickered back and forth from his chin to his eyes seemed to suggest she was afraid of what he might answer.

"Miranda, I'm not sure I understand what you're saying."

"I'm not either." She inhaled and slowly exhaled. "I'm asking you to make love to me tonight before we part ways, but I'm also asking you to leave so that we don't."

He drew her closer. "We can wait." He kissed the side of her ear, down along her jawline and then stopped, waiting for her to make the decision.

She brought both hands toward him. She stepped forward, and their lips met, lingered, parted slightly. Ren slipped his hand down her back and twitched the hem of her shirt. She froze and pulled from his embrace.

"Miranda, I'm not looking for a holiday fling. I've had enough of them in my day."

Her reaction surprised him. "Don't raise your eyebrow at me. I don't think you came here for this. Will you trust me and tell me what it is you truly want?"

When she nodded, he stepped back and reached for her hand, guiding her back toward the couch where he handed her the brandy glass and then lifted his own.

They sat with thighs touching and her shoulder nestled against him, she sipped her brandy, then said in a very quiet voice, "I don't want to be alone in the time remaining in my life."

"You won't be alone. You have your children, your friends, family."

"I don't have children. I have adults who are busy learning who they are and what they want from life. I know they love me in their way, but not the way I want to be loved. Can you understand?" She placed a hand on his thigh.

He covered her hand. He was a sucker for a sad woman, and it had gotten him into more trouble than not in his life. He would like to blame his bachelor status at the age of fifty-five for his compassion for women in need. First, as a pre-teen, he cared for his mother, then his grandmother and in between, a few women who were not related.

Putting aside his primal urges, he deposited his glass on the table beside him and wrapped her closer. "Miranda, what do you miss?" She was quiet, but he could and would wait.

"I miss going out dancing until past midnight." Then she giggled. "To be truthful, I never did go out dancing. I worked with my parents and went to school, got my license, and continued working."

"There must have been special men in your life."

"The father of my children, even though I've never met him, danced me with hope. I've met different parts of him in my children. The parts I don't recognize as my relatives or me." She sighed. "Because my children's father's sperm was in a bank, my fingers had danced through the catalogue of characteristics until I found him."

"Why did you decide to go that way?"

"I wanted children, but I didn't have time to work on a relationship. I suspected I wouldn't be very good at it. Just like now."

He stroked her hair, hoping to convey that she was doing just fine. "What else do you miss?"

"My children's arms around my neck when I picked them up from daycare. Their scent. Even today. Stacy likes the fruity shampoos and lotions while Nathan is all musk."

He had a feeling he'd miss the citrus scent of Miranda, the way she reached for his hand, her trust in him if they parted ways today. "What else?"

"Driving up my driveway with the fir trees we planted from the forestry park when Stacy and Nathan were in school. The red front door. The shimmer of light from the chandelier in the hallway."

"Out of all of that, what do you miss the most?"

"Ren, I miss me, the me I was before this. The decisive me. The button-down business me." She snuggled closer to him and laid her arm across his stomach. "Your turn. What do you miss?"

"I miss my sense of home. Until I came back this time, I hadn't realized it quite as much because . . ." He couldn't go on.

"Your grandmother wasn't there."

"Yes, that's part of it. I mostly thought it was the space and place before, but now I realize it's the people in my life. I miss the boys who used to meet me on the public soccer pitch. We never dreamt of the big time, or if we did, it was our dream, not our parents and grandparents as it is now."

"Did we have it easier in our childhood, or did it just appear that way?" She ran her fingers up and down his forearm. "I miss the safe streets we used to have."

"Me, too. We rode our bicycles from the time we got out of bed until our parents called us in for bedtime. We played on the beach and in the waves close to shore until we got tall enough and brave enough to face our mother's wrath for venturing out further. But the exhilaration was worth every moment of it."

"I miss my mother's scent," he continued. "I used to have a bottle of it, but I lost it. Or misplaced it when I thought I was too old to care." He wished she could wrap him close one more time so he could inhale the sweet, spice she called her joy. Until now, he didn't realize how much he missed his mom. He could visit her. She wasn't gone, just away.

"I miss my mother's stressed singing. Whenever she wasn't sure what might happen after presenting an offer to the client, she sang, 'Que sera, sera, whatever will be will be.' I always knew when my mother was making an offer that she wasn't convinced was acceptable."

"Do you notice other people singing under stress?"

"I do. Sometimes small business owners, sometimes health care professionals, and occasionally myself." She snorted.

"What song do you sing?" He turned to look at her.

"I used to make up songs. I sing off-key, but it helped. I mostly breathe deeply to calm myself. I know, why didn't I just deep breathe? But Stacy and Nathan would never know how important something was for me. This way, they know as soon as I break into made-up songs."

"Do you sing now?" He was curious.

"No, not now. But before you came, I wanted to. 'Ren's coming, what should I do? I like him, and he likes me, but I'm leaving tomorrow. What can we do?'"

He laughed. "Such a pretty ditty."

She gave him a playful swat. He caught her hand and held it to his chest. "May I please drive you to the airport tomorrow?"

"Oh, Ren, how can I say no? I want to. I want to say, think of your aunt, the shopping, the special dinner and sorting out your grandmother's house. But I also know that you're an adult, and you know the consequences of your actions. If you tick off your aunt and she decides to go back to Regina without completing the tasks at hand, that's on you. So the short answer after all of this rambling is, thank you. Yes."

His heart reverberated against her palm. He wasn't sure why he wanted this woman's hand on his chest. This woman's face in his mind, this woman's scent in his nose, but he did. And he was tired of denying what he wanted.

But was it what he wanted or what he needed? His aunt was right. Miranda would never give him children. She may not give him many years either, but those reasons didn't seem to matter tonight. If he had wanted children, he would have made that happen long ago. Now, he had found a woman he liked and a woman he wanted.

What if she didn't like sex? Would that be a deal-breaker? He was way ahead of himself. She had her hand on his chest, her head on his shoulder, and her legs crowding his on the couch. She liked to touch and cuddle. Would this be enough when he got home from a hard day of work? Who was he kidding? When he got back from a hard day at work, he was exhausted.

She tapped him on his chest. "Where are you, Ren? Where did you go?"

"Ahh, Miranda, I was looking into a crystal ball in my head."

"What did you see?" She leaned back and studied his eyes.

"I see that I don't want this to be a vacation friendship. I'd like to see you back in Regina, and I'd like to introduce you to the folks at the Apex Medical Centre. I'd like to show you my work. And if it works out like I think it will, I'd like you to live with me there."

"And did your crystal ball show you what I would do?"

"Unfortunately not. It reflects my wishes, but not if they are granted."

"Let me consult my genie." She rubbed his arm as if polishing a lamp. Then she waved her hand in front of her eyes as if clearing smoke and gazed wide-eyed. "What's that you say? I can't understand you." She turned with a puzzled look. "She's speaking genie, and I can't understand her. I think we'll have to play it by ear."

His relief at her humor and acceptance caused his chest to tighten while he tried to contain a chuckle. But he couldn't hold it in. Laughter exploded from him. He wrapped his arms around her and hugged her close.

She sighed deeply and then she yawned.

"I know you'll have a big day tomorrow winging your way home." He loosened his hold and slid away from her. "I'll come at eleven, and drive you to the airport. On the way, we'll plan for our next date."

She bit her lip, and then a tear escaped down her cheek. He laid his thumb in the tear's path. "That will be nice. I'll be ready."

"Thank you for the brandy," he said.

"My pleasure."

He held out his hands and helped her stand. They walked toward the door. Before he opened it, he drew her close for one final hug. "'Til tomorrow."

"If you insist." She tilted her head and smiled.

On his walk home, the seabirds called to one another, and couples lingered in the shadows. What would he rather be? A lonely seabird searching for a mate or part of a couple walking arm in arm along the shore? Even though he and Miranda were not young, he looked forward to walking arm in arm for however long they had. He whistled while he walked. He didn't have to discover the answer this evening, and he would be with her again tomorrow. They would have a future, possibly a silver anniversary.

He ran his hand along the front of a house with the tiled outer walls. Some tiles had either been knocked off or had fallen off, but it gave the house character. Like wrinkles on a face or hands, the lines that declared a life lived.

His hand slid along a stone handrail worn smooth over a century except for the dates and names carved into it. Declarations of love or a mark that the carver was there. Who was HB who loved JM? Did they remain together, or did they have a holiday romance and then drift apart? Did it matter? They had the time they had.

And that's all he was asking of Miranda. Time to get to know her, the real her, the one she'd lost and the one she'd find. He'd had glimpses of her over their time together, more so tonight as she shared with him those things she missed the most. He was sure he'd like that Miranda very much.

He passed an open door that led to a tiled staircase. The hours it would have taken to create such a passage. Would he have the time to have a relationship and continue with his craft? He thought about all the apartments and side-by-sides that would require tiled kitchens and bathrooms. He loved his job. The creative aspect, the precision, but did he love it more than getting to know this woman? Will managed to have a relationship with Tiffany, and he was as busy as a one-armed paper hanger. Perhaps there was someone who would enjoy learning the craft, and he'd free up some of his time. If he didn't change his ways, he'd be sitting alone rubbing ointment on his worn-out knees, wondering when someone would come and visit.

But Miranda may not be his answer, and he might not be her answer. He was a crab crawling along the shore, looking for a place to hide. He needed to swim toward a buoy. Maybe Miranda had been right, and they would need to play it by ear.

He walked into the house and found his aunt in the hall, her hands planted firmly on her hips, staring at the soil she had tracked into the house.

"I wondered if an animal had been digging in our garden. Then I saw the missing flowers, and I knew you are up to your old tricks again. Robbing the garden for a woman."

Chapter 19

After watching Ren disappear down the hall, Miranda placed the vase of flowers on the side table and sank into the couch. She reached out and touched each flower, unable to stop smiling. Could she stay? Could she have a virtual client meeting? It might be possible with another client, but it was with Mr. Keene. The situation demanded an in-person meeting. But her consolation was that Ren would drive her to the airport. His intentions to renew and continue their budding friendship in Saskatchewan were sincere, and of course, she would be thrilled if he called, but she knew all too well that life gets in the way of even the best intentions.

Why was she so negative? Insecurity wasn't like her. If she had had this attitude while building her business, she would never have accomplished what she did. And if she continued, she'd turn into a negative Nelly who no one would want to be near. And from Negative Nelly, it would move to Nasty Nan. The old Miranda would not spoil his wish for the future. But work-in-progress Miranda would not sit and wait for a call.

She got up and packed her meagre belongings, her new bathing suits. It was winter at home. But she had today with the sun on her body for the first time in this new future, and for this, she was thankful.

She stood in front of the mirror and marveled that she was going through her third act in life while she was physically active and able. It wasn't her advancing age that had convinced her to leave the business. Her mother's example of getting out of the way had influenced her. It allowed her to move forward with the times.

When she had dreamt of her life, work was not going to be the most important thing. Her early diary entries were about being different than her mother. But the good times were addictive, and she managed the slow times. While Stacy and Nathan were tiny, she cared for them twenty-four-seven. And she loved that she could schedule a house viewing or present an offer around their infant schedule. They may have even helped close a few deals, mostly if a woman was in charge of choosing the house. The prospective buyer would look at Miranda and recall her sleepless nights, her time at home with only children to talk to and her busy days. If the client was a single parent, she might relate to Miranda, providing food and a home for her children. When Stacy and Nathan were toddlers, and if they behaved, Miranda took them along during negotiations if the clients liked children. But if the client had ever hinted at losing a child or didn't have children, she found a sitter for the kids. As Mom always said, use what you have at hand. Miranda shook her head at her reflection. She had absorbed many of her mother's business skills.

Tonight was the last evening she would have her window open to the sea, the last night she would see fishers' boats on the horizon. It had been her chance to convince Ren to make love to her and end her virginity, but this was definitely out of her realm of expertise. Did she freeze when he reached for her shirt because she was frightened or because she couldn't toss herself overboard, at least without a life ring? As she snuggled down into her covers, she was glad he had been the strong one for whatever reasons. She wouldn't carry a memory of him inside of her, but she'd have memories of his touch, friendship, and respect.

She recalled their first meeting. That first day when he asked her if he could photograph her. She had been among what felt like a world of perfect, young bodies. But he wasn't perfect either. He was a middle-aged man with lines and greying temples. When he held her, she had experienced his muscular body from what she understood was from labor-intensive work. And he was considerate of his family, his friends, and with her. That's what drew her to him, a safe place to land. However, she had always created her own safe space, and now it was here. Tomorrow it would be on the plane and the day after, her bed in her own home with her son and daughter close at hand.

Miranda lay perfectly still as she realized the tightness that had been in her chest was gone. A sense of calm settled over her. She had always created safe spaces for her and Stacy and Nathan. The Miranda she was looking for was still here. Momentarily, she wondered if she would have had this same awareness if she had stayed in Saskatchewan. Miranda knew the decision to come to Albufeira had been for the best.

Miranda woke to the song of the seagulls as they swept across the beach and into the sea. She heard the distinct backup signal of the garbage trucks as they gathered the trash from the streets. Doors closed, and suitcase wheels bumped along the tiled floor on the other side of the wall. It was time to say farewell to beautiful Portugal.

She ate a small breakfast out on the patio, enjoying the final moments of ocean breezes and the scent of hibiscus. Already packed, she dressed and headed for the lobby.

"Thank you for your understanding." She passed her credit card over to the manager.

"We try our best to assist our traveling guests when they must return home. We hope you will come again."

"I hope so, as well," she said with a heavy heart. She found a chair to wait for Ren.

Soon, he was walking through the door, all broad-shouldered and salt and pepper hair gleaming. "Olá."

"Ren." She couldn't help but smile, happy he had insisted on accompanying her rather than some stranger in a taxi or a hotel shuttle driver.

He reached for her large roller bag, and she pulled her carryon and shouldered her backpack. "How did your aunt react when you told her you'd be away again?"

"She hit me upside the head and said I'd better not dilly dally on the way back."

"She hit you?"

"More of a love tap. I'm one of her favorite nephews and to be truthful, she's enjoying being here close to her other favorite nephews and nieces."

Buckled into the passenger seat, memories of the time they spent in the car made her smile. Once he had stowed her luggage and sat in the driver's seat, she said, "Tell me about your Uncle Tomas. Doesn't she miss him?"

"She does, but she knows he's doing the job he loves best. He is a master's master tile installer. He can fit tiles in complicated designs faster than someone who sings the alphabet."

"Did he teach you?" The midday traffic sped around them. Ren drove with an assured calm.

"Yes. Uncle Tomas is a man of passion. Calm, as if he knows a tile would accept a score without shattering. He's the same with people. He listens, really listens, then just seems to know when to speak, and with the right words needed."

She placed a hand on his forearm. "Are you like him?"

"I aspire to be." He shoulder-checked and entered the traffic circle. "It comes from life experience as well. And where he is silent, Tia Isabell creates the chatter."

The airport signs indicated they were nearing the end of their journey. If Ren were like his uncle, would he need a partner like his aunt, someone who would provide the sounds to their life? She couldn't be that. She could be up and an extravert when it was necessary, but then she needed to recharge.

He parked in short-term parking. "We're here."

A deep sigh escaped before she had the thought to silence it. "Yes."

He put his hand on her cheek and looked into her eyes. "I will go inside with you, wait in line, and stay until you are through security. Then I will see you when I return to Canada."

He was more like the man he described, his uncle, than perhaps even he realized. He had said the right words that created a smooth break. "Yes."

Unfortunately, there wasn't a line up at the check-in counter or to go through security. Their time together, and her time in Portugal, had come to an end.

Miranda wrapped her arms around him. "Thank you."

Then she entered the point of no return, lifted her laptop into the bin, then her small bag of liquids alongside her purse. The security guard motioned her to proceed through the scanning arch, and she was officially on her way home.

Chapter 20

While Miranda's scent lingered in the car, Ren sat in the parking lot and watched people rushing in and coming out either alone, dragging their luggage behind them, or surrounded by family and friends. Or on the arm of a special someone. He couldn't recall the last time someone met his plane. Not when he arrived back in Canada, nor when he arrived here. Now, without his grandmother, what reason did he have to come back? His friends had changed their lives with wives, partners, children, and careers in other towns or cities. His cousins had built their lives surrounded by family, yes, but more importantly, friends. The older generation that held everyone together was slowly dying.

A TAP Air Portugal plane flew overhead. Miranda had left this vicinity, but not his heart. He hoped she believed him, but her eyes held doubt that he had been more than a helpful tour guide. If she only knew, he hadn't shown anyone around in years. What was it that had compelled him to photograph her that first day?

He opened his phone app to the first picture of her intent on doing something as ordinary as reaching for her shoe. He had connected to her aloneness. He continued to scroll through photos he had taken over the days they were together. He laughed at their selfie with the two most massive ice cream sundaes in front of them and the awnings and displays of T-shirts and towels in the background. He had also felt her strength. Her aloneness might have been the first siren call, but her strength was what had made him come back and stay.

He clutched his phone as a horn blared repeatedly. He

craned his neck and spied an impatient man waving and shrugging his shoulders in the hope that Ren was leaving right now. Ren started the engine.

He drove the secondary highways home. When you knew your way around, all roads seemed to lead to your destination. At the first traffic circle, Ren smiled. He enjoyed the roundabouts, actually missed them when he was in Canada. They were an efficient way to control traffic but once a country or society decided on one thing, it was hard to change them.

Was it hard for his relatives to approve what Ren knew was right? Hard for them to change their way of thinking? It mattered, of course, it did. His family was as much as his foundation, as was his talent he'd learned from his culture. He recalled Miranda's story about passed down traditions from generation to generation without knowing the actual reasons.

He had learned different ways of doing things like obeying the many traffic signals in Canada. Even his patterns and colors of the tiles he now designed had changed. His pallet consisted of yellow for crops, blue for the sky, and green for trees, brown for the winter, and red for the sunrises and sunsets. He had learned to source his product from other places rather than just the factories he had known. He could change or not change. He knew what he wanted and accepted who he'd become. But of course, Miranda would also have to be willing to accept his offer of love. Perhaps years weren't as important as a deep commitment for as long as they had.

As he drove through town, he decided he would be the man his aunt wanted him to be for a few more days. He would sort, pack, and deliver Avó's things and work hard. But after he got on the plane, he would discover who he was without his family calling him back.

"Renato." His aunt reached for his hand as soon as he

entered the kitchen. "Come and tell your tia what is going on. You have never been so unfocused as you have been since I arrived."

He followed her to the kitchen table, where two espresso cups waited along with an assortment of cheeses, meats, and crackers. After he sat, she bustled around and poured coffee into both cups. Then she sat and waited.

He sipped his coffee and placed the cup on the saucer. "I must decide if I should cut the ties with this place of my birth."

"But why?" Her brown eyes teared up with concern.

"You know, I mostly came back to visit with Avó and then saw my cousins and friends. But now," he spread his arms. "I have her things, but she isn't here." He placed his hand on his heart. "She's here. I carry her everywhere I go."

"But what will you do with the house? Your heritage, inheritance?" She lifted her apron and dabbed her eyes. "It's that woman, isn't it?"

"Miranda? In a way, yes. There are things I want to do, but they are not what you expect of me. I will not be marrying someone who is half my age and have children. I will be going back to Saskatchewan and work in the career of my passion, but I'm also going to take another step."

"Renato, you have always been a gentle man. If there was an injured bird, you brought it home. You even chased the mice out of the house rather than catch them. It is no wonder she is attracted to you, your empathy. Mama," she implored toward the ceiling. "What should we do?"

"I'm sorry."

"Stop right there. You have become like those Canadians who apologize at the turn of a dime."

"I have not been taken in by her weakness but rather by her strength."

"Strength, smength. She has hoodwinked you, boy."

"That's where you're wrong, Tia."

"If I'd known this, I would never have allowed your uncle to fill in for you with his bad knees. You would have had to go back and work hard, and then perhaps your head would be on straight."

"But, Tia, you don't understand. My life isn't here anymore."

She hit the table with the flat of her palm. "Do not blaspheme in this house."

He stood and pulled her to his chest. "What can I do to help you? I've left you alone to cope. I'm—"

She held up her hand. "No more *sorry* while you are here." She pushed the plate of meat and cheese closer to him. "Eat, then we will get ready for our guests for dinner and tomorrow we will go through the linen closet and give what you don't need to the poor. You will drive it there in the afternoon, and it will be out of the house."

He nodded, and then to satisfy her, he piled slices of prosciutto and Havarti cheese on a cracker.

Ren chopped and stirred, set plates and condiments, changed into a clean shirt and readied himself to entertain and be entertained by family and the book carrying young woman. Perhaps Eduardo would be someone she would be drawn to. Ren might try a little matchmaking of his own.

~ ~ ~

After the guests returned to their homes, He checked the time. Miranda should be in the Lisbon airport waiting for her flight back to Canada. He texted her Portuguese number and asked for her Canadian number. He didn't want to lose her.

He walked to the end of the street, one of his favorite spaces. Leaning against a wall, he stared at the sea. Would she answer him? He began calculations for setting floor tiles, starting with the dimensions and finding the center distracted him until the familiar text notification *binged*.

He hesitated before opening the message. It could be

from anyone, possibly someone needed a sub player in a pickup soccer game or game of bocce, or Eduardo wanted him to give scooter lessons again. Or Katia. He wouldn't know until he pressed the message bubble. He was acting like a teenager who was afraid of rejection. Like ripping a bandage off a wound, he closed his eyes, pressed and then opened them.

Just about to board. Miranda's message included the familiar area code and seven numbers.

He hadn't shared his Saskatchewan cell number, so he added it and a hug emoticon then pressed send.

Opening his wallet, he removed his ID section and, tucked behind his birth certificate, found a tiny scrap of paper where he wrote her number. Then he sent himself an email containing the contact information. He wasn't taking any chances. When he closed his eyes again, he felt as if there was a secret pattern to a part of himself that had closed off so long ago he had forgotten.

When his phone sounded again, he didn't grapple for it. He allowed it to hold whatever message or request was there while he thought about the juxtaposition of his life. His family wanted him to find someone who knew their traditions, but he was linking with someone only familiar with his new life, his Canadian life.

Ren opened his eyes when a seagull landed next to him on the walk. It tapped on the stone with its beak. He looked into the dark eyes and then scanned area for something that might be attracting this scavenger. Nothing. The bird appeared to smile before it hopped to the edge and spread its wings and flew away. Fascinated, Ren couldn't recall anything like that happening before.

~ ~ ~

The next morning after washing the breakfast dishes, he listened as his aunt climbed the stairs, and the familiar sound of slippers on the treads brought a lump to his throat. The women in his family raised him to be who he was, but now they wanted him to be different. He couldn't be. Wouldn't be. But he also didn't have to push it in their faces. He would quietly go along with the plans and then return to Apex. Life was like the mortar he worked with, malleable, a versatile and tactile medium. For the next few days, he would be what was needed here.

He went to the basement and brought up some of his grandmother's baskets. "Let's put the things we want to donate in here."

"But, Ren, those are good. Maybe someone in the family will want them."

"But the poor can also have them, Tia. I don't like to donate to the poor with garbage bags. They get enough of that in their lives."

"Renato, where do you come from?"

Placing a hand on his aunt's shoulder, he said, "From the strong women who raised me."

"But you've been away longer than you ever were with us."

"When you have a good foundation to build on, it can only get better."

She placed a hand on his heart. "You are so much like her." Then she shook out a colorful patchwork blanket she had been holding. "Stay or go?"

"Go. Someone will be warm tonight."

They worked sorting the linen closet and then the cupboards with assorted ornaments until the church clock indicated the half-hour. "If I'm going to deliver these before the thrift store closes, I must go now."

Isabell rubbed the small of her back. "I admit, I'm tired. But we did a lot."

She lifted a smaller basket filled with ornaments wrapped in tissue paper and followed him out to the car.

He smiled at her. "I barely have room to sit. But the charity will be happy."

"Some of those things are pretty fine pieces."

"Then the charity will make more money to help the poor."

"I know you are right. Whoever is the next owner will have my mother's spirit added to it, too. Drive carefully."

He kissed her damp cheek before getting into the car

When Ren drove up to the shop, two women came out to meet him. The first looked past him and into the car. "Your aunt called ahead."

The second woman put her hand out toward him. "Renato. I heard you were back in town."

He cocked his head. His mind scurried for a reason to know her.

"Oh, I have the advantage. I knew you were coming, although I would have recognized you. You haven't changed since grade school."

"I'm sorry. I can't place you."

"Maria. Maria Santiago."

He still didn't make the connection, so he shrugged his shoulders.

"We were sweethearts in grade five."

He recalled that ten-year-old boy. A slow smiled crept across his lips, and he gripped her hands tightly. "Of course, Maria." He looked into her eyes and saw the girl she was so very many years ago. "But we called you Terry."

"Yes. There were so many Marias when we started school, so the teachers addressed us by our middle names. Mine was Theresa and there were a few of those as well, so I became Terry."

The first woman cleared her throat. "Maria, hurry up and help Renato empty his car. We have to close up soon."

Maria rolled her eyes. "Yes, Katherine." She turned so that only Ren could hear her. He felt her breath on his neck.

"Give some women a little power and suddenly they're the CEO of the company."

Something in his memory tried to surface. When Maria touched his arm, he knew he had been in this situation before. It hadn't ended well. He didn't believe in déjà vu.

"Want to meet for a drink after the Major hangs the closed sign on the door?" she cooed.

"Sorry, Maria-Terry."

She smiled at his stumble over her name.

"As you may have heard, my grandmother passed away, and I'm here trying to sort out a few things."

"I could help," she all but purred and rubbed her leg against his.

Ren stepped away from her touch.

"Still so serious even after all these years. You never would let me kiss you behind the soccer fence."

He chuckled. "Perhaps, still an introvert."

"When you're bored with all the old lady stuff, give me a call." She reached for his palm and wrote her number with a marker.

The black bled into his lifeline. He removed the baskets from the car, depositing them on the sidewalk as fast as he could. Then, he swung into the driver's seat and snapped the door closed. He couldn't speak, but he waved out of politeness. He'd have to ask his aunt about her. Or perhaps his cousin Eduardo or Katia instead.

Both of his cousins were almost like his children. He felt the age difference. This year more than ever. They could be his children if he'd started raising a family very early. But he hadn't, and he'd always been careful to use protection as much for himself as for the possibility of a pregnancy. He knew that some of his friends paid for the support of children they no longer recognized. But they were the responsibility of the father even if it was also the law. The women he'd dated had deserved his caution.

Chapter 21

Miranda watched the safety demonstration as the attendant fastened a seatbelt, indicated the emergency exits, the lighting on the floor, the floatation devices, and ended with instructions on who in a family should place the oxygen masks first. If she passed out, there wouldn't be anyone to give her assistance. Her option was not to pass out. When Stacy and Nathan were youngsters, she knew she must don her oxygen mask to be capable of protecting her children.

Even though her first inclination was to protect her children, she should have trusted them to find space for her. In her heart of hearts, she knew she was giving them their wings, but what if she could be there, unobtrusively assisting them? What if horses really could be unicorns and fly?

Using her Canadian phone, she had captured a photo of the screen with Ren's number. Was it him who gave her the thoughts about life again rather than her children? The crew dimmed the cabin lights, and many passengers had their eyes covered, ears plugged and wrapped in blankets, their bodies at odd angles trying to be comfortable for hours. Her seatmate was a man she guessed to be younger than Nathan. A game on his tablet, where bombs exploded and charaacters ran helter-skelter, captured his total attention. His thumbs frantically pressed buttons. She was glad she wouldn't have to make small talk or that he would even pay the slightest bit of attention to her.

Tucking her phones into her purse, she drew the shade and lifted the blanket to her shoulders. The passenger in front of her reclined the seat and invaded her personal space.

Taking deep breaths, she glanced over in time to see her seatmate stop in mid-motion and roll his eyes at her position. She shrugged. Of course, she could recline her seat as well, but then the person behind her would be affected. Instead of fussing she closed her eyes and scrolled through the memories of the moment when everything changed.

The moment Ren asked her permission rather than barging ahead and snapping her image and then walking away. Her loose-fitting pants were fluttering around her calves and her feet were bare, with her back against the weather-worn rock. Her orange gift cradled in her palm. The sea had lulled her, and she hadn't thought about the future or the past. She had sensed someone near her, but she was on a public beach. It wouldn't be unusual for someone to pass through her place in the sun. She eventually looked up into the face of a man she would never forget. He could have stolen her image, and she would never have known until perhaps one day she might have seen it on the internet. But he hadn't. Then he had joined her for dinner at the tiny outdoor café, and the next day, he had ridden up on the red scooter to give her lessons.

The scooter. Miranda smiled at the memory of the stylish woman and the thoughts of emulating her. When she got back home, she would add color to her wardrobe and wear styles similar to younger entrepreneurs. Stacy and Nathan always looked good but not buttoned-down like she had.

Would it change Mr. Keene's opinion if she turned up in a muted watercolor, silk skirt? Perhaps for that day, she could be button-down. He was one of her first clients and was used to seeing her one way. And she must inspire confidence. However, she would not meet without Stacy or Nathan, or both in the room. She was there in a consulting capacity. The clients would have to get used to doing business with her children.

She fell asleep with the memory of standing at the wall at the end of the earth. Ren silently supported her for who she was right at that moment.

She was startled awake by a loud snort. The passenger in front of her was in a deep sleep. Her seatmate had turned off his game and slept. She lifted the shade and peeked out at the sky. A quick check of her watch told her they should be approaching Toronto. After going through customs, it would be back to a lounge to wait for the flight home.

Miranda's decision to return as soon as Stacy called might not have been the best. She wanted to be there for her children and her clients, but she also wanted a different life. One where she embraced her courage for another chapter with endless possibilities rather than a bottomless pit of not knowing who she was without work. She thought it would be easier to get used to a new life while she was away, but it had only brought on further questions. She was back on Canadian soil when the wheels hit the tarmac.

After she cleared customs and found her way to her gate, Miranda powered up her Canadian phone. It binged and flashed like four-way flashers on an emergency vehicle.

Nathan had texted her not to come back. Just like him not to use her out-of-country phone and provide his advice when she couldn't see it. He would say they could have handled whatever Mr. Keene needed. She was too tired for this. Stacy had texted updates and emailed a link to Dropbox with the proposal in it.

A storm in another part of the world delayed the Regina flight. Miranda found a café with an open table and ordered a muffin and coffee. She would have preferred a glass of wine in an outdoor café and a certain handsome man with brown eyes and a ready smile sitting across from her, occasionally touching her knees with his.

She opened her laptop with a sigh and made sure she was connected to her data and not the open Wi-Fi. This material was too sensitive for phishers to catch. The server delivered her muffin and a carafe of coffee along with a jug of cream and sugar. The first sip said, welcome back. Everything would be okay.

She clicked through and read Stacy's proposal and checked the numbers. The offer was perfect. What had caused him to be cautious? She read Stacy's notes from the meeting. Could it be that Keene wasn't ready to accept her educated and experienced children because he remembered them growing up in the business? Miranda scrutinized Stacy's vocabulary and then Nathan's. But perhaps she was too familiar with them and understood their nuances. Some clients had a difficult time communicating with the next generation.

When she heard the announcement for her flight, she closed her laptop and pulled her carryon to the departure gate, where other bedraggled passengers waited. Suddenly, her silk skirt and yellow blouse looked out of place among the heavy parkas, scarves, toques, and winter boots. She recalled the times she thought negatively about passengers who arrived from other climates inappropriately dressed. But her attire had been the furthest thing from her mind when she chose her travel outfit. She had dressed to impress Ren.

As she watched passengers trundled by and babies cried, parents admonished children, and young people sat on the floor near an electric outlet charging their devices, her phone vibrated. Dragging it from her backpack, she took a deep breath and tapped the envelope. A glass of wine, a face sporting a pair of sunglasses, and a jaunty wave greeted her. Ren. As if thinking about him had conjured him up.

In all the times they had been together, he had never given any indication that he was not trustworthy. She had shared her insecurities, and he had been a gentleman. He hadn't realized the effort it had taken her to suggest that they be intimate. But perhaps he had, and that was why he didn't take advantage. Maybe he was hoping for the right time in the future.

~ ~ ~

Miranda felt conspicuous in Regina with her name on a placard as if she were a stranger. She approached the car driver and introduced herself. He reached for her carry-on and followed her to the luggage carrousel.

When her suitcase fell out of the shoot then onto the belt, she pointed it out to him. The slight man struggled to lift it onto the floor. He extended the handle and with both bags in tow, he led the way out of the terminal. The cold air took her breath away. He opened the warm car, showed her a blanket and closed the door firmly. Miranda texted Stacy to say that she was with the driver and was on her way home to shower, find her warmest PJs, and crawl between her flannel sheets.

Welcome home, Mom. Food and milk in the fridge. Catch you later. Love you.

Stacy's thoughtfulness extended to fresh flowers on the dining room table. Miranda quickly texted a thank you and then sent a sleeping head and home emoticon to Ren. She had no idea what he would be doing in Albufeira and was too exhausted to calculate the time difference.

When she came out of the washroom, she had a message. She was happily surprised to see it was Ren. She laughed at floating hearts. He was creative. She hugged the phone to her wildly beating heart while she twirled around and dropped onto her bed. Fifty-five years old and she felt like a teenager. If it was jet lag, she didn't care. She simply enjoyed the moment.

Another message binged before she put her phone on the bedside table. She opened it to find a recording. When she pressed the button, the ocean waves lapped onto the beach. The short segment ended with seabird calls. She closed her eyes and played the recording over and over.

Chapter 22

Ren sat in the chair across from his avó's rocker. Isabell was out with her friends, no doubt discussing strategies to convince him to return to Albufeira and find work and a relationship. He thought about the benefits of the ocean being a couple of blocks away, and the consistent weather without the "dry cold" and the intense heat. He liked having coffee bars and pastry shops on every street and the ability to eat out of doors most of the year. There was also the convenience of outdoor markets and fresh fish. He thought of Terry at the charity shop. She was interested in connecting with him. And she might be lonely if she returned to Albufeira from wherever she had been. Her loneliness wasn't his concern, and neither was the reason their long-ago friendship disappeared.

His work was in Saskatchewan. He enjoyed being a mentor to men and women who wanted to learn his craft. He liked being a contributing member of the local service club. The biggest drawback to living in Albufeira? Miranda wasn't here. The adjustment of leaving family and friends was difficult, and, unless she was comfortable with her plan, she should spend quality time with the people who knew and loved her. He didn't know if she'd want to become a part-time Portuguese resident.

He wanted to be with her, though. People would call him foolish and just aiming for heartbreak, but he had a good feeling that the time they shared would be worth any pain. As the saying went, you live every day and only die once. If Will Cleaver and the people in the Apex accessible neighborhood taught him anything, it was that people had to keep going.

He wondered about her children. Would they have a say in how she lived her life? She had run away from them to find a way to be firm in her resolve. He may not understand her reasons for leaving the business, but he respected her choice. It came down to the fact he enjoyed her company and wanted to spend more time with her. Perhaps, eventually, they could both give each other what neither of them had had, a wedding.

He smiled at the thought. Will and Tiffany were getting married. He was part of the wedding party, and he wanted to be there to celebrate with them. When Will set his mind to a project, he went for it one hundred and ten percent. Ren could learn a lot from that attitude.

His phone vibrated on the side table. Miranda's number popped up with a house symbol and an emoticon with the zzzz surrounding it. She had reached out to him. As if she knew he was thinking about her.

He replied with floating hearts. He thought about Miranda leaning against a rock and gazing out to sea. He searched his saved recordings for one of the sea gently lapping against the sand and ended with the sea birds calling. She had often said she liked to listen to the ocean through her open window. He hit send.

He felt inspired. For the next few days, he would take videos of the streets and the ocean. The recorded moments would be two-fold. He would have them for his memories when he returned to Saskatchewan, and he'd have someone to share them with now. He wished he could capture the scent of an orange orchard or almonds in bloom or even olive trees. He may not be able to take the real thing through customs, but he might be able to bring a sample of the best oil or a bottle of wine.

He shuffled off to bed with a plan to win the woman's heart. In the meantime, he would work with his aunt and complete the tasks she asked of him. It wasn't fair to her or the rest of the family. The clearing of memories was his responsibility. He would speak to Katia about the house's value and the possibility of selling it when he was ready.

Isabell's solid shoes clicked against the tiled floor, and he could hear her humming softly. She would want to return to Uncle Tomas soon. Ren wouldn't slack off until she was happy they had done everything they could. Perhaps he could escort Tia back to Saskatchewan, make sure she got home okay. What was he thinking? She'd flown there on her own without a problem. She would probably look after him and still have energy left over for whomever else on the plane might require a bit of assistance. And his family wondered where he acquired empathy. Ha.

Tia's arrival home reminded him of the times he would be waiting for his avó to come home. She hadn't gone far, the church, the relatives, the community hall to play cards or quilt, but he always felt better when Avó was back in the house. She did the same for him. Long before mobile phones, they had to trust one another. He wouldn't call out to his aunt because she wouldn't want to think she kept him awake. He thumped his pillow and settled in for the night.

The sunlight streaming through the slats in the blinds woke him. He recalled his promise to help his aunt until the house was what she wanted and needed it to be. She knew the drill for passing on and sorting out personal belongings. He would focus. No one could erase the memories of his grandmother from his heart. Even though there had been aunts and uncles with children almost the same age as Ren, his grandparents were the first to step forward when his dad died, and his mom could not cope. He might have enjoyed being in a houseful of cousins, but Grandpa and Avó had loved him to his core. They had given him a sense of himself.

What was he going to do with the keepsakes he wanted? Waterproof containers in the basement until he decided where his future home would be. With firm decisions made, he rolled out of bed and prepared for the day.

Isabell interrupted his perfect rendition of a Portuguese song when she exclaimed, "Ren, you made breakfast. I can't recall the last time someone made me breakfast. Perhaps when I had my hip surgery."

"Then consider this the second time. Have a seat, and I'll bring you coffee." He set the espresso cup filled with the black liquid in front of her.

"Come," she said. She wrapped her arms around him. "I may not want you to marry anyone. I'll keep you for my old age, instead."

"I'll always be where you need me, Tia." He turned back to the stove and plated the omelets and toast. "I didn't know if you would prefer preserves or salsa with your toast and eggs."

"As I'm queen for breakfast, I will have both." She reached for the salsa and dropped a spoonful on her eggs and then spread preserves onto her toast. "Come and join me."

"Be right there," he said. "Would you like another cup of coffee?"

"Who taught you to make coffee like this?"

"Avó taught me about beans and brewing the coffee. And I've had a lot of practice in Saskatchewan. It was hard to find a coffee I enjoyed that reminded me of home."

"The coffee houses try. And I must admit, I do give them a chance about once or twice a week."

"Me, too. The barista at Regina Beach is learning how to make a pretty good espresso. I admit to giving him a few hints."

"That's what it takes, helping those understand the things we need." She began to eat enthusiastically.

After she finished, she placed her knife and fork across her plate and turned to Ren. "Are you bribing me because you want to gallivant around again today?"

"No, it's my way of telling you I'm here for you all day so that we can do what we need to do. When I take things to be donated, I will pick up some waterproof containers for the treasures I want to keep."

"I was right. That Canadian woman was causing you to be away from your job."

"You were, and you weren't, Tia. I wanted to be with her, but now she has gone back to Canada. I hope to see her when I'm back there again."

Tia sighed. "She's closer to your age. And if you wanted to father children, you would have done so by now. Are there any fertilized eggs that led to children that you haven't shared with your family?"

"Tia!" He had always known her to be bold in her thoughts and actions, but this surprised him. "No one has told me that I have a child. And I always took precautions."

"You are a man who didn't allow your passions to run away from you."

"I admit that sometimes in the heat of the moment, it seemed unimportant, but Avó's face always seemed to appear, reminding me of my responsibilities."

Ren waved Tia away, and he cleaned up the breakfast things before joining her. It was hard moving from room to room with all the memories. Turning his head and seeing Avó's dog-eared Bible on the end table almost broke his heart. He put his hand on it.

Tia came up behind him. "I can't seem to move that either. It's been there as long as I can remember. Perhaps when Ester is up to it, she will be the strong one. My sister always was."

The worn leather edges and broken spine from lying

face down was proof that Avó had believed her readings. He'd decide what to do with it later.

He noticed his grandmother's keyring on the holder on his way out with a box of books. He had been using the spare key, unable to find her set on the St. Christopher's ring. Tia must have found it when she was going through Avó's purse. Memories of Avó maneuvering into her little parking space flooded his brain. She loved her red car. However, over the years, she had used it less and less, relying instead on her two feet. He swallowed hard, palmed her medallion of St. Christopher, the patron saint of travel, then dropped the set into his shirt pocket over his heart.

The little things gripped his core now and again through the process of dismantling the house. When it came time to sort through all of her kitchen pots and pans and spices, he would have to hold a tight rein on his emotions or he'd take them all back to Saskatchewan.

He headed out the door for another trip to the charity shop. As he buckled his seatbelt, his phone binged. He opened it expecting to see his aunt's familiar opening, *It's me*. And a list of items he had forgotten.

But it was from Miranda. She'd sent a picture of pristine snow outside a window. *See what you're missing*.

He wished it was a picture of her, but he'd have to be content knowing that she had thought of him. He shivered slightly. Soon, he'd be back in the land of snow.

The next tone was from his aunt, asking him to come back into the house. He wished for one short moment that he had driven away, but then he remembered his promise to be available today.

He quickly found the emoticon wearing a pair of sunglasses and added a sun for good measure. *See what you are missing*. Two friends were staying in touch. Jogging back into the house, he felt lighter, knowing that he didn't have to hold onto his avó's life. He had one to form of his own.

"Here, Tia," he called from the kitchen.

"Come. Up here," Isabell replied.

She sounded breathless, winded. Isabelle was old, and perhaps she had a heart attack. Ren sprinted up the stairs two at a time.

When he broached the top stairs, she was peering into a box in the linen closet. "What is it, Tia?"

"I think my mother had a secret life."

"What do you mean?"

"This box is filled with old coins. They are from all countries and different years."

He crouched down beside Isabell and lifted the box from her hands. "I haven't seen this in forty-some years. When I was around ten, I wanted a hobby. Avó asked all of her storekeeper friends to save foreign coins for me. We had fun placing the coins on a map of the world, but then, as most boys do, I got tired of the game."

"Was that the year you had those terrible growing pains and couldn't play soccer?"

"Yes, now I remember. I spent a lot of time here. Mom and Dad seemed to be too busy for me."

"I've heard so many stories of children clearing out their parents' home and finding things they hadn't known about and most times didn't want to know."

"Mystery solved. I'll store these with the few things I'm going to keep. I might find a kid who is into something like this. It will be a treasure trove."

Ren placed the lid on the box and tucked it under his arm. For a moment, he wondered if the map with his childish handwriting would turn up as well. But probably not. It wouldn't have real value, whereas these coins might have.

"Don't be too quick to give them away to a stranger." His Aunt Isabell put her hand in his, and he steadied her as she rose, "You might not have children of your own, but you could be a grandpa if someone you marry has children, someone like that Miranda."

Her words surprised him. "What are you suggesting?"

"We've been talking, the other aunts and cousins and me."

"Tia." The women had been discussing him. Why was he surprised? He now had a house with a carved chimney, no less. But still. Another thing he liked about Canada, if Tia talked to the relatives about him, he never knew. And there wasn't any chimney on his roof to advertise his wealth and availability.

"Don't get all in a huff. We do it because we love you." Tia patted his cheek.

"You do it because you want a big extended family, but some of us just didn't catch the right boat at the right time to catch the right fish," he said.

"Or you needed a different kind of bait," she continued the metaphor.

"Since you discussed me, what was the consensus?"

"It was not unanimous. The younger ones thought you should choose who you want to share your life with if you want to. But you might prefer to be alone. But my generation says no man should be alone."

"Thank you. Both sides of the discussion are correct." He pointed toward the stairs. "Let's take a break, and I'll make coffee."

"Can you make plain Canadian filtered coffee?"

"Yes. I'd enjoy a cup of our new life, too."

He must remember that his aunt was away from a life she'd made over thirty-five years ago as well. He had followed them soon after they'd immigrated. Uncle Tomas helped Ren adjust as much as he could. From the time Ren had flown to Canada, he had planned to return to Albufeira. Remarkable how life changes in a single photo frame. He wondered if Miranda would think less of him because he hadn't stepped up to become a business owner as she had. He was beyond middle age, beyond hindsight. There were only the decisions and consequences in the past.

His childless state, for one. He hadn't thought about being tested for infertility because he had always taken precautions. Would it have made a difference if he had been? There weren't many cool stories about middle-aged men who weren't married and childless by choice. He didn't make a conscious decision to remain single and childless. It was circumstance. He hadn't met a woman he wanted to be with for life. For men like him who worked mainly with other men, there wasn't a place to talk about how being single and childless might affect him. On days when families or relationships were in trouble, then they envied him and the paycheck that he could spend on himself. But on the days of the soccer championship game or the dance recital, or special holidays, they may have pitied him. He could have his biological child with a younger woman, but would it be fair to the mother and the child?

"Is that coffee ready?" Tia called from the porch.

Chapter 23

Miranda stifled a yawn. She used to be able to bounce back from zone changes without hesitation. What was different this time? Perhaps because she didn't want to return. In the past, when she was away, she'd always stayed in contact with the office, available for clients day or night. However, the business was no longer her responsibility. But she had promised assistance if they were concerned about a long-term client, especially one that may not be as technologically savvy as the new young owners. Sometimes Stacy and Nathan forgot to slow down for the ageing baby boomers.

Keene was just the type of client who needed special treatment. And if that included sitting with him and pouring tea from a Royal Doulton teapot, asking if he took one or two lumps as well as milk, so be it. She did so because she had learned to respect the way he did business. Stacy considered pouring tea archaic, but it was an art form. Miranda often measured a client in the way they held their teacup or coffee mug.

Thinking about coffee and mugs, she added to her must-buy list a set of espresso cups, well perhaps just two. Ren hadn't told her the exact date he planned to return to Canada, but she'd be ready when he did.

Time to think of Ren and future possibilities later. She knotted the scarf around her neck, her business persona in place. She clutched her briefcase, ready to beard the lion or comb its mane.

The leather crackled when she slid into the driver's seat. Her luxury sedan was very different from Ren's grandmother's little car, but in Regina, they had room to park on the streets, and there were many parking garages. The vast difference between the historic Albufeira and the new world. As she drove to the office, she couldn't help but compare the two. These neighborhood houses provided an illusion of privacy, but the design also isolated neighbor from neighbor.

She needed to stop thinking about Portugal and prepare herself to clarify what the company's client required. The ownership belonged to Stacy and Nathan now, and she was their mentor, their sounding board, their guide, not their captain. Not even the wind in their sails, nor their rudder. Was she rudderless? Perhaps, but for the first time in five decades, she was excited to find out where the currents would take her.

The door chime signaled her arrival. The receptionist looked up. "Miranda, welcome home." She rounded her desk and advanced with her arms open. "You have a tan." Shelley stood back and looked at Miranda. "And a new hairstyle."

"I'm still me, but yes, I changed some things before I went away and a few things while gone."

Looking around, Miranda noticed her certificates of achievements had been replaced by Stacy's and Nathan's.

"Miranda, welcome."

Miranda wished the agreement for them only to address each other by name when at work would disappear. She placed her briefcase on the desk and extended her hands to Stacy.

Her daughter stepped into her arms. "Thank you, Mom, for coming."

Miranda closed her arms around her firstborn and breathed deeply before stepping away. "Let's go into your office and talk about Mr. Keene's contract."

Gone was Miranda's solid grey and chrome desk, a modern glass desk in its place. Gone were the ocean oil paintings, replaced by abstract accent pictures from a designer collection. Her heart lurched. She was gone. She sat in the client's chair while Stacy sat behind the desk. Straightening her spine, Miranda stared out at the familiar view out of the corner office, which was comfortingly the same.

Stacy opened her computer to the proposal and Mr. Keene's concerns.

Miranda nodded and leaned in attentively before offering the suggestions she had compiled at the airport between flights and her thoughts through the night when her body clock was saying it should be awake. A beam of sunlight flooded over her.

Stacy jumped up. "Sorry, Mom. I'll close the shade."

"No, please don't." Miranda stretched like a satisfied cat. The glint of light reminded her of the shimmer of sun on the moving ocean. The ocean had been the beginning with a bump against a hard head. The hopes for a new life became a possibility, and along with it, another desire she wanted to fan like a spark—a chance at love with Ren.

"Mom, are you listening to me?" Stacy had come around the desk and touched her arm. "Nathan said this was too much pressure for you."

"It's not stress. It's a dream." Delight filled her. "Sorry. Back to business. I suggest that you meet him and accompany him to the office. I'll boil the water for tea. I know just how he likes it." Stacy raised her eyebrows. "It's okay, honey. Sometimes I massage the boundaries a bit. But you don't have to."

Stacy nodded. "As long as a foot massage isn't in the deal."

"No, it isn't." Miranda looked at her daughter pointedly, business etiquette in place.

"I'll wait in the reception while you work your magic and accompany him in." Stacy stepped out of the office.

Miranda discovered the external signs of her office had changed. However, the well-supplied kitchenette still contained packages of Mr. Keene's favorite jellybeans, and the teapot and various mugs and teacups she had used to woo a few of her clients.

She rinsed the pot and poured boiling water over the black leaves. Then she set the coffee table with the candy, the teacups, milk, and sugar while the tea steeped. The intercom buzzed. Her senses attuned, she heard the slight swish along the carpet. She turned to face Mr. Keene.

"Miranda."

She extended her hand. "Jack. Please have a seat."

Stacy moved toward a chair on the opposite side. Miranda tilted her head as a signal to come closer. Then she poured the tea and placed it on the table. "Cream, no sugar?"

"Yes, as always." He turned and lifted an eyebrow toward Stacy. "Thank you for requesting Miranda's presence. Should we get down to business?"

Miranda discovered the big picture items Stacy and Nathan had negotiated were rock-solid, but for some reason, the small, inconsequential details were the sticking points. "Jack, what is your bottom line?"

He chose a green jellybean. He was ready to sign.

Popping the candy into his mouth, he nodded and smiled. "You found it."

After Stacy had escorted Mr. Keene to the foyer, she skipped back into the office and grasped Miranda's hands. Jumping up and down, she said, "Mom, you did it. You saved the business."

"Stacy, I may have nudged the close, but you had it almost done."

"But I don't get it? Mr. Keene's foot wedged the

metaphorical door open. There was something he wanted, but we didn't change anything."

"We did, sweetie. The difference was we gave him what he wanted, some deference and respect to his position. Even if you don't realize it, for some of our clients, this is important. I'll make notes on who needs this assurance that they matter."

Stacy rolled her eyes.

"I know you may think it's beneath you, but sometimes don't you want someone to do something extra nice just for you?"

"But this is business, Mom, not a tea party. Don't tell me there are more men for whom you act like the perfect hostess?"

"Yes, and a few women, too. I may have spoiled them, but they kept the roof over our heads during lean times. I said thank you by offering something they enjoyed."

"I have so much to learn, Mom. Do you want your office back?"

Miranda's heart sped up. She'd been here many times in the past when all looked lost, but then with luck and kindness and negotiation, she had managed to forge ahead. She looked around at a space that reflected the business of today. Sure there were a few deep-pocketed clients, but most were older than she was and would be handing their portfolios over to their successors. "No, Stacy, this time belongs to you and Nathan."

"Mom, you're back." Dressed in jeans and a plaid shirt, Nathan strolled into the office. "Wait until you see this." With his arm slung across her shoulder, he directed her toward Stacy's computer. He popped in a memory stick and tapped a few keys. On the screen was a fabulous presentation of a property for sale in a beautiful small town.

"How did you do this?" She was mesmerized by the presentation.

"Drone photography. I dabbled in it during my last semester, and then I took a course. Money bags here"—he pointed to Stacy—"liked my proposal and doled out the cash."

"Is this why your sales numbers have been so consistent?"

He looked at Stacy, and she nodded. "Yes, Mom."

"What was that look for?"

"We just remember that you were averse to taking chances."

"Not all the time."

They began their usual "Oh, yeah," in unison, but perhaps maturity stopped them. Or their love for her. "Then I'm glad I stepped as far away as I did. And as soon as I did. You both made decisions to benefit the company. I like the idea of my cushioned retirement income." She'd made the right decision to leave. Now she'd have to stay away unless called, like now. However, she knew it would happen less and less.

Her phone vibrated in her pocket. "Unless you need me anymore today, I'm going to go home and catch up on some sleep."

"No, you go ahead. We'll handle this, right, sis?"

"Are you sure, Mom?"

"Of course. What have we always promised each other?"

"Honesty is the best policy in a family business."

"Come here." Miranda wrapped her arms around them. "Catch you later." She gathered her briefcase and chose a red jellybean from the bowl. It was time to go.

Once in her car, she leaned her head onto the steering wheel and let the tears trickle down her face. She was so darn proud of Stacy and Nathan. She swiped a tissue across her face, and she hoped this was her final hiccup of grief about losing her place in life. Her phone vibrated again. She discovered it was Ren requesting FaceTime. One more quick wipe to rid any traces of sorrow, and she hit open. "Ren."

"Hi."

"Hi, yourself."

"Did you sleep well?" He looked concerned.

Trust Ren to see the remnants of her grief. "Oh, I'm not tired. I've just had a little reality check."

"And?"

"And my reality is changing pretty quickly."

"It seems to happen at our age."

"I always promised myself that I wouldn't hang on by my fingernails."

"You'll need fingers for my idea. When I get home, would you go ice fishing?"

"What would I need to do?" She had never been ice fishing.

"Dress warmly. While in a shack on the ice and holding a rod, you dangle a hook and bait down a hole. And hope a fish doesn't bite."

"How warm?"

"There's heat. But remember, we are on the ice."

"Yes. I'll come."

"Then it's a date." He blew a kiss. "Until then, *querida*."

She caught the kiss in her palm and placed it on her heart, blew a kiss back, and waved goodbye.

Miranda drove home, her mind once again on Stacy and Nathan. The drone presentation, the Keene proposal, showed how far they'd progressed without her and also because of her. They had spread their wings and were flying. Yes, there was the odd hiccup, but they would work those out. Clients would learn that these two next-generation entrepreneurs knew the market and the business; they might even forgo their tea. Or Stacy would recognize that it was not servitude but courtesy.

When she entered the house, she knew that Laura, her housekeeper and cook, had been and gone. A casserole was in the oven, and the house had a lived-in scent. But it was empty. She switched on the stereo and walked through the rooms.

After Stacy moved out, Miranda had turned the room into a private gym. When Nathan moved into his apartment, she hadn't decided how to change it. Miranda knew the housing business. If she were to put her house on the market and start again, she would stage her home to show off many uses. It was big, comfortable, and close to schools, parks, and transit routes. A family should live in these rooms and bring them to life again.

Miranda shook her head. Always a realtor. She headed for the kitchen. Although the casserole smelled delicious, she turned off the oven and placed her dinner on the counter. She needed a rest more than food right now.

She flipped back the edge of her purple comforter, kicked off her shoes and crawled into bed. She was probably suffering the results of jetlag. After she rested, she'd seriously look at Nathan's room and the possibilities.

The sound of a snowplow's blade on the pavement scraped her back into consciousness. Her mouth felt as if the plow had dumped the dirty, gravelly snow into it. Stretching, she checked the clock on the bedside table. The travel gurus advised that it usually took a day for every hour of difference in time to get back into a before travel routine. Sitting on the side of the bed, she didn't have to hurry her body clock along. The future was wide open. She had as many days as she needed to slip back into her old life or move toward the new one.

She glanced over at her bookshelf, filled with self-help manuals. The books she would read when she began paring down. Maybe she'd pick a self-help book and start. But not right now. She was hungry for food and something else.

At the stereo, she lifted the Age of Aquarius from the record sleeve and placed it on the turntable. The arm raised itself and dropped the needle onto the groove, and the song burst forth. Miranda raised her arms and swayed and sang along to the long-forgotten song about harmony, understanding and love. Had she ever honestly believed that sentiment?

Her mother was pragmatic and hardworking and wanted the same for her. Mom's theme became her theme. Work hard and retire early. Miranda hadn't believed the business would ever become her responsibility until she waved goodbye to her mother in her RV, all set to travel the world. Not exactly the whole world but North America until she found a place to block the tires.

That was the keyword, independent. Miranda had been self-sufficient for so many years, thanks to her mom. When Mom and Dad went off to conferences and speaking engagements, Miranda either remained at home or in a hotel with a caregiver until she had been old enough to attend, even if she was bored or the topics were above her skill level. Miranda became the woman her mom wanted her to be. But now it was her time. She could decide who she would be.

Chapter 24

Ren boarded the plane with a box of confections for Miranda rather than wine or oil. He had texted Miranda his estimated time of arrival and was confident that she would be there. They had been texting and FaceTiming over the past days while he lived and completed his errands around the ocean's edge, and she sat in the sun cascading through the window safe from the minus double-digit winter. He shivered. His body would need to make a quick adjustment. He would be back at work, but he would also have a woman in his life that he wanted to know more than anything. He had upgraded to first-class so that he could sleep and would arrive rested.

Isabell had chosen to stay in Albufeira and suggested that Tomas visit their home city, especially since they had a place to stay. Ren had convinced her that this was a perfect plan rather than allow the house to be empty. Katia had agreed. In her experience, time to decide after a loved one's death was wise, and there was no need to rush. Avó would never have wanted her house to be empty for long.

He reclined, covered his eyes with an eye mask, clamped on noise cancellation headphones, and turned on his resting playlist. He drew the thin blanket up to his chin and drifted off.

The flight attendant gently shook him awake and told him it was time to prepare for landing in Toronto. He was back on Canadian soil, closer to the life he had established. Once through customs, he found a quiet spot in the corner of a restaurant and ordered breakfast.

People rushed by in parkas and heavy winter boots, dragging winter scarves. Some were in their shorts with pale legs and colorful shirts, ready for their trip to the sunny holiday. There was always a buzz of tension in terminals. Passengers checked for arrivals and departures and sudden gate changes, which usually meant someone had to run. Anxious calls for a passenger that the doors on their departing plane were closing added to the overall noise.

The Western sandwich met the requirements of a breakfast with the omelet between two pieces of brown toast. He hadn't had hash browns since he left Canada. The differences in cuisine always surprised him when he either returned to Portugal or came back to Canada. He sometimes craved what each country did not have. Different tastes, sounds and traditions in both his homes. Yes. He acknowledged that he had two homes. That gave them each the respect they deserved and the credit for what they brought to his life.

The muffled voice calling his flight number interrupted his musings. He slipped a tip under his plate then withdrew his debit card and took the check to the till. He had time, but he preferred to arrive early rather than minutes before the plane was going to close the doors. He didn't have much to stow, but he wanted his box of pastries to be safe. This time he didn't have flowers with roots encased in the soil. The image brought a smile to his lips. The cashier brightened and wished him a nice day.

The seat beside him was empty. He felt as if he scored a lottery win. After he buckled his seat belt, he lifted the center armrest, and his body relaxed. Once the safety demonstration was over, he covered his eyes, secured his headphones and settled in for another three hours. He drifted between being awake and sleeping, dreaming that Miranda was at the airport. When she saw him, she opened her arms and he stepped into them. They held each other tight.

It would be the first time anyone had met him at the airport for a very long time. But not just anyone, Miranda. He wanted it to be this woman. He'd heard stories of people who knew they were meant to be with each other after a few hours together, but he'd never believed them until now.

The rough landing startled him awake. He waited impatiently while the plane taxied to the terminal, surprised at how jittery he was about Miranda meeting him there. Finally, the aircraft came to a stop and the sound of seatbelts clicking open filled the cabin. Ren shouldered his backpack, carefully lifted the box of pastries and waited while the passengers ahead of him struggled with cases stuffed into the overhead compartment.

At the top of the escalator, he could see the arrivals area. And there was Miranda, wildly waving. His heart faltered at the sight of her in a bright red toque and matching puffy jacket. For a moment, he worried if she would be different here, in her environment where she had been successful and well-known. Was he a different person at home, where people knew him? When she opened her arms for him, all doubts disappeared.

"Ren, welcome home."

"Thank you, Miranda." He leaned his head against her forehead, "It's home for me now."

The string on the cardboard box twisted around his finger. He lifted his arm. "I brought a memory of your adventure."

"Yum. Will you come to my house for coffee and a delight?"

His stomach flipped when he realized she had only said delight, not afternoon delight. He caught her blushing. "Coffee and a pastry would be perfect."

"Ren, you forgot your suitcase."

He shifted his knapsack. "No, this is it. I travel light. Everything I need in Albufeira is there, and everything I need here is in Apex. But I will need to rent a car to get me out to Apex."

"Not a chance, I'll take you."

"If you've got the time, I'm your passenger. Perhaps you can meet my Uncle Tomas." He handed her the bakery box. "I'll trust these with you now."

"Let's go. My car is right out front. It's running to stay warm. I'm still not adjusted to the cold."

"Just a minute." He dropped his pack on a bench and dug around until he found the jacket squished into a small sack. "My emergency kit."

"You are a Saskatchewanian." She laughed, and his heart sprang in his chest.

After zipping up the jacket, he tugged a toque around his ears and leather gloves on his hands. Reaching for her free hand, he said, "I'm ready if you are."

"I just have to pay for parking." They lined up and waited in comfortable silence while other passengers jostled suitcases and carts filled to the brim. Miranda confidently inserted her ticket and cash, and as soon as the cancelled ticket spewed from the slot, she tucked it into her pocket and then wrapped her hand back around his. He felt the heat through her glove as well as his. The box swinging from her other hand kept time with their walk.

She popped the trunk of the luxury sedan, and he stowed his pack. She placed the pastries on the floor in the rear seat. As soon as they buckled-up, she poked the seat-warmer buttons on her side as well as his. Then she maneuvered the streets with the practiced ease of years in her home city. He hadn't ridden around Regina often. Ren usually drove while others relaxed.

She hummed softly along with music playing on the stereo. He listened carefully and smiled. "Miranda, you've thought of everything. Fado. The folk song that talks about leaving one shore for another."

"I didn't know the story, but I felt the emotion."

They entered an older residential area. Miranda drove up to a double car garage and pressed the remote. The door opened to reveal a pristine area, everything in its place. "Sorry to bring you in through the garage entrance, but I'd rather keep the car warm during this nasty stretch of cold weather."

He unclipped his seatbelt and hurried to open her door for her. "I will follow you," he sang off-key.

She laughed and slid her legs out of the car. With her feet planted firmly on the cement, she accepted his hand. He closed the door.

"Wait." She opened the back door and picked up the confection box. Then she led him up a few stairs, keyed in a code, and opened the door into a bright yellow kitchen with gleaming white appliances and bright sunlight beaming through the patio doors and large window. The aroma of coffee met him while he untied his boots.

She opened a closet and handed him a hanger for his jacket. "Come on in. There's a bathroom down the hall and to your left for you to freshen up while I set out coffee."

He reached for her and kissed her gently. "Thank you."

She reached up, pulled him close, and kissed him. "You're welcome." Then she turned him toward the hall.

He padded down a carpeted hallway and located the assigned door. Straight ahead was a glimpse of Miranda's bedroom, with subtle lamp light flowing onto a deep purple spread. He was intrigued. But in the bathroom, he discovered a toothbrush with his name on it and a sea-breeze scented soap. She must have been, or perhaps still was, a force to be reckoned with when it came to convincing someone they needed the home she was presenting. He was ready to accept what she wanted to offer on any terms.

Hold it there, fella, he cautioned his image in the

mirror. Miranda was offering friendship. But the phrase the hospitality of love captured his mind.

There was also a razor and shaving cream with a question mark on a note next to it. Running his hand over his jaw, he declined the shave. He wanted to be in her company rather than wasting precious minutes. But he did brush his teeth and wash his hands and face. A quick inspection told him that he had left everything as he had found it and he returned to the kitchen.

She was standing at the patio doors looking out into her backyard. "Miranda, you thought of everything."

Turning to him, she stepped closer and ran her hand across his jaw. "Not the right type of razor?"

"I didn't want to take the time away from you." He decided he would be as they had always been to each other, honest.

"Thank you. Let's sit down. We have pastries and strong coffee." She patted the back of the chair next to her.

They sipped their coffee and watched sparrows cling to the feeder, eating a few seeds at a time.

"How often do you have to fill the seeds?" Ren hadn't thought of feeding the birds in the winter.

"Depends on the time of year and the migration. I hired a high school student to top up the feeder every day while I was gone. I didn't want the birds to think I had forgotten them."

"Do the same birds return every year?"

"I don't have any way of knowing. I think they have an underground information service that they pass from one flock to the other about where to locate food." She nudged his foot. "I think I'm on their list, and I didn't want their location finder to be disappointed."

Ren winked. He cupped his mug in his hands, feeling warm and comfortable in a way he hadn't before. He loved the way the lines at the corners of her eyes crinkled when she smiled. Had she always been as playful, even during her busiest time?

He reached for her hand. "I like your fanciful ideas, Miranda."

"I've been discovering them myself. I don't have to adult every moment of my day, and now my imagination comes out to play."

She had probably worked more than played. He squeezed her hand. "And a poet. So, are you comfortable driving back in the dark?"

"It's a double lane highway all the way. I'm fine." She glanced at the clock and sighed. "We should go. I'm sure you're anxious to be back in your place and touch base with your colleagues."

"I promised Tia that I'd have Uncle Tomas on the plane to her by midweek."

"Do you work weekends as well?"

"Depends on how much work there is."

"If you need someone to watch you work your magic with tiles, I'm your woman."

"I'll certainly take you up on that offer." He stood and cleared the table while she covered the treats.

"I've kept one, but I'll box the rest for your uncle. I'm sure he'll appreciate a taste of his first home."

"They might tempt him to leave faster than I want him to."

"Going on an adventure is enticing. But working side by side with you might be attractive too."

"I'm sure Tia Isabell has been talking to him and telling him not to hang around longer than necessary."

Chapter 25

Miranda watched through her eyelashes as he stacked the mugs and plates on the counter while she tied up the box with the left-over cakes. She learned more about Ren during their texting and Facetimes, but a tiny voice had whispered this wasn't a business deal. It was life. He was here, in her kitchen, waiting for her to take him home. She approached him from behind and placed her hands on his waist. "I'm ready when you are."

He turned to face her, taking her hands and squeezing them. "I'm so comfortable. I'm not sure I want to leave and go out into the cold."

She read self-help books on relationships, and although one advised that she should leap into the unknown, what if Ren meant it literally, that he didn't want to get cold. What if he was suggesting something else? She shook her head and cleared her thinking. Her pulse raced. "You could stay the night, of course. I have a spare room. But I believe you're anxious to relieve your uncle and continue your project."

Ren's deep brown eyes searched her face. "You do know how to read people."

"I've acquired a certain amount of skill over the years of helping clients find their next home." Had she guessed correctly? "Let's get the show on the road."

He slipped on his jacket, toque, and gloves before she passed him the box of pastries. Then she followed him into the garage and opened the garage door. He opened her door and only after she was in, with her seatbelt buckled, did he move around to the passenger side. She could get used to Ren's care and attention. She hoped driving in the dark wasn't an omen. Next time she picked up a man, she'd take him home when the sun rose just to make sure the relationship would continue. She smiled to herself.

"What's bringing a smile to your face?" Ren asked.

"It's silly, but I was thinking that since I was taking you home in the dark, I hoped it wasn't an omen. I promised myself that the next time I drove a man home, it would be at sunrise."

"When do you suggest?" he said. "I don't work twenty-four-seven."

"I'm glad we're on the same wavelength." Miranda laughed as her insides tingled in new places.

The highway signs directed the way to Apex while the snow-covered fields and the leafless trees stood guard beside the evergreens.

"I missed this expansive view," he said. "The only thing that comes close to it in Albufeira is from a boat on the ocean with nothing to see but more water. This landscape is equally as beautiful."

"Whenever I have the opportunity to drive the highways, it astounds me," she said. "I try to calculate the distance to the horizon."

"At least there are landmarks on the prairies. The ocean fishers depend on their instruments and their instinct about the water. It's as if it's inherent in the soles of their rubber boots."

"It may be as easy to get lost on a frozen lake as it is on an ocean in bad weather." Miranda nodded to herself. "I may have been a bit lost myself. Out to sea, you might say."

The seat leather crackled as Ren settled back. She glanced over. The heated seat and the warm air must have lulled him into a deep sleep. She remembered how tired she had been after arriving back from Portugal. She lowered the radio volume and hummed softly along as she kept her speedometer within the legal limit.

All too soon, the sign indicating Apex came into view. The temptation to pull into the rest area and watch Ren sleep was strong, but it wouldn't accomplish anything. She may as well get him to his destination and then resume her retired life, discovering the new Miranda and, hopefully, a new relationship. He might be too busy in the next while to even contact her, and she had promised herself she would not check her phone every few minutes.

When she slowed to turn, he yawned and sat up. "Sorry, I dropped off."

"I'm glad you felt comfortable enough to sleep."

"When you get into Apex, you'll turn onto Main Street and then follow the signs to the medical center. From there, you'll see the townhouses and the apartment building. I live in one of the townhouses, and I expect Uncle Tomas will be there by now."

He sat forward. "Turn in this driveway."

She did. They could see a TV reflected in the picture window.

"I was right. Tomas is here."

She shifted the car into park.

He reached over and squeezed her hand. "I'll be busy during the day catching up on things, but I'd like to call you in the evening if you're available."

"I'd like that."

"I'll also get all of the information I can on the ice conditions and who might be willing to lend us their shack in the Last Mountain Lake ice fishing village."

"I'm going through things at home now, so I'll search for warm clothes and boots. Will I need to buy a rod?"

"Some fishers use a cut off hockey stick handle, with the line wrapped around the end."

"So is that a no?" She wasn't sure if he was joking or not. He shook his head. "Do we use bait?"

"Worms don't last, so it's minnows. We thaw them out and then as they wiggle, we attach them to the hook.

"Ok, now you're kidding, right?"

"Yes, and no, but you'll have to wait and see. I'll arrange everything, and you find your warmest clothes. And no high heeled, fancy boots allowed."

Miranda pictured the over the knee, steel shank boots she'd tucked away in her basement years ago. She would find those boots just for this adventure.

Through the window, she saw a man carrying a plate.

"Uncle Tomas must be having the time of his life. Tia Isabell would not allow him to eat in front of the TV," Ren said.

"And you're going to spoil all of this by sending him over to her. Quick, we can still make a run for it."

He laughed. "Miranda, I love my work, and I'll be happy to get back to it. Uncle Tomas is over seventy years old. He's probably lonely and wants company while he eats."

"Why do we always have to defer to our seniors?" Miranda pretended petulance.

"Because they love us and we love them."

Miranda's belly flip-flopped. Did she love her mother? Or had her mom transferred to the business partner category? Another question to analyze.

"Where did you go?" Ren turned her face toward his.

"I want to think about something you said. This retirement gig is giving me all kinds of new experiences and new ideas to consider. I'm not sure I'll like it as much as working under pressure all of the time."

"That's a real first world problem, Miranda."

Was he criticizing her? She felt judged. "You're right, but I live in the first world, and it's my problem."

"Whoa, let's not leave each other on a sour note, please? I'm sorry. I'd rather kiss you and take that with me throughout tomorrow."

Ren's observation wasn't her losing a deal. This was about Ren, who wanted to kiss her. "After our kiss, you'll leave. My unpleasantness might return. So hurry up and kiss me."

They reached for each other, but the center console was in the way. "Would your uncle mind if I walked you to the door, and we necked under the lamplight?"

"I'm sure Uncle is involved in his TV and his dinner. But there are a few neighbors who would be interested in seeing me kissing on the doorstep."

"Is that a yes, Ren? Are you worried about what your neighbors think?"

"Hell no. Are you?"

Her pulse quickened. She didn't know anyone in Apex and she was trying new experiences. "Hell no." She echoed him.

They got out of the car as if on cue, closing the doors quietly at the same time. She smiled as she popped the trunk and he retrieved his backpack and the pastry box. He led her up the walk and under the light on the front landing. She stepped into his embrace. Their lips met hungrily. She ached to open her coat and then reach inside his to share their body heat.

The light flicked on and off.

Ren leaned his forehead against hers. "We've been seen."

"Your Aunt Isabell probably told him to watch out for the cougar."

Ren laughed. "He'd get a gun because he wouldn't know any other definition than a big cat on four legs prowling around the neighborhood."

"I'd better go." She stepped away from him and felt the winter air trying to cool her. She hugged her coat tighter, gathering in all of the warmth she experienced and shielding it from escaping.

"I'll walk you back to your car."

"No, please don't. Because then I'll want to walk you back to your door, and neither of us will want to be the one to leave."

"Did you always put your needs last?"

"That too is something I'll think about while I search for my high heeled boots." She floated down the stairs and along the walkway, aware that he was watching her. When she arrived at the car, she blew him a fist full of kisses. He caught them in one hand and sent her back kisses. She held her palm with the captured kisses to her heart.

All the way home, Miranda sang songs from her teenage years at the top of her lungs. When she didn't recall the words, she filled in the lyrics with something she made up on the spot. "Ren, Ren, what songs did you sing while you gyrated on the floor with the girl with the curl in her hair?" She laughed. All the questions that she fended off all those years from people who assumed she wasn't a happy single surfaced. But she had been happy in a different way. She enjoyed her life, her work, her children, and her success. Her choices. And now, she treasured these special feelings and entertaining the idea of dare she hope—she pressed the garage opener—love.

The garage door slid open. Once inside the house, her mind said, google ice fishing. But her heart said no, borrow a book. She would go to her neighborhood library tomorrow and search the old fashion way.

Tonight, she was going to put on her warmest PJ's and snuggle under her blankets and dream like a teenager.

Opening her closet to hang up her clothes, she stared at the many outfits she had accumulated over the years. She had needed to dress well, that had always been her reasoning. And the European fashions were different from what other realtors wore, helping her stand out in the crowd. But in this new life, this new chapter, she didn't need them. Other women, however, did. She could bring warmth and joy to many women in her city.

She began checking pockets and scanning for cleanliness. Her scent was on collars of things she'd worn recently. She sorted two piles, one to go immediately and one to be cleaned before she donated. She carried the sorted clothes and placed them on Nathan's bed. Tomorrow, she would find sturdy suitcases and pack the clothes and coats into them. Another bit of weight lifted from her shoulders. She was making progress and that's what counted for a good night's sleep.

The next morning, while she brewed coffee, she scanned her kitchen shelves. Here too, she could downsize. When was the last time she had clients in for dinner? It just wasn't done anymore. People met in a restaurant, a place where no one had more power than the other. And it wouldn't be her decision but rather Stacy and Nathan's call where meetings took place.

Taking her coffee and the pastry she had kept for herself, she moved into the living room. The pastry flaked on her tongue, and she remembered Ren's hand full of kisses he gave her. She laughed.

Her phone binged. A message arrived. Closing her eyes with a wish and a prayer, she opened them to a text from Ren.

Uncle to the airport Wednesday at two. Time for coffee?

She knew her calendar was wide open, and she couldn't wait to see him again.

Yes. Meet you at departures Wednesday at two.

Emoticons of a thumbs-up and shining suns were his replies.

She answered with a kiss and hug.

Many smiley faces floated across her screen. It felt terrific to be lighthearted.

When Miranda finished her coffee, she tackled the kitchen. She wrapped glassware and extra dishes. Then, she purged the treasures she had brought home from various trips she had taken with the kids over the years. If the souvenir was extra special, she snapped a photo. She hoped that donating her mementos would bring someone joy.

She packed her car with the boxes and suitcases. A quick trip to drop off at the cleaners, Goodwill, and a stop at the library, then she was back in the house to meet Laura. She and Laura made a pasta sauce that, when she tasted it, rivaled any she'd eaten on her trip. The rest of the day sped by with chores and reading up on ice fishing.

That night, while she surfed channels, she received Ren's message saying he was thinking about her. She sent him a picture of her feet with fluffy slippers and the TV screen. *Waiting patiently.*

The downsizing bug persisted, and the next day Miranda purged more items she would never need in her new life. She found decorative boxes in the basement that would be of no use to anyone and packed away more of the old Miranda. After a quick shower and a lunch of leftover pasta, she packed her car, picked up the dry cleaning and dropped everything off at the thrift store. Another trip to the library for more ice fishing research and then back home.

She spent the evening watching borrowed DVD's about fishing and reading about warm weather gear. Snuggled under a blanket with a glass of wine at hand, in her past, she wouldn't have considered being near an ice shack. But the thoughts of Ren in close quarters brought goose pimples to her arms. She couldn't wait to see him again.

She sent him a picture of a clock. *My arms will reach for you tomorrow.*

Before she fell asleep, he sent her a ticking clock and hearts and kisses.

On Wednesday morning, she roamed through her house with a laundry basket and filled it with decorative pillows that hid in various corners. Surely someone would appreciate accents in these colors. But her mind was on Ren. If she arrived early at the airport, she'd have the advantage of watching Ren, a sturdy man with solid steps and a gentle heart.

After a light lunch, and unable to sit still much longer, she drove to the airport. She would have skipped to the departure area, but she didn't want to fall and hurt anything that might postpone or interfere with meeting Ren and his uncle.

Families pushing carts piled high with cases and everyone with backpacks from toddlers to seniors filled the airport. Most were wrapped in their winter gear, reluctant to let it go, but if their destinations were somewhere warm, they would boil until they reached their hotel. That was always the dilemma of traveling from the frigid prairies.

Perched on a bench close to the entrances, Miranda watched both the parking area and the inside. She spotted Ren the moment he stepped out of a black half-ton truck. She watched as he hoisted the kit bag on his shoulder while a man with a thatch of grey hair, presumably Uncle Tomas, spoke quickly and excitedly. The two men turned and walked toward the entrance.

Her eyes teared. She hadn't expected this reaction. When had she become so foolish? Her belly flutters were a physical indication that she'd fallen in love. If this was love, then she was holding on with both hands. She was good at closing a deal. Blinking quickly, she stood and waited so that they would see her immediately.

Ren dropped the bag and wrapped her in his arms and spun her around. "Hi."

Deep clearing of a throat brought them back to their surroundings. With her hand secured in Ren's, she smiled at the man who had allowed Ren to stay in Albufeira and gave them a chance to discover each other. Miranda stretched out her hand and felt the calloused roughness of Tomas's against her palm.

"You must be the woman who turned Ren into a head of dry garlic."

She looked questioningly at Tomas and then at Ren.

"It translates sort of like being distracted," Ren answered with a smile.

"The monkeys are biting me." Tomas swallowed a laugh.

Again, she looked at Ren.

"Roughly translated, it means he is surprised." Ren picked up the bag. "We need to get you checked-in if you're going to make your flight or Tia Isabell will have little monkeys in her head."

"She's always suspicious of the decisions we men make without her help," Tomas said while he made his way to the check-in kiosk. He scanned his passport, and his boarding pass clicked out. "All ready. Let's have coffee."

Ren fastened a name tag to the bag and carried it up the escalator, his hand on the small of her back while she rode one step above him. Dry garlic and monkeys. Perhaps she would spend more time in Ren's birth country and learn about the origin of some of their unique phrases.

Chapter 26

Ren balanced the tray with three take-away coffee cups and a box of mini doughnuts. "Here we go."

Uncle Tomas snagged the box toward his side of the table. "I want to make sure I have a few to take on board with me. I never know what they will serve." He grinned.

"The whole box is for you," Ren said. "Are you ready for espresso when you get back to Albufeira?"

"Of course. The backward adjustment is easy because it is the most remembered." He opened the box and passed it toward Miranda. "Please, I was breaking the dishes."

Miranda tipped her head and looked at Uncle Tomas. "Is this another one of your sayings?"

"You caught me. It means I don't want to cause any problems. Have a treat. Ren tells me you shared some of the pastries which he brought for you with me."

Ren smiled at his uncle, teasing Miranda. His smile deepened when Miranda slipped her hand over his thigh. Sitting with her excited him and he sensed she felt the same.

Uncle Tomas's lips twitched before he bit into a doughnut. The man missed nothing.

Miranda toyed with her cup. "Was the work challenging, Senhor Tael?"

"Tomas, por favor."

"Obrigada, Tomas."

"A piece of cake. But like my nephew, I wish they would use more color in their designs."

"As a woman who sold many houses, I know builders keep everything neutral to attract potential clients. They suggest adding color with things that can be changed easily. Tiles are permanent."

"In our culture, color is permanent and neutral is for the things we can change."

Ren's heart swelled. His uncle treated Miranda with respect. "Also, Uncle, the houses at home remain in the family longer than they do here."

"That, too, is changing." Sadness passed over his uncle's face.

Ren understood that his avó's house, his house, was still a hot topic for the relatives.

The intercom announced a gate change for his uncle's flight. "Time for me to leave you." Ren and Miranda stood. Tomas placed his arm through Miranda's. "Welcome to the family. Make sure you invite me to your wedding."

"Uncle Tomas, I haven't asked her to join the family." Ren couldn't look at Miranda. Instead, he hefted the bag onto his shoulder.

"I know you. You will. But first, you must convince Miranda to answer yes. You deserve a good woman."

Ren glanced at Miranda, who looked like she was holding back a smile. He followed them as they walked arm in arm to the security entrance.

Miranda kissed Tomas on both cheeks and then stepped back. Ren hugged his uncle before he handed over the bag and watched the man enter the lineup.

Ren wrapped his arm around Miranda's waist while they waited for Uncle Tomas to weave his way through security. He turned and waved at them.

"He's a charmer. Are we going down that road, Ren?"

He turned to face her. "I'd sure like to. Are you game?"

"We don't know each other very well. And you did suggest we could live together."

"True, but we will know more and given time, I'll know what side of the bed you sleep on."

"I like what I know so far. So yes, I'm game. Where to now?"

Love and marriage. Ren stumbled, and Miranda was right there to keep him upright.

"By the way, I sleep on either side."

The idea of a relationship for life had been percolating since the moment he spotted her leaning against that rock. He pulled her to his chest and kissed her. She bracketed his face in her palms and smiled. They both had arrived at a new road.

Reluctantly, he stepped away as more people milled around them. Hand in hand, the door slid open and the cold air brought him back to the present. "I have to return to Apex. Will and I need to talk about the construction and the wedding details," he said as he walked her to her car.

Miranda turned to stare at him. "Pardon. Shouldn't we talk about our plans first before you discuss them with your boss?"

He pulled her close. "We'll discuss our wedding plans, I promise. It's Will and Tiffany who are getting married. I'm a groomsman in the wedding party." He squeezed her tight. "I hope you'll be my date."

"Who are you going to disappoint if I go with you?"

"Not one person, I was going solo. I've been to many weddings on my own."

"Me, too. When Stacy and Nathan were younger, they accompanied me, but then they grew up."

"I don't want to return to Apex alone. My townhouse has two bedrooms. Are you up for another vacation?"

"I'm decluttering my house, and I should stay at home for a while longer."

"I'll come in as often as I can. But be forewarned, I may have to stay over."

"I have an extra bed." She tweaked his jacket and pulled him toward her. Their lips met.

"If I don't leave you now, I'll be a garlic head, and I won't get anything done."

He stepped away from her, creating distance between their bodies.

"Until we meet again." She smiled up at him.

He reached around and opened her car door, and she slipped inside. He'd carry her warm smile in his heart until they were together again.

On the drive home, he reviewed the work that he had to complete. Uncle Tomas and the team had finished nine out of the ten apartments. He and the team, less the new father, could tile the kitchen and bathroom in a couple of days. Then the pressure would be off until after the wedding.

He struck his forehead with his palm. His suit needed the final fitting. Then he chuckled. He had another reason to go into Regina, soon, very soon. He'd text Miranda, and she could help him choose a shirt. Tiffany, the bride-to-be and an artist, had dictated the tie and sock color.

He parked in the nearest open space next to the snowmobiles outside of Chuck's Coffee Shop and Gas Bar on Main Street. The first order of business was preparing for his ice fishing date with Miranda. He'd beg, borrow, or rent an ice-fishing shack from one of the fishers inside.

After paying for a round of coffees and donuts, he had secured a luxury ice shack for this Sunday. The owner even promised to show him how to operate the underwater camera monitor if they wanted it.

Next up, his meeting with Will.

Ren tapped on the open door of Will's office.

Will turned his chair from his corner window. "Ren, glad you made it back."

Ren walked over and extended his hand. "Tomas is on his way."

"If I'd known Tomas was as good as he is with the tiles and the men, you could have stayed the month."

"I'm sure Tomas would have been just as happy to be in the wedding party."

Will slapped his forehead. "Oh, yeah. That is a slight hitch."

"As if you've forgotten." Ren moved to the architectural plans pinned up on the wall.

Will joined him. "The seniors from Regina will arrive on Monday. The cleaning staff has followed the floor installers, so eight of the ten apartments are ready. If I understand, the tiles in nine are setting and the floor people can move in tomorrow while you begin on ten."

"Yes, Tomas brought me up to speed and I helped sort out a couple of issues. Everyone has worked hard and fast to make this happen."

"I'm proud of the staff and the new apprentices. Tomas had an affinity with a couple of new students. They might not take to you."

"I've already started to win them over with my charm."

Will laughed. "You're looking relaxed and tanned."

"I am, thanks," Ren said.

"So, you inherited a house in Albufeira. Are you considering returning?" Will sat in a nearby chair and studied him.

"Not anytime soon. Going back to the place I grew up is tough. There are family expectations." Ren perched on the edge of the desk.

Will raised his eyebrows.

"The matriarchs want me to marry a younger woman so that I can be a father."

"Understandable."

"I'm safer here."

"Glad to hear that."

"How are the wedding plans coming?"

"An architect and an artist decided to marry. One likes to plan, the other likes to create. The planner steps back. And the artist shines." Will pushed himself up and positioned his crutches, ready for a longer walk than across the office. His alarm rang on his phone. "Time for another wedding detail conversation."

Will's smile told Ren everything he needed to know. He wanted that kind of relationship. Miranda could make him smile like that. "I'll leave you to it while I check on the supplies for the work tomorrow. I want to check the measurements."

"What's the hurry?"

"I may want to travel to Regina more often than I used to. And I have a date for ice fishing on Sunday."

"I thought you looked different. You've met someone, haven't you?"

"Yes, I'll have a date for the wedding."

Will pounded Ren's shoulder. "Good for you. I look forward to meeting her. Wait until I tell Tiffany, she's been thinking of matchmaking as well."

Ren shook his head. "Women."

"I was considering candidates."

"Not you, too."

"When you're as happy as I am, I just want everyone to have something similar."

"You've read too many of your mother's romance novels."

"Why not. Happily ever after is a pretty solid goal."

Ren pumped his fist in the air and then chucked Will on the shoulder in a rush of adrenaline. "I'm working toward it."

"You can always show her the color of your tie, and she can wear a matching dress."

"Isn't that what the bridesmaids do?"

"Right. Complimentary, then."

"I'll leave it in Miranda's hands."

"Smart man."

"If there isn't anything else, I'll keep you up to date on our progress."

After Ren returned home, he printed off his avó's Cataplana recipe and made a list of ingredients on his phone for easy reference. Then he texted Miranda to check if she was available on Sunday for their fishing adventure. He whooped when she answered yes.

Ren changed into his overalls and steel-toed boots. Since his body was still adjusting to the time difference, he'd continue to do simple things his brain didn't need to engage in fully. The rest of the team had gone home for the evening. He turned on the lights in each completed apartment and re-examined the quality of the work. The seniors would be pleased to be living in this space full of light. Each door width could accommodate mobility devices, and the reinforced ceilings would sustain overhead tracks if residents needed assistance moving from place to place. He ran his hand over the tiles Uncle Tomas had placed. His pride in his uncle's part of this accessible neighborhood project grew. He wanted to show it off to Miranda.

He heard footsteps in the hall and turned to find Max, the resident nurse practitioner, standing in the doorway. "Hey, Max, how are you?"

"I'm checking your progress. Emily's Uncle Harold is going to be a resident in the memory wing by spring."

"He's very lucky. Will sure had a great idea."

"You know that it all started with the projected potash mine." Max looked out into the darkness with the light reflecting off the snow.

"Ah-huh, until prices went south and construction stopped, but Will and the community went ahead." Ren joined Max at the window. "That's when I came in. He's a convincing man."

"Will's motto. Give everyone a chance and they will

succeed." They both turned when they heard the familiar thumps down the hall. "Speak of the silver-tongued man."

"I spotted you guys through the window. What's up?" Will leaned on his crutches.

"I'm admiring the completed work," Ren said.

"And I'm curious. Spring isn't too far away, and Emily's uncle will be coming to live here," Max said.

"Let's go down to the rec room where it's more comfortable."

"Not if you're going to talk wedding." Max bumped shoulders with Will.

"And they say guys don't talk." Ren turned off the lights and followed the two men to the elevator.

Once in the rec room, Will clicked the starter on the gas fireplace.

"Tiffany is working hard on the final arrangements. I'm trying to do what I can. I'm the receiving agent for the online orders of chair covers and bows, table centerpieces and who knows what else." Will settled into a recliner, dropping his crutches on the floor beside him.

"That's what you get for tying yourself up with an artist," Ren said, folding himself into a club chair.

"I can't wait to see her walk up the aisle," Will said.

"What about your handsome groomsmen at your side?" Ren said.

"You're not even in my sightline until the party."

Max stood leaning against the fireplace mantle. "I'm going to be taking notes. Emily and I should be next in line. Ren, did you know there's something in the water around here?"

"Where can I get some?" Ren sat up.

"It seems to be in the aquifer between here and Regina Beach," Will said.

"Is anyone bottling it yet?" Max laughed.

"No, it's our secret," Will said. "First Jake and Robbie, then Nick and Anna, now Tiffany and me. And Max and Emily have each drank their fill, then Ren, you and your special woman may be next in line."

"Congratulations." Max reached over to shake Ren's hand and then sat in the chair opposite. "Whoa, wait a minute. When did this happen? When you were in Portugal?"

"Thank you. Yes." Ren ran his fingers through his hair. "It would be hard to top all the parties. Any of you think about eloping? My family's in Portugal and my friends are here. A wedding will create quite a challenge."

"That's easy," Will said. "Two parties. Lots of food, lots of wine, lots of friends."

"Sure, and when did you want all of the work completed on this project?" Ren asked.

"Okay, you can't tie the knot until we've completed the unit for Emily's uncle. Right, Max?"

"Definitely. Emily won't rest until Uncle Harold is safe, and then there's harvest."

Ren wanted Miranda to be his wife as soon as possible. "I'm not waiting that long."

"When are you seeing her next?" Max asked.

"Sunday, we're going ice fishing."

"I'll get you a jug of that water."

"You're serious?"

"We sure are," Both Will and Max said in unison.

"How can I say no? I'll take all the help I can to persuade Miranda that we'll be good together."

"You're a braver man than I am. I gave Emily a year to get to know me."

"I'm also older and wiser," Ren said.

"Time to call it a day for me. Anyone else?" Will got to his feet.

"Right behind you," Ren and Max said.

Chapter 27

Miranda checked the linen closet for the silk sheets she'd purchased on her last trip with the kids. She had been saving them for a particular time when she needed comfort, but now they may be for a special sleep-over friend. Dancing down to the laundry room, she wondered if Ren liked silk sheets. Who wouldn't want soft, smooth sheets? While the washing machine did its job, she went back into her bedroom and assessed the purple duvet that reminded her of lavender fields, the yellow tub chair in the corner with a mauve toss cushion, and the blackout blinds. No, not too feminine.

She moved down the hall and stood on the threshold of Nathan's room. She had told Ren that there would be an option. To honor that promise, she stripped the bed and headed back down to the laundry room. She chose fresh sheets and a spread, and she tried to recall the last time someone had stayed in the room. When the last time her kids had stayed over? They had their lives. The knowledge was like a slow-growing vine, she'd watched it and nourished it, and then one day, it was full and mature.

She plumped and positioned the accent pillows onto the plaid duvet cover. If Ren chose to sleep there, he would at least be comfortable. Miranda ran the vacuum and dusted all of the surfaces in both bedrooms. What ever his choice would be they would be together. She trusted that he wouldn't take advantage of her. Trusted that he would want to explore their connection at a comfortable pace.

Next on her list was to locate the thigh-high boots as a joke for Ren. Labeled totes filled the basement shelves.

She would have to tackle these next in her downsizing. She scanned the totes and opened one marked winter footwear. Nothing. In another, she found warm mittens and a hat, and from another tote, she chose thick socks. On a whim, she checked the tote labelled souvenirs. There they were. Soft, black leather with stiletto heels that she'd purchased in Sicily because of the craftsmanship and the texture. She'd wear skinny jeans to show off these boots. Laughing to herself, she pictured Ren's face when he picked her up. She was having fun.

As she passed into the kitchen, she ran her fingers over the growth marks etched in the jamb. A tangible record of Stacy and Nathan's journey from toddler to teenager. She leaned the boots against the wall, poured herself a glass of wine and perched on the kitchen stool next to the island. The house deserved to have more people creating noise and memories. Like retiring from the business, it was time for her to move on. She'd speak with Stacy and Nathan before putting it on the market. It was the home they'd lived in, but she didn't think they'd have an attachment to it. Through her years working with potential buyers and sellers, she was always surprised by who seemed reluctant to leave the memories behind. Ren was also dealing with the memories of Avo's house. Leaving home was tough.

Her phone beeped. She heard it but couldn't find it. It could be in any of the rooms she'd wandered through. The notification stopped. Not important. She sipped her wine and scanned the newspaper real estate section for condos on the market. A change would be good. And this house needed a big family, not a retired lady with the occasional male house guest.

The phone binged again. With her wineglass in hand, she went searching for it. This time, the message signal continued. She followed the noise back to the kitchen. She opened the flatware drawer and, next to the corkscrew was her phone. Ren was requesting FaceTime.

She opened the app. "Hi, there. You were hiding beside by knives and forks."

"Pardon?"

"I misplaced my phone"—she held up her glass—"when I opened a bottle of wine."

"Are you toasting anything special?"

"Change." She lifted her glass and sipped. "Shifting goals." Sipped again. "Modifying my behaviour possibly because of meeting you."

"Then I wish I had a glass of wine, too."

"Can we drink wine and ice fish?"

"Yes."

"Then I'll pack a bottle and two glasses. Anything else?"

"Just the warm clothes I suggested. I'll pick you up about nine."

"Do fish get up that early?"

"The early fish catches the worm."

"I think that's a bird. Will I see you before then?"

"I'm hoping. I have the final fitting of my suit for the wedding. Can I count on your style sense to help me out tomorrow after dinner?"

"I'd like that. Where should we meet?"

They discussed a time to meet at the men's store and if time permitted, they would grab a quick coffee before Ren returned to Apex. He had no idea how quickly she could shop when she had a reason. Sitting across from this dark-eyed man and getting lost in his smile would be reason enough.

~ ~ ~

The next day, Miranda worked methodically through rooms, selecting and packing items. Without all the stuff, the rooms began to show off their true qualities. After a simple dinner, she drove to the men's shop and waited for Ren. Her mind went blank, but her heart did a happy dance. It felt as if it had been a week since she'd seen him.

She waved. "Ren."

He opened his arms and kissed her on both cheeks.

She nudged him with her shoulder. "Ready to shop?"

"If I must." Ren shook out a raspberry pocket square. "The bride's wedding color."

"Let's do this." She hooked her arm through his and held him tight to her side.

Miranda was reminded of the men in the old movies who sat in the chair while the woman came out modeling a lovely dress. She watched from her perch as the tailor measured the cuffs, tucked the back, and accentuated Ren's shoulders and then she blushed when he looked to her for approval of the fit of the seat of the trousers. She nodded and caught Ren's smile in the mirror. The tailor removed the suit jacket and tweaked the vest, which showed off his muscular chest and arms. The raspberry hue was perfect for Ren's olive skin and salt and pepper hair. She looked forward to meeting Tiffany and complimenting her on her color choice.

Ren emerged from the dressing room in his jeans and jacket. Holding out his hand, he helped her stand. "I think you enjoyed that way too much."

"It was my pleasure. I'm glad I could be of assistance." She snuggled close to him. "There isn't time for coffee, is there?"

"No." He wrapped his arm around her waist. He was tall and strong, everything she hadn't realized she liked in a man. She thought someone as large as he was would want to dominate her, but not Ren.

"Walk me to my car?"

"Of course, querida"

When they reached her car, she turned to him. "What should we do now?" She enjoyed the slight confusion on his face before she winked.

He smiled. "We could stand and neck beside the car?"

With her finger on her chin, Miranda slowly gazed at the surroundings. Then she reached for his face and pulled him down to meet her lips. He pressed her up against the cold metal. With his arms around her waist, his warmth seeped into her. An unfamiliar protected feeling astonished her.

"Darling?" Ren wiped a tear that trickled down her cheek.

"Oh, Ren." She shivered.

"You're cold." He reached behind her and opened the door. "We must be sensible and part."

"Must we?" She sat when he insisted.

He crouched down and slipped his arm between the seat and her back, drawing her close again. "You're lucky I have strong thighs, or I'd be kneeling in the snow."

"I'm a fortunate woman to have traveled to the sea to find you. Ahh, are you a merman?" She tipped her head toward his legs.

"Yes, but my tail is quickly falling asleep." Ren gripped the doorframe and stood.

"I'm looking forward to seeing you in your raspberry vest, tie, and pocket square. You'll be the most handsome man at the wedding."

"I'll be the proudest man there, waiting for you to join me for dinner and a dance."

"But first a day outdoors, ice fishing. We need to see if we're compatible in the cold." She winked. She really couldn't believe she could be so flirtatious. She was heating up just imagining him keeping her warm. "I'm looking forward to discovering your heating powers, merman."

"Okay, siren, I have to go, or I won't get my beauty rest. Then I'll be all thumbs, and the tiles won't fit together, and I'll be a grouch, and my team won't work."

"A grouch. I can't let that happen. I'll see you in my dreams."

"You're tempting, but because I'm all grown up, I've learned to appreciate waiting for dessert." He closed the door.

She rolled down the window. "Drive safe. Text when you get home."

He blew her a kiss. Then he pretended to fling a fishing line and reel it in.

She felt like wriggling at the end of the line. Miranda didn't know anything about landing a fish except what she saw on the library's DVDs. The big fish put up a fight. When she thought about Ren, she didn't want to fight. Tomorrow, she'd shop for a dress for the wedding from her closet. Then she'd continue purging her space. If the opportunity arose, she wanted to be close to Ren, where he could come home to her in the evenings. She'd spend her time becoming domestic. Now there was a word she hadn't thought would ever enter her vocabulary.

She had never been domestic, but she did have children, an experience she wouldn't trade for the world. Could Ren be happy without children? Maybe the females in his family were right and he should be looking for a younger woman. Should she even consider a relationship other than friendship? Maria's comments about Ren being a kind man who helped anyone in need sprang to mind. Could he be helping her adjust to her new way of life because he wants to help an injured bird? Had she been a desperate older woman?

She inhaled deeply and released the breath slowly. She was overthinking. They had a date on Sunday. Spending a whole day together would provide opportunities to talk about the kind of relationship they wanted. Nothing had to be decided tonight.

The next day, while she sorted, tossed, and donated, an idea bubbled inspired by her bowl of oranges on the kitchen island. She held the orange and recalled the warmth of the one gifted to her in Albufeira. Her race to the ocean to save them as Ren stood at the rock waiting. His kindness and generosity.

Then, she remembered a dessert she'd ordered at Paulo's Pizzeria. An orange scooped out, filled with ice cream and the top put back into place. A perfect hiding place for an unexpected treasure. Dressing quickly, she drove to the nearest mall.

Chapter 28

Sunday was one of those prairie days where the sky was a big blue bowl without even a drift of clouds. That also spelled frigid weather.

When Ren knocked at her door, and Miranda greeted him wearing her skinny jeans, puffiest jacket and over the knee boots. She'd slung a fishing rod she'd found in the basement over her shoulder. "Come on in, Captain." She saluted.

Ren's jaw dropped. He backed up and looked at the numbers on the door again. Then, he smiled. "If I hadn't promised to meet Joe at the pier at ten . . ."

"Oh my Captain, I have my heart set on a fish fry for my dinner."

He opened his arms. "Captain Renato at your service."

Miranda dropped the rod and closed the distance. He drew her close. She lowered the zipper on his jacket and wrapped her arms around his back, feeling the warmth radiate. "Oh, Captain," she whispered into his neck.

He nuzzled her hair.

She tipped her head. Their lips met.

Ren broke away. "Miranda, even though I appreciate your choice of clothing, I'd appreciate it if you would save this outfit for another occasion."

"Aye, aye, Captain." She stepped out of his embrace. Opening the closet and pointing to a parka, winter outdoor pants, and sturdy warm boots, she said, "I'll be right back."

As she strutted into the kitchen, Ren whistled, and her heart sang. With the cooler in hand, she returned and handed it to him. She sat on a chair and tugged off one boot, then the other. She was fully aware that his eyes followed her every move. She stepped into her winter outdoor pants, then drew on thick socks before her sturdy boots.

He placed the cooler on the floor and stepped forward to hold her parka for her while she slipped it on. She heard a guttural word. "Say that again?"

"*Gostosa.*" He smiled. "I will allow you to translate for yourself." He reached for the cooler. "*Querida*, darling Miranda, we must go, or Joe will fish by himself."

The truck glided down the highway between fields covered in snow. Miranda watched the scenery go by, fully aware of Ren sitting beside her.

"Have you had to save the day, again, since your return?" Ren asked.

"No, just that once." She was quiet for a moment, thinking of Stacy and Nathan and their ability to run the business. "They're doing great. They've modernized the company in a short time. If it had been any other client, I might not have had to return."

"I'm glad I had you to return to." He reached over the console and cupped her shoulder.

She reached up and covered his hand. "If you hadn't been coming back to Apex, I'd have been sad."

"How do you feel about the progress Stacy and Nathan have made?"

"Proud. Surprised. Jealous." She covered her mouth with her hand. Miranda recalled the jubilation she felt when her mother drove away in her RV. Now she wondered if her mother had had these same emotions. She stared straight ahead. "But I needed to get out of the way and let them fly. I always told myself, they needed both roots and wings."

"I suppose they're too busy to see you very often."

"Yes. Stacy texts or calls more than Nathan, but they're excited. They remind me of my mother and me. Now I understand why she bought an RV and drove until she found a new home." She allowed Miranda to find her wings and fly.

"I'm beginning to realize how much Mom and I are alike. I didn't acknowledge it before. Mom started in the business with my father until he passed away and then she continued to succeed without him. I was beside her until she transferred the business forward and got out of my way."

Miranda turned to look out again at the snow-covered fields. How had she not seen that she was continuing to walk in her mother's footsteps? She glanced at Ren. But instead of an RV, Miranda had found a man.

"Will I meet her?"

"Yes, I'd like that. Mom visits every spring."

When they arrived in Regina Beach, Ren drove down Centre Street to the main pier. A man in a brown jacket, snow pants, and toque stood beside a rumbling snowmobile with a sled hitched to the back. Ren waved. "Joe's going to give us a ride out to the shack on his snow machine. "I'll ride in the sled and you can slide in behind Joe."

They got out of the truck and once Ren had the cooler in hand, they met Joe.

"No time for small talk. Time's a-wasting."

Ren climbed onto the attached sled, while Miranda took her place behind Joe. She recalled the scooter lesson and her position behind Ren as he drove her around Albufeira. She smiled at the memory.

Joe instructed Miranda to hold on tight. He drove onto the ice and stayed on the path worn clear by many machines. She looked around in awe and squealed with excitement when he climbed the ice ridge. Miranda hoped Ren was hanging on tight. Joe drove toward a cluster of sheds of all sizes and shapes.

He parked beside a shed that had smoke coming out of the chimney and a sign on the door that read, *Fishing is not a hobby; it's a way of life.* Miranda snapped a quick photo of Ren in the sled before he climbed out.

"Hurry, Ren. We don't want to melt the ice." Then Joe opened the door and heat radiated toward her.

Miranda gasped and turned to face Joe. "Will that happen?"

"Nah, I'm kidding around." Joe waved them both inside.

"Now, I've drilled the holes for you, and there is enough wood to last you for three hours. There's coffee brewing if you take it black—a rod for the lady and one for you. The fish finder is below. If you want to check it, turn it on here." Joe pointed to the screen. "Good luck. See you later." And he closed the door. The snow machine motor revved, and he was gone.

"I've been a guest and ice fished with experienced guys. We can do this." Ren dropped the cooler next to the table. "Choose your battle station."

Miranda opted for the padded bench leaving Ren with the old recliner next to a radio playing country tunes. A container of thawed minnows sat at his feet.

"What next, Captain?" Miranda peered into the plastic container. "I'm certainly glad you've done this before."

"We slide one of these onto the hook and then drop it in the water." Ren pinched a minnow between his forefinger and thumb and threaded it onto the barbed hook. He presented the rod as if it was a precious gift.

Miranda dropped the fishing line into the hole and watched it sink into the clear, cold water.

Ren baited his rod and then did the same. The sound of the wood expanding and contracting, the smell of the woodstove mixed with the bitter aroma of boiled coffee and Ren's lingering musky scent lent to the surrealness Miranda was experiencing.

"Thank you, Ren," she whispered, not wanting to disturb the song of the ice shifting beneath their feet.

Chapter 29

Ren divided his attention between the line down the hole in the ice and the beautiful woman sitting comfortably on the bench across from him. He wouldn't want to be anywhere else at that moment.

"Are we supposed to jiggle the line, to make the minnow dance, look alive?"

He loved how excited she was over the experience. "Can't hurt. I suppose it matters how much you want to catch a fish."

"Do you mean we have an option?" She frowned. "I thought that was the purpose of the day."

"Or we could sit back and talk. You could tell me about you, and I could tell you about me. And if a fish happens to see the minnow and the bell on the rod jingles, we could try to reel it in. But then we'd have to take it off the hook, kill it and fillet it."

"Are you telling me you are a fraidy cat of a little old fish?"

He pointed behind him toward a three-foot stuffed pike hanging on the wall.

She looked from the fish to the hole in the ice and back to the fish. "You're kidding me."

"No. This lake has so many species, and that's one of them."

Miranda yanked up the line and held the hook up to Ren. "Take it off, please?"

After winding up his line, he removed both minnows and dropped them into the water. "We could turn on the fish finder and watch the fish or we could see what you packed for lunch."

Miranda scrambled off the bench. "Let me."

"Let's set up the table, then we don't have to look at Peter Pike." She pointed upward.

"Sure." He unzipped his coat. "It's getting warm in here."

She wiped down the table with a wet cloth and then spread a fish-printed tablecloth over it. She unpacked flatware, disposable dishes, colorful containers, two wineglasses, and a bottle of wine. "Ready, sir."

"Again, you've thought of everything." The ice under his feet cracked.

"Are we safe?"

"Of course. The ice must be a foot thick. The water under it is moving, and ice fluctuates. It's going to make some noise. Now, what are you going to share with this hungry man?"

She patted the seat beside her. "Come and join me."

He put his hand over the glass when she went to pour the wine. "I have to drive."

Her eyes twinkled as she pushed his hand out of the way. "Non-alcoholic."

They dined on hot chicken soup from a thermos, an array of crackers with choices of cheese, sliced ham, and party picks with shrimp and scallops. She had brought enough to feed an army.

When she offered the plate of cheese, Ren shook his head. Then, he leaned forward and kissed her. "That was amazing. You're amazing. You know, when we first met, my heart seemed to follow you like a magnet to metal. It wanted to be near you. It was right." He tapped his chest. "It wants more."

"Ren, are you sure? There won't be any children to carry on your name."

"When we were clearing out Avó's things, I discovered my coin collection. I wanted to give it to a great-niece or nephew, but Tia Isabell suggested I keep the collection if I become a step-grandpa."

She licked her lips, and her throat worked as if swallowing something big enough to choke her.

He hoped she wasn't getting cold feet about their relationship. "What is it, Miranda?"

"Do you remember the oranges I carried when we first met?"

"You held them as if they were precious objects."

"They were. The woman at the restaurant seemed to understand that I was struggling, and she shared those freshly picked oranges, still warm from the sun. She placed them on the table as if it was a promise that everything would be alright."

She nodded to herself. "I've thought about my oranges a great deal since I've returned. I know oranges are a symbol. After the blossom of life is over, there are many promises for the fruit and the endless possibilities waiting for me." She reached into the cooler and brought out two oranges. "The oranges, the promise that everything would be all right, I should have trusted. I didn't need to go to Portugal to find myself, I've been right here all along. I went to Portugal to find you." She presented the orange on her palm. "This is for you."

Ren touched her cheek. He accepted the orange and noticed the altered peeling. When he lifted the top, instead of ice cream, which he would have received at home, he saw a plain gold band.

She lifted it from the pulp, turned his palm over and placed it inside. "Ren, I'm a woman who is ready to make the promise of love if you will accept it."

He folded his hand over the ring. "Miranda, are you sure? I'm a working man who enjoys what he does, and I hope to do it for many more years. You're a successful woman who has earned her right to travel and live wherever she wants."

She opened his palm and kissed the ring. "I promise to love you. I accept you for who you are right now. My heart wants to be with you, too. When I'm not with you, I think about you. Can we try?"

"Miranda, when I imagined a marriage proposal, other than Uncle Tomas suggesting it, and we agreed to think about the possibility, I thought I'd talk to perhaps your mother before I asked you to formally join me in my life."

"I've learned to cut out the middleman."

"But."

"Are you having second thoughts?" She blinked.

"No, my darling. No." He drew her to his side. "When a Portuguese man approaches the family, it is a sign of respect. Because your father is no longer with you, and your mother is away, I'd like to meet the other two people in your heart."

"Stacy and Nathan."

"Yes, please. And the sooner, the better."

"I will demand their attendance wherever and whenever you want, love."

He slipped the ring on his right ring finger. She tipped her head. "In my family, we wear our wedding rings on our right hand."

"I have a lot to learn, and I will, I promise."

"Miranda, for me, you don't have to change one hair, one eyelash, nothing."

"So, is that a yes?"

"Sim."

Ren reached into his jacket and brought out a flask. "I've been told this water has special qualities." He poured it into the flask top and offered it to Miranda. Smiling, she brought it to her lips. "Anything for you, Ren." She swallowed in one gulp and passed it back.

He filled it and drank the cool water. Reaching for her, they sealed their promise with a kiss.

The rumble of the snowmobile motor interrupted them. They quickly jumped up and dropped their lines into the hole. Miranda scurried onto the bench, and Ren slumped into the chair before the door burst open.

"Any luck?"

The bell on Miranda's line jingled. "But there isn't any bait on the hook?"

"Hurry, woman, wind up the line. Ren, get the net."

A small fish emerged from the hole in the ice. "Can we let it go?"

"Ahh, a softy. I should have known." Joe removed the hook from the fish and dropped it back into the water. "What have you two been doing? Mark down the way has caught his limit." He picked up the full container of minnows.

"We've been fishing in a different stream," Ren replied and winked at Miranda.

Joe shook his head. "Pack up. I'll take you back to your truck. There's still a couple of hours left for me to catch my dinner."

As he walked up to her house, Ren said, "A wedding will be a complicated event with your family and our friends here, but my family back in Portugal."

"We could elope and then have parties on both sides of the ocean."

Precisely what Will had suggested, Ren smiled. "You'd do that?"

"Ren, I want to be with you. But what about you, what have your dreams been for your special day?"

"I've been a member of a wedding party four times, counting this one, twice as the best man and twice as a groomsman. The part I remember most is seeing the love in the couple's eyes when they say their vows to each other. That's the part I want the most."

"Will you come in tonight?"

He held her tightly. "When I think about you in your tight jeans and boots, my body says yes, but my heart says we'll have a lifetime to consummate this love. I'll text when I get home."

"As soon as you tell me when, I'll gather my darlings in one room."

"A kiss for the road."

"Only one?"

Ren practically skipped down the steps and into his truck. Who knew he had been waiting all this time for the right woman to want him for who he was?

The highway home belonged to him and a few truckers. The sky was a dome of starlight. And he was in love. He couldn't wait for the many adventures and journeys with Miranda.

He rubbed the pad of his thumb over the gold band. It would have to come off when he went to work. He wanted to keep this precious gift to himself until he met with Stacy and Nathan. He'd loop it through a leather lace he had and keep it next to his heart.

At the wedding, they would dance together as a couple. Wait a minute, did Miranda dance? She had music in her soul. She made up songs. And if she didn't, it wasn't a deal-breaker. She accepted him for who he was right now, not knowing everything there was to know, and he would do the same for her. And like riding the scooter or eating Cataplana, it would be one more thing he could introduce to her in her new life.

~ ~ ~

On Wednesday evening, Ren drove to Miranda's. Stacy and Nathan would join them for an after-dinner drink and coffee. He was nervous. He hoped they'd give their permission for him to marry their mother.

Miranda greeted him with a hug and a long inviting kiss. After she hung up his coat, they walked hand in hand into the living room.

A young man in jeans and a flannel shirt stepped forward and offered his hand. He had Miranda's eyes. "Pleased to meet you, Renato, I'm Nathan, Miranda's son."

A beautiful young woman, the image of her mother, followed. "Pleased to meet you, Renato, I'm Stacy, Miranda's daughter."

"Let's have some brandy and coffee." Miranda gestured for everyone to take a seat.

The conversation flowed smoothly. Ren could tell they were personable and confident. And so like their mother.

Miranda scooted closer to Ren and reached for his right hand. The gold band shone in the lamplight. "I asked you here to meet Renato. And to tell you that I've asked him to marry me. He said yes."

Glasses stopped mid-sip. Then they lifted and toasted. "To our mother, the best closer we know."

Was that it? "Wait a minute." All eyes focused on him. He cleared his throat. "Yes, I accepted, but I would also like to ask your permission to become part of your family."

Stacy winked at Miranda. "He has class." She turned to him. "We want whatever will make Mom happy, and she's chosen you."

Nathan placed his glass on the table, walked across the room and offered his hand to Ren. "Thank you for asking, Renato. And welcome to our family. I'll finally have another male to offer support."

Stacy hugged her mom. "I'm so happy for you. I knew something was up when you were reluctant to leave Albufeira. Welcome, Renato. Future family discussions will prove interesting. I'm sure Nathan will put up a fuss just to try it out."

"Right now, I'm on Miranda's side. Whatever she says goes. And please, call me Ren."

"Oh, oh, Nathan, it's us against them." Stacy put her arms through Nathan's. "Sorry to drink and run, but we've got a busy day tomorrow. We're very happy for both of you."

He and Miranda walked them to the door. Ren stood back while Miranda said her goodbyes and the kids congratulated them again.

The door closed. "My love, I need to leave, too. Tomorrow we need to seal all the tiles and then we'll pack up until after Will and Tiffany's wedding. Friday evening is the rehearsal party." He pulled her to his side. "I can't pick you up for the wedding. All hands are on deck to help with the decorations."

"No problem. Just tell me where to meet you and I'll be there."

"Pack an overnight bag, will you? I would prefer if you stayed safe with me and didn't drive home."

"Can I bring my other winter clothes?" she asked. "Maybe a few books and my laptop too." She wagged her eyebrows at him.

"You can bring whatever you want and think you'll need for the foreseeable future."

"Ren, an overnight bag will be sufficient for Saturday. And then we'll talk on Sunday. I love you."

"And I love you, Miranda. The days are slow and monotonous without you."

"My days are filled with the scent of hope." She pointed to a bowl of oranges on the entry table, on the accent table in the living room, and she tugged him around the corner and pointed down the hall. And there in the center of the bed was a bowl of oranges.

He tugged a baggie from his jean pocket. "And I have mine right here." He held up the peels from her gift to him.

As he pulled on his coat, he said, "Miranda, could you come before the ceremony? They're having photos taken while there's good daylight, and I'd like to have a photo of us together."

"What a wonderful idea."

He nuzzled her hair before he bent and drew her to him. He didn't know where he ended and she began. "I'll text you the details."

If she hadn't opened the door for him, he wasn't sure he would have had the strength to leave. "Good night, Ren."

"I'll text when I get home, my love."

~ ~ ~

Saturday was bright and clear. Ren worked with the bridal party, setting out bronze chairs beside tables adorned with candle centerpieces and covered in silver clothes. Candles lined the aisle between the chairs, and they hung fairy lights along the outer edges. At noon, everyone departed the recreation hall in the complex, and he went home to change.

The photographer had called the last picture. Ren didn't think he could smile any longer, but when Miranda drove up, his heart jumped and he beamed.

After speaking with the photographer, he raced toward Miranda while the others dispersed. She wore a green, wool full-length coat with a matching hat and gloves. "Miranda, you are beautiful."

She curtsied. "As you are, Ren."

He directed her toward the cluster of trees that hadn't been a background for the wedding photos. The photographer nodded. Ren drew Miranda close, and he placed her palm over his heart. The gold band gleamed. After a few photos, the photographer asked Miranda to stand in front of Ren for a few more.

When they finished, they walked to Miranda's car hand in hand. He couldn't remember the last time he had been so happy. She drove them both to the Recreation Complex, where a fresco mural of the town preserved in time greeted them.

He turned to her as they entered the hall. "I have to leave you here."

She straightened his tie and dusted off an imaginary snowflake. "Go. I'll be fine, I promise."

When the crowd turned to see Tiffany in her long-sleeved wedding gown walk down the aisle, Ren only had eyes for the woman in the third row smiling back at him.

Their life together was about to begin.

Also from **Soul Mate Publishing** and **Annette Bower**:

WOMAN OF SUBSTANCE

"You will never understand what it means to be fat." With those words, grad student Robbie Smith begins the Fat-Like-Me project. In order to support her thesis, she puts on a fat suit to measure people's reactions to the new her.

Accused of embezzling funds, Professor Jake Proctor returns home to spend quality time with the only father he has ever known. There, he meets an intriguing overweight woman who reminds him of his late grandmother. She's witty, charming, and cares deeply for those around her, including his dying grandfather.

When Robbie meets Jake while she's in disguise, she deceives him for all the right reasons. But how long can she maintain the deception before Jake discovers that she is not who he believes her to be?

Available now on Amazon: <u>WOMAN OF SUBSTANCE</u>

MOVING ON

Anna is a mysterious young widow who just moved to Regina Beach. The residents of the small town know everyone's business and they are very keen on discovering Anna's secrets. She meets Nick, a Sergeant in the Canadian Army, until a horrific accident sent him home to recover from his injuries sustained in an IED explosion. He helps Anna feel safe and comfortable in her new environment, just as he has always done for his men in strange, dangerous places. Meanwhile, he focuses on preparing for his future physical endurance test to prove that he is capable of returning to active duty. Because Anna doesn't talk about her past and Nick doesn't talk about his future, she is shocked to discover that his greatest wish is to return to active duty. Afraid of getting hurt, she won't love a man who may die on the job again. Intellectually, she knows that all life cycles end, but emotionally, she doesn't know if she has the strength to support Nick.

Available now on Amazon: <u>MOVING ON</u>

FEARLESS DESTINY

Tiffany George, riding high on her commission as a fresco artist, returns home for some deserved rest and relaxation.

The drive proves uneventful until she rescues Will Cleaver on the side of a highway. While savoring memories of a kiss and a well-formed butt, her future goals do not include a romance.

Once in town, she discovers the hopes and dreams of her community hinge on the development of a new resource mine and Will's designed neighborhood. Her parents demand she give up art and resume her working partner role in the family business.

Tiffany finds herself pulled by her community roots and stretched by her newly discovered independence.

Will knows about taking charge of destiny. He models the courage she uses to become the woman she needs to be.

Available now on Amazon: <u>FEARLESS DESTINY</u>

PONYTAILS AND PROMISES

Emily Lange is a fourth-generation farmer with fields to seed, machinery to fix, grain to sell, and a lot to prove to a community who doubts her abilities. But in the heart of the Canadian prairies, family always comes first. Her aging uncle, whose dementia is worsening, needs constant supervision and Emily is forced to hire a caregiver to see to his needs during spring seeding.

Max Fraser, a nurse-practitioner, has his future mapped out. He's set to begin his new position with the Apex Medical Center and settle into his new life, which hopefully includes finding the woman of his dreams and beginning a family. That is, until he meets Emily and she convinces him to take a detour, move to the farm, and care for her uncle.

The lines of their temporary business arrangement begin to blur as their attraction grows. But neither of them are prepared to abandon their dreams. Not even for each other.

Available now on Amazon: **PONYTAILS AND PROMISES**

CPSIA information can be obtained
at www.ICGtesting.com
Printed in the USA
LVHW080856150322
713481LV00008B/292

9 781647 162603